I0891510

A Pale Horse

A Mediaeval Mystery

C.B. HANLEY

The Mystery Press

First published by The Mystery Press, 2025

The Mystery Press, an imprint of The History Press
97 St George's Place
Cheltenham, Gloucestershire, GL50 3QB
www.thehistorypress.co.uk

British Library Cataloguing in Publication Data.
A catalogue record for this book is available from the British Library.

ISBN 978 1 80399 666 0

Typesetting and origination by The History Press
Printed and bound in Great Britain by TJ Books Limited, Padstow, Cornwall.

FSC www.fsc.org MIX Paper | Supporting responsible forestry FSC® C013056

Trees for Life

For K.C.
Friend and librarian
par excellence

And I looked, and beheld a pale horse:
And his name that sat upon him was Death.

Revelation, Ch. 6, v. 8

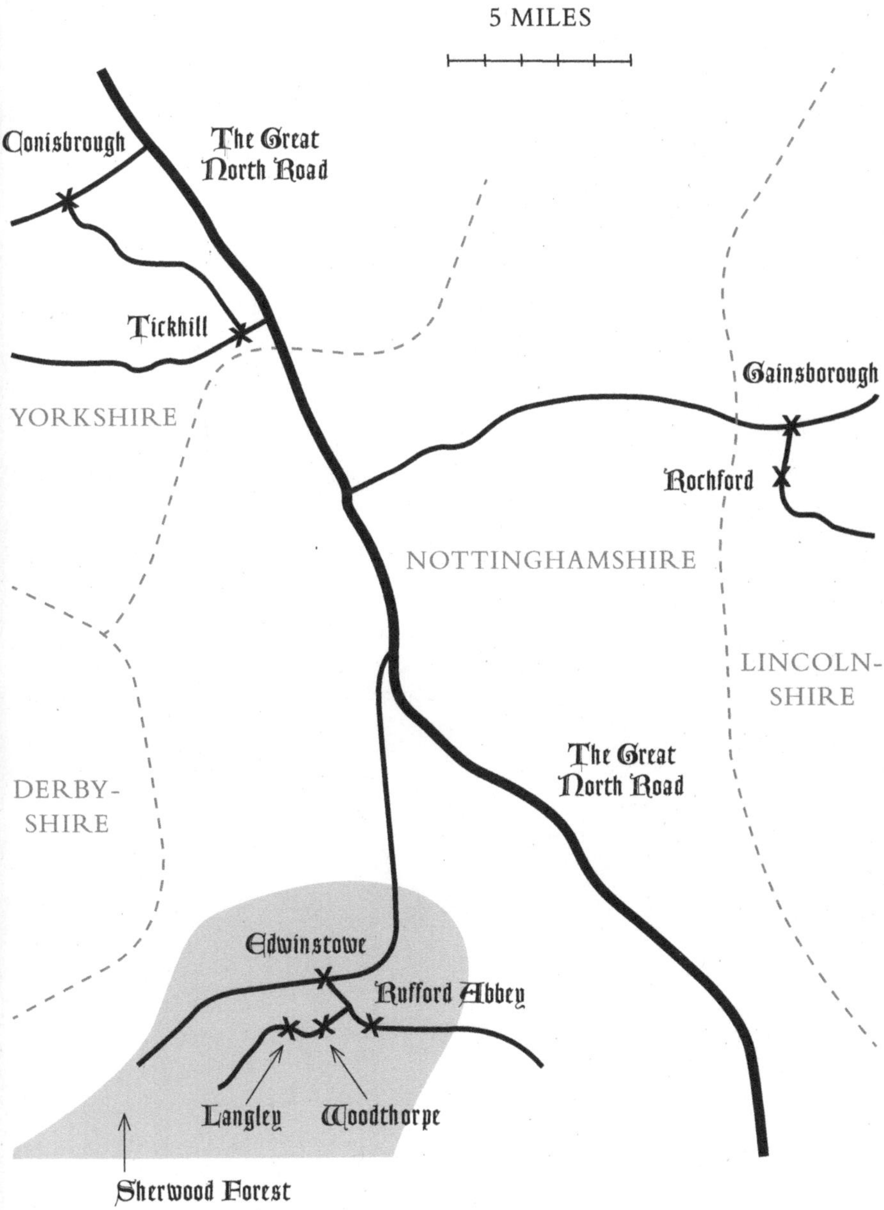
5 MILES
Conisbrough
The Great
North Road
Tickhill
YORKSHIRE
Gainsborough
Rochford
NOTTINGHAMSHIRE
LINCOLN-
SHIRE
DERBY-
SHIRE
The Great
North Road
Edwinstowe
Rufford Abbey
Langley
Woodthorpe
Sherwood Forest

Prologue

Sherwood Forest
June 1221

It wasn't particularly comfortable, standing in this ditch, but the wait wouldn't be for much longer. The target would be coming along soon, and then it would all be over.

Evening was approaching, and the shadows were lengthening. Was the level of light going to make a difference? Perhaps. But it wouldn't have any effect on the *angle* of aim, which had already been checked several times: the road was above this hollow, but not much, and it was close enough that the arrow could be loosed on a flat trajectory, not needing to fly up into the air in a high arc in order to gain distance. That meant it would travel faster, with more power, and it would thump all the harder into the target.

The intention was to shoot as the rider approached, aiming at the broad torso that was the clearest target, because there would be no second chance. There was only one arrow, because that had been easier to conceal than a whole quiver, so the shot needed to be true enough to kill.

Cramp was going to be a problem soon, if the wait were much longer. But stay – what was that? The sound of hoofbeats? Yes, it was.

Best to check first, just in case the approaching rider was someone else. *You've only got one arrow.*

There he was. Riding at a slow walk, which was all to the good, and on such a familiar road that he wasn't really paying much attention to where he was going. The horse ambled with its head down, knowing its own way, and the reins were slack. Even better.

The arrow was nocked. The setting sun was casting dazzling spears of light through the trees, but at least they were coming from the side rather than straight ahead and into the eyes. Begin the draw, now. Silently.

Stop! A sudden cawing of crows had made the horse raise its head at exactly the wrong moment, blocking the line of sight to the rider as it flicked its ears in the direction of the noise. If the arrow had been loosed it would have hit the animal, causing disaster, but fortunately there was just time to react, and the arrow was still safely on the string.

The horse, which was merely curious rather than frightened, hadn't stopped and was now almost level with the hollow. *Come on, put your head down again so I can see him properly.* Yes, that's it. A reassuring pat, and you can relax. Think of the stable waiting for you.

Thankfully the horse's head had dropped once more, but by this time the rider was nearly past. It was time to shoot lest the chance be lost. His flank presented a much smaller target than his front – was it too risky? But everything was a risk, a gamble; that was how life advanced. *You have to shoot now, or you'll lose your chance.*

There was a clear line of sight to his exposed right side, and no time to waste. Draw – *calmly, now* – and then loose.

The arrow flew smooth and true, the spinning broadhead tearing into the target's body exactly as it was supposed to. He cried out, just once, in pain and surprise, and his steed reared.

The rider toppled, crashed to the ground and lay still.

The horse bolted.

Had the shot been successful? Surely it had. The arrow was visible even in the waning light, still embedded in the bleeding body. The target wasn't moving, and there had been an audible thump when his head hit the ground.

Don't go near the road. Not yet, at least, just in case anyone else might be coming. But there was no need: he really was dead, wasn't he? The intoxication of the thought was almost too much.

Think, though. The frightened horse would run straight home. That wasn't far, so men would soon be here, searching for the lost rider. It was time to go. Time to run, although with exhilaration rather than fear. Success! The gamble had paid off.

The plan was nearly complete. After all this time, it wouldn't be long now.

Chapter One

Conisbrough Castle, South Yorkshire
June 1221

'*Requiescat in pace*.'

Edwin uttered the time-honoured words along with everyone else in the castle chapel, his head bowed and his eyes closed as he asked God's mercy for the dead man.

It was strange to be attending a funeral where there was no body to bury. But then it wasn't really a funeral, was it? More of a memorial service, because although they'd only heard the news yesterday, Sir Roger had been dead for many months. He'd perished in a place unimaginably far away and exotic, a city called Damietta, in Egypt, a land Edwin had only ever heard of in Bible stories and couldn't even begin to visualise. And there, under the scorching sun of Outremer, he would lie at rest until Judgement Day.

Edwin called Sir Roger's face to mind as he prayed. The knight had been a good friend and a fine and honourable man and, having met his death while on crusade, he was sure of the mercy they were all praying for. Edwin was confident that Sir Roger would soon be in heaven where he belonged, if he wasn't there already, meeting up with the old friends and comrades who had reached it before him.

Edwin concluded his prayers and opened his eyes to find that he was the last to do so, the others already crossing themselves and getting to their feet. He was at the back, nearest the door, so he jumped up and made way for everyone else to leave: the lord earl, followed by his clerk Brother William and Conisbrough's castellan Sir Geoffrey, then Sir

Martin, having to duck under the lintel, and finally the squires Adam and Hugh and the little page, Wil.

That just left Father Ignatius, and Edwin moved to assist the priest in putting away the vessels and folding up the altar cloth. As he did so, he noticed the strain on the other's face. 'Courage, Father. I know we're all sorry that Sir Roger's gone – and I'll certainly miss him – but he died doing what he wanted, and the Lord's work too, on crusade, so we should be glad for him and his soul.'

'Oh, I am,' replied the priest, in a tone that sounded anything but, while he looked around to check that everything was safely stowed. 'And although he was only a young man, he'd already achieved a great deal and he was much loved. How many others can say the same, when their time comes?' He sighed. 'No, I'm afraid the weight on my shoulders is that I'm going straight to another funeral, down in the church.'

Edwin recollected. 'Oh yes, of course…'

'Burying children is part of my lot as a parish priest, but it never gets any easier, no matter how many times you do it.' Father Ignatius gestured for Edwin to leave the chapel first, and then genuflected before turning to follow him through the empty council chamber and into the cool stone stairwell.

'A drowning, I heard.' The words echoed.

'Yes. Fire and water, Edwin, that's how the Lord chooses to bring children home to Him when they aren't suffering from any illness. They drown, or they stray too near the hearth. It's His will, of course, but I confess I don't always understand it.'

Edwin remembered what he'd already seen of the parents' grief, although his mind shied away from the question of how he would ever survive if anything happened to one of his own beautiful children. The *pain*… it was just unimaginable. A village boy of seven or eight years old, full of life and splashing in the river with his friends, was within an hour pale, lifeless and gone forever. Edwin shivered.

'At least with water,' continued Father Ignatius, puffing a little, 'you can sometimes bring them back. If they haven't been under too long, the Lord shows His mercy and you can pump it out of them so they can breathe once more.' They reached the keep's outer door. 'But with fire, all you can do is pray for a swift death so as not to prolong the agony.'

Both of them had to close their eyes for a moment as they stepped out from the dark stairwell into the full glare of the late-morning midsummer sun. Then, shading his face, Father Ignatius moved off towards the gate, while Edwin drifted in the direction of where the earl and most of his attendants were standing.

'… and so, it would hardly be worth him having, wouldn't support him properly even if there wasn't this cousin with a claim,' the earl was saying to Sir Geoffrey. 'But we'll find him something else, never fear. One or two other estates will no doubt be falling vacant before too long, and back into my hands to bestow as I see fit, which will give him something at least until he gets his own inheritance. His father remains in robust health, I gather?'

'Yes, my lord, or he was the last time I heard.'

'Good, good. Haven't seen him for years, but he's a fine man, always has been.' The earl nodded and clapped. 'Now, as to – ah, there you are.' He'd spotted Edwin.

'Sorry, my lord, I was just helping Father Ignatius.'

'Never mind that.' The earl waved his hand, seemingly in a good mood despite the mournful event they'd just marked in the chapel. 'I won't need you for the next few hours. We're going to ride out, and Brother William says no new correspondence has arrived today as yet. So, go about whatever other business you have, and report back here a couple of hours before sunset.'

'Yes, my lord.' It was the feast of St John the Baptist, the first day of the season for hunting hart, the great stags of the red deer, and the talk in the earl's senior household had been of little else for days.

Edwin made his way through the outer ward, spotting Sir Martin outside the stable, giving brusque orders while men rushed to obey, and then he strolled down the hill towards the village. He'd just reached it when he was overtaken by the mounted party, swelled by the presence of a dozen garrison members and huntsmen accompanying the earl and his attendants.

Sir Martin nodded to Edwin as they passed, standing out from the others not only by his stature but also by the startling white colour of his magnificent new horse, Blanchart. Sir Martin always called it 'grey', for some reason, but it was definitely white, and Edwin had joked that he might as well put a target on himself if he ever had to ride into battle.

'Wouldn't need one,' had been the knight's terse reply, and he was right. He'd always been unusually tall, but now, at twenty-one, he'd grown into his full strength as well, and a punishing daily training regime with armour and weapons had given him the muscles and solidity to match. Mounted on the gigantic horse, the only one in the castle stable that would carry him, he could hardly be missed even if it wasn't for the colour.

But ownership of such a beast made Sir Martin a little happier, and the Lord knew he had some need to be after all he'd endured in the last few years. When he was with his beloved steed, or with Edwin and his family, he could unwind and become more like the real Martin, but with most others he was short-tempered. Edwin noted now that the garrison men in the party were keeping their own mounts well away from him. Occasionally, Sir Martin really needed to work out his frustrations, and although Edwin couldn't exactly approve of his method of doing so, he did at least understand it: young men living in the area who were violent bullies or who were credibly accused of assaulting girls often returned from the woods covered in blood and bruises at times when Sir Martin was known to have been out riding. At least it saved his sparring partners in the garrison from further injury.

The group rode through the village and out the other side, eventually becoming no more than a cloud of dust, and Edwin turned towards the church. He took off his hat as he entered, and bowed his head at the piteous sound of a mother's anguish.

After the sad service was over, he was sorely in need of the comfort he'd find at home, so he made his way there, attempting to fix a more cheerful expression on his face as he went.

It was busy at the cottage, as it always was. Several of the girls who worked for Alys were outside, taking advantage of the sunshine as they spun the wool she needed for her weaving, their hands busy as they chattered and as the clouds of fleece were expertly turned into thread. Edwin greeted them but had no need to ask where Alys was, as he could already hear the steady beat and thump of the loom.

As soon as he crossed the threshold of his home, his smile was genuine. How blessed he was in his family: there was his loving and beautiful wife, frowning in concentration at the intricate pattern she was halfway through; next to her was the cradle containing their healthy eight-week-old son; and over in the far corner were the two giggling little girls. Edwin was glad to note, remembering Father Ignatius's words, that they were well away from the hearth. Even in this warm weather a fire needed to be kept burning all day so that the grain in the pottage had ample time to simmer and soften before it went into those little mouths.

It was Edith and Matilda who spotted him first, and they toddled over to clutch at his legs and beg to be picked up. As they were not much past two years old, he could still sweep them both up at the same time, and they shrieked in joy and covered his face in wet kisses. Strangers often took them for surviving twins – a rare occurrence and one that merited comment – and indeed they had been born within days of each other, but Edwin never tired of explaining that he had received the different but no less miraculous blessing of a daughter and a sister in the same week.

The sound of the loom ceased, and Edwin caught the scent of flowers as Alys came to embrace him. 'Come and sit down, my love. The service in the castle must have finished some while ago, and if you've been to the church as well, then…' she tailed off and ushered him to a seat by the open window. 'I did hear the bell, but I was feeding Robert at the time, and I didn't think it would be right to appear like that, in case it upset them even further.' She crossed herself. 'Anyway, I'll get you something to drink, and you can take your ease for a little while.'

She always knew, thought Edwin, as Edith and Matilda slipped off his lap and ran back to their game. It was like she could see into his thoughts. And the way she cared for him? Truly, he was the most fortunate man in the world.

Edwin was just taking a first refreshing sip of home-brewed ale when, to his surprise, he saw Sir Geoffrey approaching the cottage on foot. He experienced a moment of alarm at such an early return from the hunt, but the knight was smiling and easy, nodding to the girls outside, so surely there was nothing wrong. Edwin moved to the door, which was standing open in the fine weather.

'My horse pulled up lame,' were the knight's first words. 'The lord earl is perfectly well attended with the others there, so he bade me return. I've already been up at the stable, so I thought I'd make the most of my unexpected free time.' A wide smile creased his lined face as he looked past Edwin at the children, and Edwin happily moved aside to let him enter.

'Are you coming to Papa, then?' Sir Geoffrey swung Matilda up into the air, and they both laughed.

Edwin sat down again, thinking to himself how odd this would all look to anyone who didn't know the circumstances, who weren't aware that his widowed mother had married Sir Geoffrey not long after he himself had married Alys, and that both women had given birth at the same time. Mother's death in childbirth had hit all of them very hard indeed, and it had taken Sir Geoffrey a long time to get over his guilt, but he loved his daughter to distraction, and hearing her call him 'Papa' was the greatest joy in his life.

It was a pleasant interlude for a couple of hours – all the more precious for being unforeseen – and Edwin and Sir Geoffrey managed to squeeze in a game of chess, with Edwin's makeshift scratched-out board and home-made pieces, while they also kept enough of an eye on the children to enable Alys to concentrate properly on the difficult part of her pattern. But all such joys were fleeting, and when the sound of horses' hooves became gradually audible, the two men exchanged a glance and got up to leave.

'A sad business about Roger,' began Sir Geoffrey, as he shut the garden gate. 'I didn't want to speak of it while we were in your home, didn't want to cast a cloud on Alys or the children.'

'Yes,' agreed Edwin, a little of the earlier weight returning to his shoulders.

'You know, I suppose, that the lord earl was going to make him the next castellan here?'

'I didn't,' replied Edwin, 'but, all things considered, it doesn't come as a surprise. He did have that practice here while you were away that time.'

Sir Geoffrey snorted. 'The less said about that the better. Still, give him his due – he did learn from the experience, and we were sure that this crusade would give him a new perspective on matters. I thought he'd make a very good castellan, in time.'

There was silence for a moment while Edwin wondered how to bring the subject up tactfully, but Sir Geoffrey forestalled him. 'And when I say "in time", I should add that I'm not yet so ancient that I'm considering retiring and taking to my bed.'

Edwin didn't know exactly how old Sir Geoffrey was, though he must be more than halfway between sixty and seventy. However, in some respects he was ageless; he merely became tougher and harder as the years passed, like a good oak beam. He was perhaps a mite slower on the stairs than he'd been in his younger days, but he still stood as straight as an arrow and had sinews of rope and fists of iron.

'There's plenty of time for the lord earl to choose someone else, then,' Edwin said. 'I wonder if…'

The knight shook his head. 'I know what you're thinking, but Sir Martin is too young for that just at the moment, and his temperament… well, he's a fine knight and one of the most fearsome combatants you could hope to see, but being a castellan is a very different thing. Staying in one place, men to command, to know, to *understand*. The patience required. I'd like to say that if I kept him in hand for a few years he'd come round to it, but even then I'm not sure. I think his path will lie in another direction.'

Edwin made no reply. It was complicated, probably much more complicated than Sir Geoffrey realised, but now wasn't the time to delve into it too deeply.

They arrived in the outer ward just as the earl's party were dismounting. The boys were set to unsaddling and assisting the grooms, and the earl gave his horse a final pat before calling Sir Geoffrey over as they made their way up to the inner ward.

Edwin fell into step with Sir Martin. 'Good hunting?'

'No kills today,' came the rumbling voice from a foot above Edwin's head. 'But we caught enough scent to know where to look next time, and Blanchart got himself some good practice.'

'You're getting to know each other better?' Edwin had little interest in horses except insofar as riding them was sometimes preferable to walking, but Sir Martin lived for them. 'And he's getting more used to…?' he indicated the artificial hand, made from metal, that took the place of Sir Martin's missing left hand.

'Yes, he's got used to the way I hold the reins, and…' The enthusing continued until they reached the keep, and Edwin tried to look interested.

The earl still took his evening meal in the great hall, in the old-fashioned manner: other noblemen had apparently started to withdraw to a private space with their families, but there was none of that here, and the earl preferred to remain visible to his men in the way his father had done. Besides, he had no family, and neither did any of his close household, so with whom could he withdraw in any case?

There was not one woman living in the castle. Sir Geoffrey was a widower, of course, as was the earl himself – his wife had died almost as long ago as Edwin could remember, leaving no children, and he'd never married again. Sir Martin was not yet established enough to support a wife, and besides, he'd had his heart broken a few years back when the girl he loved was sent away to marry someone else. Brother William was a celibate monk, and the officers of lower ranks, Humphrey the marshal and John the steward, were single.

The only other household member apart from Edwin who had a family was Matthew, the bailiff, who oversaw law and order in Conisbrough and on several of the lord earl's other estates, but he (sensibly, in Edwin's opinion) chose to reside with his wife and children in the village. Down there, among the wattle and daub and thatch, there was colour and warmth and life and family; up here, the surroundings might be richer, but everything was grey and cold, except for the occasional heated outburst of the earl's famed temper.

Edwin tried to shrug off the feeling of gloom as he sat next to Brother William at one of the lower tables and tucked into his stew. There was some chat around him, and he made an effort to join in, noting that the banter was in stark contrast to the high table, where the earl sat flanked by Sir Geoffrey and Sir Martin, served by the three boys, and all in a silence that was as stony as the walls.

After the meal there were a few bits of business and correspondence to deal with, and then Edwin was released once more. It was still light as he made his way down the hill, a balmy summer evening with the aroma of wildflowers mingling with woodsmoke, and the setting sun illuminating the fields bursting with crops. Edwin gave thanks that they were growing well, and that the village would enjoy a year of plenty. All was, in fact, right with the world, and he knew that he should be more grateful and more at ease. But the very serenity of life at the moment was making him worry that it couldn't last, that something was bound to go tragically wrong sooner rather than later. He quickened his step, anxious to get home and hoping that he would be able to shake off this dark sense of foreboding when he got there.

It was early the next morning when a hammering sounded at the door, but Edwin and Alys were already up, baby Robert having woken on several occasions during the night. Each time he heard the crying Edwin was caught between groaning and relief, because at least it meant that the child was alive. The nightmare of every parent in the village, and one that came true far too often, was to awake to a cold, still silence from the cradle.

It was Sir Martin, and Edwin's dark thoughts immediately returned, but his friend was smiling broadly. 'Sorry to call at this hour, but I'm due to drill some of the men this morning, and I wanted to come down and give you this first.' He held out a sack and then looked over Edwin's shoulder. 'Morning, Alys. How are you, and how's my godson getting on?'

At their invitation he stepped inside. As ever, he seemed to fill the whole space – and, as ever, Edwin felt that he had to tone down how happy his family life was. Sir Martin had long got over the jealousy that had caused him to act rashly a couple of times, but Edwin still felt obscurely guilty that he had so much while his friend had so little. Which was a very odd thing, given that he was a commoner and Sir Martin a knight, but given the choice of status or family, Edwin knew which one he valued more highly.

'I should've brought this yesterday,' began Sir Martin, thumping his burden down on the table. 'But I didn't get time, sorry.'

'Well, it was the first day of the hart-hunting season,' said Edwin, eyeing the sack warily in case it contained a deer's head or something. But no, it was the wrong shape, didn't stink, and besides, they hadn't killed anything.

'Yes, the feast of St John the Baptist,' continued Sir Martin, with a knowing glance at Alys. Mysteriously, she seemed to catch on to whatever he meant, and she gave a little gasp before smiling.

Edwin looked from one to the other in some puzzlement.

'Tsk, are you losing all that famed cleverness?' asked Sir Martin, giving Edwin a clap on the shoulder that nearly sent him flying. 'The feast of your birth, as well as the saint. It's an easy day to remember. I know that you don't pay it much heed since your mother – well, anyway. I've got you something.'

By now Edith and Matilda were clamouring round the knight's legs, and he bent to pay them some attention. 'Open it, do – I haven't got long before I have to get back.'

Intrigued, Edwin reached in and pulled out a magnificent chessboard, the polished squares inlaid in dark and light wood and surrounded by a carved border.

There was silence, as he was so overcome that he could do nothing but stare at it for several moments. Then, with shaking hands, he extracted a bundle of cloth and unwrapped it to find two sets of playing pieces, exquisitely fashioned from black and white materials that he couldn't immediately identify.

'That's ivory,' explained Sir Martin, trying to point while also holding both girls. 'The merchant said so. And the black ones are made of jet.' He paused, before asking in a rather hesitant tone, 'You *do* like it?'

Edwin was, quite literally, speechless. He opened his mouth to say something, and no words came out. He just stared and stared at the most wonderful items he'd ever owned, or ever would.

'Shall I take that as a compliment?'

Alys laughed in joy. 'Yes, you should. Look at him!'

'Martin,' croaked Edwin. 'I mean, *Sir* M– but where did you get them from?'

'It was when I was with my lord in London, last autumn. You can get anything there, you know – it's amazing. Food and goods from all over the world.'

'But how could you possibly afford… I mean, sorry, that's none of my business, but I hope you didn't–'

Sir Martin shrugged. 'My lord pays me a daily allowance now I'm a knight, and what else do I have to spend it on? I don't have to pay for lodgings or buy my own food.'

'But your own family–' began Edwin.

'Never mind that,' was the swift and curt reply, and Edwin shut his mouth.

'I knew we were going to London,' continued Sir Martin, 'so I asked Alys if a new chess set might be something you'd like, and she said yes, so I went looking for one. And I've kept it safe ever since, because it was to be a surprise.' He grinned and, just for a moment, the boyish old Martin appeared.

'It's wonderful,' said Edwin, still overwhelmed. 'And never to say a word all this time? Why–' He stopped himself just in time, before he could add 'normally, your every thought is written right across your face' and made a quick recovery into 'why, that just adds to the value of the gift. I'll think of you every time I use it.'

'Good. Just don't ask me to play against you! When I next see Sir Geoffrey I'll tell him, and say that he'll have to come down and christen it with you. I might just catch him before he goes out – he's taking part of the garrison out on patrol, and I'm to drill the rest while he's gone.' Sir Martin put the girls down. 'Which reminds me, I need to go.'

'Please do come back later, when you have the time,' said Alys. 'Edwin and Sir Geoffrey have no attention to spare for anyone when they get going, so you can sit and tell me all about your new horse.'

Sir Martin grinned and ducked out of the door, leaving Edwin to contemplate, once again, how lucky he was.

'I wonder if I might speak with you about something?'

Edwin had spent much of the morning at the castle, helping Brother William with the earl's correspondence and then going through some old parchments relating to various local estates with Matthew the bailiff. Surprised at Matthew's hesitant tone, Edwin turned to face him. 'Of course. Is there something I can help you with?' He gestured to the documents.

'Oh, not all this. It's just… well, I might as well come out with it.' Matthew took a deep breath. 'Your father was the lord earl's bailiff for many years.'

This was an unexpected beginning. 'Yes?'

'And, when you were younger, you probably expected to take over from him.'

Edwin understood. 'Ah. Yes, I did, when I was a boy, and for a while when he was in his last illness I did take over some of his duties. But you know that my position in the household changed long before you arrived here, and if you're worried that I might resent–'

'I know you don't. You're a generous man.' Matthew paused. 'But… now you have a son of your own.'

Edwin was taken aback. He hadn't thought of this before. Having a son was still so new a situation that he hadn't even begun to consider the fact that Robert would need a career planned out for him. And now

Matthew's diffidence made more sense. 'I see. And you're worried that I might want the position to come back to my son in due course.'

'Yes.'

'While you have two of your own.'

'Yes. And Thomas is eight now, so I need to start planning for his future. I always knew that young Matty would have to find his own way, as a second son – as I am myself, of course, which is why I need this position as my lord's bailiff – but I always thought that Thomas could follow in my footsteps. Father Ignatius tells me he's made good progress learning his letters and his Latin, and it would be time to start him on some early work, but… I wasn't sure what your intentions were, and it wouldn't really be fair to the lad to begin training him and give him expectations of a position if it's never going to be his.'

Edwin was silent.

Matthew nodded, and then sighed. 'Very well, I'll–'

'No, wait! Sorry, I didn't mean to say – you just took me by surprise, that's all.'

'So you don't…?'

'To be honest, I haven't given the matter one moment's consideration, not yet. He's still so young, and we need to make sure he's going to surv–' Edwin pulled himself away from that line of thought. 'What I mean is, the position of bailiff is yours, and it's right and proper that your own son should be brought up to it. I have no idea what the lord earl has in store for me in years to come, and there's plenty of time yet to worry about what Robert will do when he's older.'

Matthew's face creased into a smile, and he shook Edwin's hand with warmth. 'And any other sons you might have.'

Edwin held on to that pleasant thought all through dinner, and when he was able to slip away for a short while in the early afternoon he decided to make a quick dash home to see how they were all getting on.

He'd hardly made it into the village when he heard screams. There was also a distinct smell of burning, much more than would be expected from the hearth fires, and then he saw a belch of black smoke appearing above one of the houses.

He started to run, shouting and hearing other cries of 'Fire!' in return.

One of the cottages that bordered the village green was ablaze – the one where the reeve lived with his wife and two children, a tot and a baby. The hearth fire must have spilled or cast sparks, and in this hot, dry weather the thatch had caught and now the whole place was rapidly turning into an inferno.

'Who's in there?' was the first question Edwin yelled as he got there.

'Nobody,' came a reply. 'Reeve's out in the fields, and she's gone to the mill – she'll have taken the young 'uns with her.'

That was some relief, but the danger to property and possibly also to life was still extreme. The house was almost certain to be destroyed, and it would only take a few more sparks being blown on the breeze for the fire to spread and the whole village to go up in flames. But how was he to manage? All the able-bodied men were out at work, and it would probably take some while before any of the garrison noticed the additional smoke. Edwin might hurry that along, at least: he grabbed the nearest two boys and told them to run to the fields and the castle to raise the alarm. In the meantime, he did his best by starting to organise the women and children into a bucket chain from the well, but it was going to be slow.

Then there came shouts and the drumming of hooves. Edwin looked up from throwing a first and totally ineffective bucket of water at the raging fire to see, with huge relief, that Sir Geoffrey and a dozen garrison men were speeding up as they came towards the village and saw what was happening.

Sir Geoffrey threw himself down from the saddle and took immediate charge. He asked the same question as Edwin and then commanded two men to take all the horses away, frightened as they were by the flames, and to raise the rest of the garrison as soon as they got to the castle. The other soldiers he set to fetching water, though he ordered it cast at the neighbouring houses. 'This one is already lost,' he called to Edwin, shielding his face from the furnace and shouting to be heard over the roaring. 'Best to leave it if there's nobody inside, and work on saving the others.'

By now the heat was intense, the flames roaring up through the gaping hole in the centre of the thatch. Sir Geoffrey was wearing his mail armour, which must have been getting unbearably hot, and Edwin was about to suggest that the knight should step back when several things happened so fast that he could barely take it all in.

The first was a piercing scream from the other end of the street, as the reeve's wife broke into a run, dropping the bag of flour she was carrying. It was difficult going because she had a baby strapped to her, but she made incredible, desperate speed.

She had the baby with her.

One child.

One.

As if in response to the shriek, a wail came from inside the burning cottage. At first it was indistinct, but then Edwin and Sir Geoffrey, who were nearest, heard it coalesce into 'Mama, help me!', followed by a long, despairing 'Pa-paaaa!'

Before Edwin could even think about moving, Sir Geoffrey plunged through the flames that were by now licking the doorway and into the heart of the burning room.

Edwin caught hold of the frantic reeve's wife, who seemed about to do the same, and managed to fend her off into the arms of several women and the horrified priest, who pulled her away even as she continued to struggle and shriek.

A moving shadow inside the cottage caught Edwin's eye, and he was just in time to react and dive to catch the child, tightly wrapped in a blanket, who came sailing out through the flames that now filled the doorway. As he did so he fell and rolled, trying to keep her safe and put his own body between her and the fire. And it was a good thing he did, for it was at the same moment that the entire roof, with its heavy, burning timbers, collapsed into the inferno, sending the biggest flames yet roiling up into the blue summer sky.

Chapter Two

With fire, all you can do is pray for a swift death so as not to prolong the agony.

Edwin recalled Father Ignatius's words as the last embers were finally extinguished and they were able to retrieve what was left of the body. It certainly had been swift, that was the one mercy: Sir Geoffrey must have seen that the roof was about to collapse, realised he had no time to run back to the door himself, and flung the child out of danger as his last act before he was crushed by the flaming timbers. It would all have been over in moments, the heavy beams enough to kill him even without the intense heat that had fused his mail hauberk into a solid, charred lump.

The reeve and his wife were both there now, looking at the ashes of their home and shaking and gulping with the shock as they embraced their two unharmed children. Yes, unharmed: Sir Geoffrey had not only saved the little girl's life, but had done so in time to prevent her suffering from agonising or scarring burns.

Father Ignatius was on his knees praying for all of them, and through his own tears Edwin thought that Sir Geoffrey was another man who would go swiftly to heaven, thanks to his good deeds. What was that Bible verse? He'd heard it many times over the years when the reading came round in the cycle of Masses: *Greater love than this hath no man, that he lay down his life for his friends*. And if the sacrifice had been for an innocent child, so much the better, surely.

Edwin himself was little more than singed, his face and arms red and sore, but no worse, and his tunic covered in soot. Alys stood by him, having arrived while the fire was still blazing, after telling the girls who worked for her to run out of the village in the opposite direction, taking the children with them and as many others as they could collect on the way. They grasped each other's hands, silently, too overcome by the horror for speech.

It had taken several hours to put out the fire and wait for it to cool sufficiently for anyone to pick their way over the ashes, and longer still to free the body from the debris. By that time, the entire population of the village and castle was standing around the ruined house in a subdued circle. Even the lord earl looked shocked as he surveyed the scene. Later he would no doubt demand explanations, but for now he simply shook his head in disbelief and murmured prayers along with everyone else.

'Don't look,' Sir Martin had cautioned Hugh and Wil, as the first call came that the men had found what they were looking for. Edwin wished with all his heart that he could turn away too, but he owed it to Sir Geoffrey to be braver than that, so he stepped forward along with Sir Martin and Adam to join the garrison men in taking the knight on his last journey.

Gingerly they manoeuvred the blackened corpse on to a stretcher, and Edwin wondered if he was the only one who was trying not to be sick. A cloth was produced from somewhere, and they covered it – *him* – decently, so as not to expose the women and children to the horror of the sight as they passed. Then they lifted the stretcher and took pains to match their strides so they could convey it the short distance to the church with as much dignity as possible.

It was cool inside the stone building. Gently, the six men laid their burden on the floor and stepped back to pay their last respects, then parted as the earl came to stand with them and gaze down at the covered form.

He cleared his throat. 'We will have more to say in his honour later,' he began, 'but for now let us all remember that he was a good man, a brave knight and a loyal retainer.' He crossed himself, and Edwin and the others did likewise. 'Sir Geoffrey has lived at Conisbrough for many years,' continued the earl, with the hint of a shake in his voice, 'but he had a home of his own, and I have heard him express a wish to be buried there when his time came, alongside his parents.'

Edwin nodded. After Mother had died, Sir Geoffrey had ordered her buried here at Conisbrough, next to Father, her first husband, and he'd told Edwin that he wouldn't disturb their peace by seeking to join them whenever his own time came.

'Have a coffin made,' said the earl, to nobody in particular. 'One that can be properly sealed, and we'll have him transported back to his manor.' He took a last, long look at the covered form, then turned on his heel and left.

Edwin watched everyone else file out, so that eventually there remained only Father Ignatius and himself, just as it had been in the chapel yesterday – Lord, had it only been yesterday? How much more death was to be visited on one small community?

The priest glanced at him, tactfully stepped back and busied himself with other matters, leaving Edwin alone with the man who had been both his stepfather and his own father's best friend. *I will look after Matilda for you*, he said, in the silence of his mind. *I will love her, protect her and watch her grow up into the woman that you and Mother would want her to be. I swear it.*

Then he went home. Alys was already there, having fetched all the children; she was trying to speak cheerfully to them as she cradled the baby and watched the girls eat, but she wasn't succeeding very well, and they all sensed that something was wrong. Every so often Edith or Matilda would pause to pat Alys's hand, and Robert grizzled, unable to settle.

It was all too much. Edwin couldn't help them, couldn't speak the words of comfort that he knew they needed. For what comfort was there to be had after such a dreadful loss? He sat down, heavily, and gazed at Matilda's worried little face and then at the beautiful new chessboard, the pieces already set out in preparation for his first game with Sir Geoffrey. And then he put his face in his reddened, soot-covered hands and wept until he could weep no more.

It was the earl, unsurprisingly, who recovered himself first. The following day, he gathered an extended household group in the council chamber: Sir Martin, Adam, Hugh, Wil, Edwin and Brother William, as usual, but also Matthew the bailiff, John the steward, Humphrey the marshal and Tom, an experienced garrison man who had been promoted to the position of castle sergeant-at-arms the previous year.

There was an empty space where Sir Geoffrey normally stood.

Brother William was giving Edwin the sort of significant look that implied he wanted to communicate something, a warning, but there was no time to speak as the earl's gaze swept them all from where he sat in his high-backed chair. 'I have made a number of decisions,' he began, without preamble. 'They concern some of you personally, and the rest are here to bear witness – Brother William will write your names, and you'll all make your mark.'

There was a silence as everyone looked at each other, and at the empty place by the wall.

'First, the castellanship.' There was a slight pause before the earl continued, speaking a little faster and in a manner that made Edwin prick his ears up. 'I have not yet decided who will take over, but you–' looking at Tom '–will continue with your duties and also take temporary charge until a new knight is in place.' He paused. 'Which will no doubt be soon.'

'Yes, my lord.' Tom looked thunderstruck and overawed, barely able to get the words out; but he was a reliable man, and the kingdom and region were currently at peace, so Edwin hoped he'd be able to manage his enormous promotion for the short time it would last.

Sir Martin was looking at the earl with a crestfallen expression. He didn't expect to be named permanent castellan, Edwin knew that, but surely as the only other knight in the castle he might have expected temporary command? Edwin felt his friend's disappointment and wondered at the snub.

But he was now being addressed himself. 'The child. What age is she now?'

He could only mean one child, and Edwin felt a sudden lurching sensation. 'Sir Geoffrey's daughter Matilda was two at Easter, my lord.'

'Yes, I thought it was something like that. As an orphan and the heiress to a manor in my jurisdiction, she now becomes my ward. But as I have no wife, it is not practical for her to live in my household, and my sisters are… well, anyway, she shall remain with you and your wife for the time being, until she is of an age to have her own establishment and be properly educated. An allowance shall be paid for her clothing and board and so forth.'

'As you command, my lord.' It had actually not occurred to Edwin until that very moment that Matilda might be taken away from them, and now the combination of shock and relief, felt all at once, made his head spin. He was also not a little offended that the earl should consider that he needed paying to look after his own beloved sister, but now was probably not the time to bring that up. Matilda would be safe and happy with her remaining family for the time being, and that was all that mattered.

'This also gives me the opportunity to begin to provide for you,' continued the earl, barely stopping for breath as he turned to Sir Martin.

Edwin was still somewhat dazed, and he didn't pick up on the implication as quickly as he might otherwise have done. And Sir Martin didn't, either. 'My lord?'

The earl made an impatient noise. 'As the girl is my ward, her marriage rights fall to me. I now betroth her to you. She won't be old enough actually to marry for another ten years or so, but in the meantime the betrothal will be legally binding enough for you to hold the manor and its income in her name.'

There was a stunned silence.

'Right,' said the earl, clapping his hands. 'That's that settled, then. Most of the documentation is already drawn up, so we'll finalise it now.' He pointed to the stack of parchment in front of Brother William, who shrugged his shoulders at Edwin with an expression of apology at not having been able to warn him.

Sir Martin gaped. He stood unmoving, his mouth hanging open but no sound escaping him as he stared at the earl. Edwin was equally paralysed by his own shock and struggled to think straight. Sir Geoffrey – Sir Martin – Matilda – family – marriage – what was going *on*? What in the Lord's name had just happened? The earl had spoken as though they were all no more than pieces on the chessboard, not living beings of flesh and blood. He had just altered the whole future course of their lives in a couple of short sentences.

The earl evidently considered the matter closed, and he moved on before either Edwin or Sir Martin could recollect themselves enough to speak. Edwin's eye had automatically gone to Sir Geoffrey's accustomed place in the room, to see what he made of it, and the sight of the blank wall stabbed at his heart. Never again would he see that familiar, reassuring, white-bearded face; never again would he hear the knight's wise counsel. He would have to manage on his own from now on, and with even greater responsibility. *I promised you that I'd look after her, and I will. Whatever the lord earl's plans are.*

'Once the writing is done and sealed,' the earl was still addressing Sir Martin, 'you will travel to Rochford to make all this known, taking Sir Geoffrey's body with you for burial. First thing tomorrow, I should think. And you–' he turned again to Edwin '–will accompany him. The document and my seal will need to be shown, and there may need to be more reading and writing, and I can't spare Brother William. Besides, you can look around the administration of the manor to check that everything is in order while Sir Martin familiarises himself with his new estate. Clear?'

The two of them just about managed to croak out 'Yes, my lord,' while somehow remaining upright and conscious, but Edwin didn't dare to meet his friend's eye, not yet. The room was still revolving as Brother William completed the necessary documents in his impeccably neat hand. He then added to each one a list of the witnesses – even including Hugh and Wil, who, although only eleven and eight respectively, were both the heirs to earldoms – and they all stepped forward to make their mark. Once the ink was dry, Brother William began melting wax, but adding the seals was fiddly and would take some time, so the earl left him to it, ushering everybody else out and down the stairs.

Edwin's first reaction on stepping into the fresh air was, again, to look around for Sir Geoffrey, and he wondered how long it would be before he would be able to stop himself doing it.

Sir Martin grabbed his arm. 'I need to–'

'I know. Let's find somewhere where there's a bit of space.'

Edwin's favourite thinking-place had always been one of the embrasures up on the castle's inner curtain wall. It wasn't completely private, as they could clearly be seen and various garrison members would walk along behind them from time to time, but these would know to give the two men a wide berth, and Edwin and Sir Martin's voices would drift outwards far above the moat and the ears of anyone in the outer ward.

They sat, and Sir Martin ran his hand through his hair. 'What just happened?'

The clear air and the familiar place were beginning to restore Edwin to himself. 'I think we all just had our futures decided for us, but really, you never expected any different, did you? We should be used to the lord earl by now.'

'I didn't expect him to order me to marry a two-year-old!' Sir Martin burst out, before stopping himself. 'Your pardon. I meant no disrespect to Matilda or to you.'

'I know you didn't. But let's sit and think.'

The ghost of a smile played across the knight's lips. 'Always the thinker. But what is there to consider? I've been given my orders and I must follow them.'

Edwin nodded, slowly. 'Even if your orders are about whom to marry, your life's partner – an area in which you might have expected to exercise some degree of choice.'

Sir Martin looked out towards the fields and the river, hazy in the sunshine. 'The only choice I wanted is gone, you know that.'

'I know.' Edwin hesitated, seeking to choose his words carefully. 'And I'm glad you've come to terms with that. And at least… what

I mean is, it might not have been what you expected or wanted, but console yourself that Sir Geoffrey can rest safe in the knowledge that his manor and his child are in good han–' mentally, he kicked himself.

'No offence taken,' said Sir Martin. Edwin had never realised how many expressions there were that contained the word 'hand' until they all started to sound like a bad joke at his friend's expense following the injury he'd sustained two years ago. Sir Martin had several carefully fashioned replacements, and the one he wore most often actually was in the shape of a hand, the fingers half-closed, which he needed to hold his reins or the straps of his shield. But today he had on another, the one that ended in a heavy iron ball like the head of a mace.

Sir Martin saw the direction of Edwin's gaze. 'I'm starting to get too used to the hand, and I need to practise with the different weights and balances of the others. This one and the knife could both be useful in combat, if I was without my shield. Tomorrow I'll–' he, too, pulled himself up short.

'Tomorrow, you'll be on the way to your new manor. We both will.'

'Matilda's manor,' replied Sir Martin, firmly. 'I'm only holding it for her. It's her birthright, not mine.'

Edwin felt everything sliding away from him again and forced himself to think of practicalities rather than emotions. 'How far is it from here? A couple of days, if I remember from when Sir Geoffrey first took Mother there?'

'About twenty-five or twenty-six miles? We could make it in a day if we rode hard, though there's no real reason to, and you wouldn't like it.'

'And we'll have a cart.'

'A cart? Why?' Belatedly, Sir Martin recalled the other reason for their journey. 'Oh. Yes, of course.' He sat in silence and gazed once more at the outside world.

'We'd better start sorting ourselves out,' said Edwin. 'And…' He tailed off and grimaced.

Sir Martin turned back, an expression of alarm spreading over his face as the same thought struck him. 'How in the name of God's blood are we going to tell Alys?'

Alys stared at them both with a level gaze. 'You don't *look* like you're joking.'

'I wish I was,' said Sir Martin. 'No – that is – what I mean is–'

She held up a hand. She wasn't quite as stunned as they'd been, because Edwin had said a few words to prepare the ground rather than just blurting it all out like the earl had done. But he could see that she was still shaken.

Alys paced away from them for a few moments, her eye straying to where the girls were playing in the sunshine just outside the open door. She paused, and Edwin watched the set of her shoulders.

She came back. 'Well, it could be much worse, couldn't it?'

This was better than he had expected. Edwin said nothing, but cast a glance at Sir Martin and saw the tiniest hint of him brightening. 'You're not angry?' the knight asked.

'Of course not. And even if I was, it wouldn't be with you.'

'So…'

'Matilda is an heiress – she was always going to be lady of her manor one day. And she will have no choice but to marry, and to marry whomever the lord earl tells her to. That's her lot in life as a knight's daughter, and we can't avoid it. So: much better you than anyone else.'

'You really think so?' Sir Martin sounded more like himself than at any time today, and Edwin blessed his wife.

'You will always treat her with respect.' It was a statement, not a question – indeed, almost a command – and Alys's voice had taken on a tone that was as authoritative as Sir Geoffrey's own.

'Of course. For her own sake, for yours and Edwin's, and for Sir Geoffrey. And for my own honour, obviously.'

'You will take care of her, protect her, treat her as your equal in rank and intelligence?'

'Yes.' He assumed an unusually formal air and took her hand. 'You have my solemn word on it, as a friend and a knight.'

'Well then.' Alys allowed herself to smile and squeezed his fingers. 'She could do much worse, couldn't she? There are many women of her rank who aren't as lucky as that. And she'll grow up knowing you and knowing her own fate. She'll be able to get used to it – it won't be sprung on her as a disagreeable surprise when she's older, and she won't have to marry a stranger.'

'Well, if you put it like that…'

'I do. Now,' Alys adopted a more familiar, businesslike tone. 'No more of that just at the moment. You'll both need to prepare for your journey. You'll be away at least a week, I would think, so I'd better get to mending that tear in Edwin's spare tunic, and you should go and look out what you'll need.'

She began to usher Sir Martin towards the door, where he would need to step over his future bride. 'Can you find out whether the castle kitchen will supply you both with food to eat on the way, or must I make something up for Edwin?'

The knight paused uncertainly on the threshold, then bent down and scooped Matilda up in his arms. He held her so they were face to face. 'Your father meant more to me than almost anyone else in the world,' he said to her. 'And I promise – I swear it on his life – I will do everything in my power to look after you, forever.'

She didn't like his serious manner and began to squirm, so he crouched to put her safely down again. 'In the meantime, you stay there and play with your sis–' he swallowed the word, then looked up at Edwin and Alys with a look of dawning comprehension. 'I didn't think,' he said, slowly.

'Oh, we've all done it…' began Edwin, but he stopped when he saw that Sir Martin was shaking his head.

'Not that. No, I mean, I only just realised. Don't you see? I'm going to be your brother.'

Edwin was worried about leaving Alys. It was still only two months since her confinement, and she had the girls to look after as well as Robert.

But when he brought the subject up, she was resolute. 'I'll be fine. It's summer and we're all in good health, and I have the spinsters here every day as well as your aunt nearby. You have a duty to your friend as well as your family, and he needs you more than I do just at the moment. Besides, Sir Geoffrey–' her voice wobbled for a moment '–needs to be taken home. And there is nobody more fitted to do that than you.'

She had left unspoken the fact that the earl had ordered him to go, so he wouldn't be able to get out of it anyway, but it was nice to believe that they were both acting of their own free will in the matter.

Edwin left unsaid a thought of his own, which was that he was feeling a little stab of uneasiness about the earl, and what his underlying motives might be. Under normal circumstances he would be brusque, telling Edwin to get the job done as soon as possible and to waste no time getting back, but when Edwin had attended the Sunday Mass in the castle chapel first thing this morning, his lord had seemed strangely relaxed about the whole situation. He had even told Edwin *not* to hurry, and that he and Sir Martin should take as long as they needed. This should have been welcome, but Edwin merely found it suspicious.

There was no point in dwelling on that now, as the sun was well up and it was time to go. Edwin said his goodbyes in the privacy of the cottage and then walked to the church, where a mounted Sir Martin waited. Alongside him was a cart, with Tom standing next to it holding the horse's head. The coffin was already loaded, and with a lump in his throat Edwin saw that Sir Geoffrey's sword and shield had been laid carefully on top of it.

The sergeant nodded at Edwin. 'You've driven before, I know, and he's a fine steady beast for the job.'

'And the roads are good all the way,' replied Edwin, trying not to think too much.

'Aye. From here to the Great North Road; then, after a few miles, off it again and across to Gainsborough. Then Sir Geoff– the manor's a mile or two south of there.'

Edwin put his bag on the driver's seat and then scrambled up beside it. Tom gathered the reins for him but hesitated before handing them over.

'You will… see him home safe, won't you?' He glanced at the back of the cart.

'I will.' Edwin couldn't get any more words out, but Tom understood and nodded as he stepped back. He was not the only hardened garrison man to have been deeply affected by Sir Geoffrey's death, and Edwin thought to himself that this was the best testament to his character that the old warrior could have.

'Ready?' he asked Sir Martin.

'Ready.'

And they were off.

The journey was uneventful, the dual sight of the coffin in the cart and the huge figure – unarmoured but with a sword at his side – riding beside it being enough to engender respect in anyone they passed. They made it more than halfway on the first day, staying in an inn overnight, and it was not much more than mid-afternoon on Monday when they passed through Gainsborough and took the smaller road that led southwards to the manor of Rochford. Oddly, they were now in their third county in two days: they had started in Yorkshire, passed through a part of Nottinghamshire, and were now in Lincolnshire. Edwin fell into something of a daydream as he drove, remembering his visit to Lincoln four years ago and how it had changed his life.

Sir Martin was getting edgy as they drew nearer to their destination. Edwin roused himself from his own thoughts and attempted to make general conversation, to put him at his ease, but the knight's replies became shorter and more clipped. Eventually his tension began to communicate itself to the horse, and Edwin thought he'd better tackle the subject directly.

'You're making him nervous.'

'It's just that he needs to get more used to the way I hold his reins.'

'No it isn't. You told me the other day that he was fine with that now.'

Sir Martin made no reply.

'Do you want to talk about it?'

'Talk about *what*?'

Edwin sighed. 'I'll start, then, shall I? You're apprehensive about arriving at Rochford. Of course you are – who wouldn't be? We're to tell them that their lord – the lord they've all known their whole lives – is dead, and that you'll be taking his place. You, someone they've never met, and you're now responsible for their lives and livelihoods.'

Sir Martin put his heels to Blanchart's flanks and trotted ahead of the cart for a while. Edwin drove on, giving him time.

Eventually the knight halted so Edwin could catch up. 'All right. Yes, some of that. And…'

'And?'

Sir Martin started to say something, stopped, restarted, stopped again, and then took a deep breath. 'I'm worried I'll bring bad luck. To the manor.'

'Why would you do that?'

'Well… you know.'

'I don't think I do.'

'Because I bring it with me everywhere I go. Ill luck, and death.'

This was more serious than Edwin had thought. 'I don't think–'

'Oh, you know I do, and don't pretend otherwise!' There was a mildly aggressive tone in Sir Martin's voice now. 'I've been killing people since the day I was born, deliberately or no, and there's no reason why that should change any time soon.'

Edwin had often wished that Sir Martin would not speak so of his mother's death in childbirth, for it was hardly his fault, but now was not the time to address that. He drove on in silence for some moments while he tried to work out what best to say.

'Well?'

Maybe Sir Martin's tone was more defensive than hostile. Did he need reason, or comfort? Edwin wished Alys were here, with her knack for saying exactly the right thing. 'You know,' he began, carefully, 'that I don't agree with you about death. Yes, people around you have died, but you could say the same about me, or anyone. And I think that on balance you've saved many more lives than you've cost. But–' he forestalled his friend's interruption 'what we need to think about now is the immediate situation. Yes, it will be a shock for everyone there. But, given Sir Geoffrey's age, it can't be *that* much of a surprise to them that he should have gone to God. Even he wasn't going to live forever.'

He risked a glance at Sir Martin, to see how he was taking it in, and thought that he saw the first sign of him relenting. He continued. 'If it's any consolation, I'm sure that after the initial blow has worn off, all will be well.'

'Will it? How?'

'For exactly the reasons Alys spoke about, and because I know you.'

Sir Martin cast him a glance that seemed to beg him for more, for some reassurance, although he couldn't bring himself to say so out loud.

'In a fight, you're terrifying. And people who don't know you can be scared by that, and by what you look like. And, if I may be honest, because you sometimes come across as short-tempered. But I know that when you care for people, you really care for them. Take Adam, for example. Or Hugh. In all the years you've known them, have you *ever* taken your temper out on them? Ever been unjust to them?'

'Well…'

'No, you haven't. And that's because they've been your responsibility to look after. You guide them and protect them. And soon, the people of Rochford will also become your responsibility, just like Adam and Hugh and Wil. And you'll treat them just as fairly, and they'll come to respect you and look up to you just as the boys do.' Edwin paused. 'And just as I do.'

There was silence. Sir Martin turned his face away. Blanchart took a misstep and then recovered.

They had still not resumed their conversation when they splashed across a stream, via the stony ford that gave the place its name, and then they had arrived. They rounded a corner and the main part of the manor of Rochford came into sight.

Edwin's first impression was of order and calm. Fields divided into neat strips basked in the sunshine, with the stream snaking between them and men and boys toiling amid healthy-looking crops. Past them Edwin could see a number of cottages in good repair, thin columns of hearth smoke rising lazily into the sky. A much larger manor house stood separately, with its own barn, stable and outbuildings, and in the distance on the far side of it Edwin could make out what looked like an orchard that gradually transitioned into a wood as the ground rose. It was all as Mother had described it to him after her first visit here, and he felt a pang that neither she nor Sir Geoffrey would ever see this scene of prosperity and tranquillity again. If things had been different, they could have spent their later years here together in happiness.

As Edwin and Sir Martin passed them, some of the men paused in their work. Seeing well-dressed strangers, one of them wearing a sword, they nodded respectfully and touched their hats. Then one of them spotted what the cart was carrying and bent to say something into the ear of a boy, who hared off in the direction of the manor house.

Edwin slowed his horse's pace even further, thinking that it would be better for the steward to be forewarned of their arrival. He was the man who really ran the place; Sir Geoffrey had visited his manor so seldom that he'd needed a trusted old retainer to act for him. If Edwin recalled correctly, the steward was called Aelred, and he must be the elderly man now being urged out of the manor house by the gesticulating boy.

Sir Martin reined in and looked wordlessly at Edwin.

Edwin took pity on him. 'Shall I speak first?'

The knight gave a grateful nod and waited while Edwin overtook him and drove on.

The elderly man came forward to greet them. 'Good day to you, sirs. My name is Aelred, steward of this manor. Whom do I have the honour of addressing?' His gaze slid fearfully to the back of the cart, where the tale told by the coffin, the sword and the shield could hardly have been clearer.

'My name is Edwin,' said Edwin. 'Of Earl William de Warenne's household in Conisbrough. I think you may have met my mother once or twice; she was Sir Geoffrey's wife.'

Despite his anxiety, Aelred's face softened. 'Of course. Such a kind and wise lady. And my master Sir Geoffrey, your stepfather, has also spoken of you.' His eyes turned once again to the coffin.

It would be cruel to delay any longer; the obvious must be said out loud. 'I'm afraid I'm the bearer of sad news,' said Edwin, trying to keep his voice level. 'Sir Geoffrey is dead, and we've been tasked by the lord earl to return his body here for burial.' He scanned around him. 'Although I can't see a church.'

'It's further on, over the rise; we share it with the next manor.' Aelred's shoulders drooped and he gave a heavy sigh. 'I'm deeply grieved, as everyone here will be. He was a good man and a good master, and it's our loss that we didn't see him more often.'

Edwin nodded. 'But Conisbrough's gain.'

'How did it…? But never mind that now. You've no doubt had a trying journey, and there are arrangements to be made.' Aelred moved to the cart to lay a tender hand on the coffin. 'Perhaps we might bring him inside the house for tonight, so his tenants and servants can pay their respects, and then we could take him to the church tomorrow? Or I can have the priest summoned here now?' He paused. 'I can arrange whatever you wish, sir – just let me have your orders. I assume that, as her half-brother, you will be taking over the manor in little Lady Matilda's name, until she is of age?'

Edwin took a deep breath. 'Yes, and no. Yes, please make whatever arrangements you think best, and yes, Matilda is my dear sister. But this is your new lord.' He indicated Sir Martin.

Aelred had been so concerned with talking to Edwin, and with his own shock and sadness, that he hadn't really paid much attention to the second visitor, and he now took a proper look.

Sir Martin, who was as aware as anyone that he tended to loom, dismounted. Unfortunately this had the opposite effect to the one he desired: while he was on Blanchart's back it was just possible that the excess height could be put down to the large horse, but once he was on his feet on the ground it was all too obvious that he was the tallest and most physically intimidating man any of them had ever seen. And although Edwin knew that Sir Martin's current grim expression was because he was nervous, Aelred didn't, and probably mistook it for ill temper or worse.

Still, he recovered and did his duty: Edwin watched as the steward took half a pace backwards without being able to help himself, but then stopped and bowed deeply and with dignity. 'My lord.'

'This is Sir Martin du Bois,' continued Edwin. 'A knight in the service of my lord Earl Warenne, and now betrothed to my sister, your Lady Matilda. He will hold the manor henceforth in her name. We have all the relevant documentation, which I will show you in due course.'

He realised that he probably sounded over-formal, and that Aelred was still in the first turmoil of hearing two sets of unexpected and life-changing news, so he stepped down from the cart and went to stand in between the two others. 'I'm truly happy for you that Rochford will be in such safe h– will have Sir Martin to watch over it.' He paused and then added, more softly, 'All will be well, I promise you.'

There was a moment of silence as the three men looked cautiously at each other, and at the growing group of onlookers.

Edwin waited for Sir Martin to say something.

He didn't.

Aelred, no doubt feeling it wasn't his place to speak to his new lord before he was spoken to, looked at the knight expectantly.

Sir Martin opened his mouth and shut it again.

The silence grew. Edwin rolled his eyes at his friend and wondered if he'd have to kick him.

'Er, yes,' managed Sir Martin. 'Let's go inside, and we can tell you all about it.' He waited for them to move, and it took him a moment to realise that they were waiting for him to go first. He stalked forward and ducked into the doorway.

Edwin expelled a breath. It was going to be a long few days.

Chapter Three

Later that evening, Edwin sat staring into the fire.

Aelred had been apprised of all the details of Sir Geoffrey's death and the subsequent arrangements, and had accepted them all without question. He had also wept. 'I'm sorry,' he whispered to Edwin, trying to hide his tears from Sir Martin, who was on the other side of the hearth and staring through the flames rather than at them. 'But we knew each other all our lives, and – if it doesn't sound too presumptuous – I counted him a friend as well as a master.'

'I can understand that, don't worry,' replied Edwin, keeping his voice low. 'My father was also a great friend of his, despite the difference in their ranks, and it was one of Sir Geoffrey's great strengths that he could see the good in anyone, no matter who they were or where they came from.'

'Yes.'

'My father was called Godric – and, judging by your own name, your family have been here some while.'

Aelred nodded, wiping his eyes. 'Yes, since before the coming of the Normans. The manor itself changed hands, but I understand from the records that many of the lower officials stayed in place. It made sense, I suppose, to keep things running smoothly. My father was the steward here, and my grandfather before him.'

'And will you pass the office on to your own son? Or even a grandson?'

Aelred shook his head sadly. 'To our great regret, my wife and I were never blessed with children. Indeed, I had it in mind to speak to Sir Geoffrey, next time he was here, about beginning the process of finding a successor. Once a good man was in place, we could always retire to the abbey as corrodians; we have enough saved to purchase a lifelong grant of accommodation and food, and would be certain of being accepted, at our age – indeed, they'd make a tidy profit. And we wouldn't want to remain here if we were going to be in the way.'

Edwin leaned forward to touch his arm. 'I'm sure,' he said, 'absolutely as sure as I can be, that Sir Geoffrey would have wanted you to remain here in peace for the rest of your days once you retire, rather than moving to a strange abbey where they don't know you. And I'm equally certain that Sir Martin will say the same. But perhaps you might consider putting that subject off for a little while.'

Aelred sighed. 'Yes, given the present sad circumstances, that would be best for now.' He looked across at Sir Martin, still oblivious to everything around him. 'Our new lord will want time to find his feet, and I would not wish to cause him any more difficulties than necessary.'

'That's good of you,' replied Edwin. 'And I know you're exactly the sort of man he needs. I would imagine that he won't actually spend much of his time here, at least not in the next few years, as the lord earl tends to keep him close by.'

'I can see why.'

'Although, of course, my sister will no doubt come to live here in due course.' Strange to think of Matilda being a grown woman, but it would happen one day, God willing. Sir Martin was already planning for it in one respect: he'd oiled and wrapped Sir Geoffrey's sword and placed it in a kist in the main chamber, saying it was for her when she grew up, so she could pass it on to her own sons.

There was a movement in the shadows behind Aelred, and the steward turned to beckon forward a woman of around his own age. 'My wife, Gundreda.'

Gundreda curtseyed. 'Pleased to meet you, sir. I met your lady mother three times, when she came here to visit.'

Edwin shifted uncomfortably. 'Please, there's no need to call me "sir". My mother's second marriage raised her rank, I know, and my sister will be the lady here, but none of that includes me.'

He invited her to sit, and she moved to perch on the edge of a stool. 'I was wondering if you could tell me more about Lady Matilda,' she said. 'I saw her just once, about a year ago, and she was a beautiful baby then. How has she grown? Is she walking and talking? Does she look like my master, or like your mother?'

Edwin was only too happy to tell them everything they wanted to know, and the old couple sat holding hands and smiling fondly at his anecdotes.

When he eventually ran out of things to say, Aelred spoke again. 'And Lady Matilda is now betrothed to…' he glanced across the fire.

'Yes. And don't be fooled by his demeanour today – he's a good, kind man, and honestly both my wife and I think that Matilda could hardly be luckier. And, although he'll never admit it out loud, he loved Sir Geoffrey as much as anyone and he's missing him a great deal already. It was Sir Geoffrey who brought him up since he was seven years old, not his own family.'

They all looked at Sir Martin in silence for a few moments.

'We'll all do everything we can to serve him and make him welcome,' said Aelred. 'You can be assured of that.'

Gundreda's gaze turned to one of practical appraisal. 'I think we might need to have more meat brought into the kitchen,' she whispered to Aelred. 'He must get hungry, needing to fill a frame that size.' She hesitated. 'Do you think he needs anything now? Should I ask if he wishes for more food or drink? Or if he has any other commands? I don't want him to think we're inattentive, but equally I don't want to disturb him if…' she tailed off, her voice anxious.

Edwin stood up and made his way round the fire, giving Sir Martin a sharp dig in the ribs that nobody else could see. 'Please, try to say something,' he murmured. 'This is difficult for them, too, and they're trying their hardest.'

To his credit, Sir Martin did make an effort to snap out of it, asking a few questions about the manor, though they did tend towards the contents of its stables and its defensive capabilities rather than the crops. But it was a start.

The conversation turned once again to Sir Geoffrey. His coffin had been placed temporarily in the main bedchamber, which lay off the end of the hall, and a long queue of local people had spent the evening waiting patiently to walk past it and say their prayers. After their evening meal – which Aelred and Gundreda had served up with many apologies about its modest nature, not having expected their arrival – Edwin and Sir Martin had stood for some while, watching all the men, women and children who had known and respected Sir Geoffrey, before Sir Martin said, abruptly, 'I wonder how many people would do the same for me if I died,' and turned away. It was after this that he'd sat by the fire and lost himself.

'And, of course, among his other qualities,' Aelred was now saying, 'a fine chess player.' He looked at Sir Martin with a hopeful expression. 'I don't suppose you…'

'Ha!' came the reply, the most animated expression to issue from Sir Martin's lips since his arrival. 'Not me. But if you want to be soundly beaten, here's your man.' He indicated Edwin.

Aelred brightened. 'Really? Sir Geoffrey's own set is packed away, and it would be a little disrespectful to get it out now, but perhaps at some point while you're here…?'

'I would be delighted,' said Edwin. 'I've even brought my own with me; just some home-made pieces and the shape of a board scratched on a piece of leather, so it's easy to roll up and carry, but it does the job whenever I'm away from home. If I can't find an opponent I play both sides myself.' He recalled, with a pang, the beautiful new chessboard and pieces that Sir Geoffrey would never see, and realised that he'd spend much more time playing against himself in the future.

'Do you know what?' said Sir Martin, suddenly. 'I don't think it would be disrespectful at all for you both to play. I think Sir Geoffrey would love the idea of the two of you battling it out, his old friends, thinking of him while you did so. It would be a fitting tribute.'

They were persuaded, unrolling Edwin's travelling board and pieces rather than going into the bedchamber to fetch the other, and Sir Martin was interested enough in the encounter to sit and watch. Aelred was a very good player, a little more cautious than Sir Geoffrey had ever been, but planning his moves further in advance. He was still no match for Edwin, of course, and the result of the game was never in doubt, but Edwin felt that he had been challenged to a greater extent than he had been in years.

When the game was finished, they all sat back and watched the last remains of the candle guttering in its holder.

'Shall I fetch another, my lord?' asked Aelred.

'Not for me,' replied Sir Martin, yawning. 'I'll get to my bed, if you can tell me where it is.'

Gundreda stepped forward from the shadow. 'I've made up beds for you both in the guest chamber, my lord,' she said, twisting her hands together. 'Of course, the main chamber is yours now, but…'

He spoke to her in a firm but gentle tone. 'It's still Sir Geoffrey's until tomorrow. And please: I don't really know how to say this the right way, but you don't need to be frightened of me. I know what I look like and sound like–' he cast a glance at Edwin '–but I will never speak to you unjustly or in anger. You're under my protection now, and that means something to me.' He nodded and walked off towards the chamber at the far end of the hall.

Edwin found that Aelred was now looking at him and the foundering candle. 'I'll turn in as well, and I suggest you do the same; I think we'll have a busy day tomorrow while you show us around.'

Aelred inclined his head. 'I will, in due course, but first I will spend some little time saying my farewells.' He glanced towards the door of the bedchamber, where candles were still burning and one corner of the coffin was visible.

'Of course,' replied Edwin. 'I've already said mine, so I'll leave you to it.' The man had known Sir Geoffrey for more than six decades; he deserved the privacy of saying goodbye with no other witnesses.

Sir Martin was already asleep by the time Edwin entered the guest chamber. Edwin undressed and got into bed, thinking he'd probably lie awake, but before he knew it, the dawn light was beginning to beam round the edge of the shutter.

The first task of the morning was to convey Sir Geoffrey to the local church, where he was laid to rest with all the mourning and dignity he deserved. After the service, Sir Martin reached up to fix the old knight's shield above his grave, where it hung alongside another that was faded but displayed the same device. He made a public promise that he would commission and fund an effigy to lie on the tomb and then, with a final prayer, they left Sir Geoffrey to his eternal rest and stepped out into the daylight.

Sir Martin and Edwin's education about the manor began in earnest in the afternoon. On beginning to understand their different interests and priorities, Aelred showed them both around the grange and its immediate environs, and then deputised the reeve to take Sir Martin to the stable and further out round the fields and boundaries while he himself sat down with Edwin to go through the records and accounts.

Everything was in impeccable order, and Edwin could not suggest a single improvement. Aelred had been doing his duty by Sir Geoffrey in an exemplary fashion, being thrifty and careful with his master's money where necessary, yet spending enough to ensure the health and well-being of all the people, animals and buildings under his care. Moreover, the fact that he had been able to produce all this up-to-date, well-organised material at a moment's notice, even though he had not been expecting a visit, testified to his honesty as well as his efficiency. The only shame was that Aelred's age meant that Sir Martin would not be able to benefit from his wisdom and experience for very long.

They put all the pieces of parchment away with care, and then stood outside in the sunshine while they waited for the others to return. When they did so, Edwin was glad to see that Sir Martin looked cheerful.

He dismissed the reeve with thanks, then strode up to them. 'I'm impressed.'

'Thank you, my lord. That means a great deal to me, and to all of us.'

They chatted for a few moments, and then Sir Martin said, 'You can ask, you know.'

'I beg your pardon, my lord?'

'You're looking at my hand. Don't worry, everyone does.'

Aelred coloured. 'I do apologise for my curiosity, my lord. I didn't realise I was staring. But… perhaps if I ask once, and then I know the truth, I can be of use in stopping any gossip that might arise.'

'In battle,' said Martin, holding up his left arm. He was wearing the false hand today. 'Actually, I should probably have my lord earl draw up a document or something to explain that – where I come from, a missing hand means something very different.'

'My lord?'

'My father's manor is a day or two's journey from here, a couple of miles south of Edwinstowe, in Nottinghamshire. But it sits within the boundary of Sherwood, which is a royal forest.'

'Ah.'

This seemed to communicate to Aelred all that he needed to know. Edwin had heard of the 'forest law' that applied in all those areas of England that were designated royal forest – whether they were full of trees or not – but he didn't know all the details. 'What's that got to do with your hand?'

'Poaching,' said Sir Martin. 'If you're caught killing a deer, or even with blood on your hands in forest territory, the punishment is mutilation.' He stared at the metal hand. 'Do you know, sometimes I could swear I can feel my fingers moving, and it confuses me when they don't. But the point is that if I went there, anyone who saw me – saw this – would assume I was a convicted poacher until they knew otherwise.' He gave half a laugh. 'So it's very fortunate that I have no intention of going there any time soon, if I can help it.'

Edwin wondered if he should change the subject, but Sir Martin continued. 'That reminds me,' he said, 'I got a letter from my father back at Easter – did I tell you at the time? I don't think I did. He was trying to get me to go and see him, something about discussing matters to do with his manor, but my lord was busy so I didn't mention it, and I never got round to replying. I suppose I should write to him anyway now, to tell him about my betrothal, not that he'll be even slightly interested.'

Aelred looked like he might be about to ask a question, but Edwin gave him a tiny shake of the head. The details of his friend's troubled family past did not need to be brought up just now. 'In fact,' Edwin said, returning to the previous topic, 'Sir Martin is being far too modest about his injury. He was wounded in the course of a siege, during which he saved lives at great cost to himself, including those of my wife and our unborn child.' He looked at Aelred and smiled. 'When you're under his protection, you're under his protection.'

Later in the afternoon, Edwin and Sir Martin were strolling about on their own. They paused for a while in the shade of an oak tree near to the house, listening to the bird song and looking out over the neat, prosperous manor shimmering in the hazy summer heat.

Sir Martin expelled a long breath.

'You're doing very well so far,' Edwin assured him.

'Am I? Good.' He paused. 'It's strange – I've only been here a day, and yet–' he stopped again.

'And yet?'

'And – oh, you know me, I can't find the right words. But I already feel like this could be… home? It could be a place that I belong, with a family of my own. A wife, children, friends coming and going, that sort of thing.'

'Good. It is peaceful here, though, isn't it? We're only a day or two from Conisbrough, and yet it feels like a different world. Calm. Timeless, almost.'

Edwin should have *known* that saying such a thing was dangerous, and the retribution was immediate. The tranquillity was broken by the urgent sound of hooves, and a rider came galloping along the road. He didn't see them, shaded as they were by the tree, but they recognised him immediately: it was Turold, the earl's most trusted messenger.

They exchanged a glance, and as they hurried towards the house, where Turold was already dismounting, Edwin wondered what sort of disaster was about to fall on them. The lord earl, the household, Edwin's own family…? Or had the earl somehow changed his mind about bestowing the manor on Sir Martin, just as he had started to like the idea? That would be cruel indeed.

Aelred was pointing them out to Turold, and the messenger came striding towards them. He held out a letter – not to Edwin, but to Sir Martin.

Edwin looked on anxiously as his friend took the parchment. 'It's my father's seal.'

'Yes.' Turold was a little out of breath. 'A man arrived at Conisbrough with it just after dark last night.'

'I suppose this is him reminding me that I haven't replied to the message he sent at Easter.' Sir Martin's tone was one of indifference, and he didn't seem to be in any particular hurry to open the letter.

Turold shook his head. 'He was in a real hurry. He wouldn't have known his way here, so my lord said it would be quicker for me to bring it on to you rather than for us to try to direct him, as I could get here within the day. I don't know what's in it, but I do know it's serious, sorry.'

Sir Martin frowned and stepped away. After a moment's seeming indecision, he broke the seal and sat down, his back to the house wall, so he could hold the parchment steady between his knee and left arm while running the fingers of his hand slowly along the lines of text. He wasn't a good reader, but Edwin forbore from offering to look at it for him. If Sir Martin needed help, he would ask for it.

Edwin watched as his friend's expression grew more and more puzzled. He reached the end of the letter and then started it again, shaking his head.

Eventually he looked up. 'I can't be reading this right.'

'Is something the matter?'

'It's – it just doesn't make sense.'

'Do you want me to look?'

Sir Martin stood. 'It's from my father, and he wants me to come to Woodthorpe – his manor – straight away.'

Edwin moved to stand next to him. 'So, he *is* just reminding you about his last letter? But why the urgency? Is he ill, or in trouble?'

'Well, that's just it.' Sir Martin's tone was exasperated as he waved the parchment in Edwin's face. 'This is from him – him personally, I mean – but then in this bit at the end, he says I need to hurry there as fast as I can, because he's been murdered.'

Chapter Four

'How can this be?' demanded Sir Martin. 'Have I made a mistake?'

Edwin took the proffered letter and read it himself. It did, indeed, ask Sir Martin to come immediately, because his father – referred to as 'I' throughout – had been murdered. Surely this made no sense, for how could a murdered man write a letter?

'Perhaps something slow-acting has happened to him?' asked Edwin, the only idea he could come up with straight away. 'And he knows he's going to die but that hasn't happened yet?'

'A wound? Or poison?' Sir Martin's head jerked. 'Poison would be just like a–' He swore.

In order to give Sir Martin a moment to himself to digest the news, Edwin turned to Turold, who was still standing by. 'Do you know anything else about this?'

Turold shook his head. 'I didn't speak to the messenger – he only saw Brother William and the lord earl. My orders were to bring that to Sir Martin, and to tell you my lord says to go and to take as much time as you need.'

And there was that twinge again. The little nagging feeling. Why was the earl being so even-tempered and tolerant about all of this? It was almost as though he was actively *trying* to make sure that Edwin and Sir Martin stayed away from Conisbrough.

'I'll have to go, I suppose.' Sir Martin's back was still towards them.

Edwin caught the sight tremor in his voice. 'Do you want me to come with you?'

'I… yes.' He turned round. 'I don't understand this. If something has hurt my father badly enough to kill him, why isn't he dead already?

Unless it's all a ruse – just a slight injury and he's using it as an excuse to drag me back.'

'Surely he wouldn't do that. And why does he specifically say he's been murdered? I think there's more to this than meets the eye, but he didn't want to put it in the letter. Otherwise why not say who and how and why he thought he'd been murdered? He wants to tell you, and only you, to your face.'

'Well… all right.' Sir Martin looked at Turold. 'Did the lord earl mention anything about Edwin?'

'Yes, he said that you should both go.'

'Good.' There was a pause, then the knight took a deep breath as he gathered his wits. 'No point setting off now. We'll wait until tomorrow. And you can't ride that horse you were driving on the way here – we'll have to find you something else from somewhere.'

Aelred, who had been standing in silence all the while, cleared his throat.

'Yes?'

'Pardon me, my lord, but this is your manor, and the stable is at your disposal. We can't match what the lord earl has at Conisbrough, of course, but Sir Geoffrey always kept a couple of riding horses here for estate use.'

'Oh yes, of course.' Sir Martin still looked dazed. 'Come and show me now, if you would.' He addressed Turold. 'It's too late for you to set off back, as well. I'll get someone to deal with your horse, and then we'll find you a meal and somewhere to sleep?' His tone rose into a questioning one as he looked at Aelred.

'Of course, my lord.' The steward beckoned to Turold to follow them on their way to the stable.

Edwin grabbed Turold's arm before he could move. 'There's something you're not telling me.'

A conflicted expression came over the other's face. 'I was told not to say.'

'Ah – so there *is* something.'

Turold didn't reply, so Edwin released him and watched as he led his horse away.

Neither Edwin nor Sir Martin slept very well that night, but they did not speak. Edwin knew some of what his friend was fretting about, but it wasn't really his place to start a conversation about it. In between his fitful dozing, therefore, he waited for any opening conversational gambit that might come from the other bed, but none did.

Several other thoughts had come to Edwin during his waking and half-waking, however, and when they were preparing to set off in the morning, he drew Turold to one side. 'The thing you said you weren't allowed to tell me.'

'I told you, I'm under orders not to say.'

'Well, how about if I tell *you*, then?' Edwin was as sure as he could be; it was the most logical conclusion now he'd had time to think it through properly. 'The lord earl has appointed a new castellan for Conisbrough, hasn't he?'

Turold pursed his lips but did not dare nod.

'And it's a man that my lord thought Sir Martin would object to. And possibly that I would, too, though my opinion on the matter is neither here nor there.'

There was no denial.

'So… oh dear. It's Sir Baldwin, isn't it?'

Turold could hold himself in no longer. 'Nobody's happy! Not Tom, not any of the lads, and not even the household officers, because they know what he's like.'

Edwin had to agree. Sir Baldwin was a knight who owed service to the earl, whom Edwin and Sir Martin had encountered during the business at Tickhill two years ago, and a couple of times since. He was impatient, violent and cruel, and couldn't really be a greater contrast to Sir Geoffrey if he'd tried. The thought of him being in charge of all the garrison men, not to mention being the one who trained and effectively brought up the pages and squires…

But what could Edwin do? Turold was gazing at him as though he expected him to come up with an instant solution which would somehow solve the problem. 'If the lord earl has made his decision…' he began. Then he glanced over to where Sir Martin was coming out of the stable. 'Don't say anything to him, please, not now. Go back to Conisbrough and encourage all the men to get used to the situation, if they can. You never know – it might prove better than expected. And if it doesn't, we'll see if there's any room for negotiation when we get back.'

Edwin didn't hold out much hope, but there was one small glimmer: if the earl had felt strongly enough to make sure that Sir Martin was out of the way when he made this announcement, it meant not only that he anticipated an objection, but also that *Sir Martin's objection would have mattered*. Any lesser being who dared to raise his voice in protest would be either ignored or summarily silenced, but the earl knew that he wouldn't be able to do that in Sir Martin's case. The young knight's influence was growing along with his physical skill, and that might well turn out to be useful in the future. And, who knew, maybe he might soon have the life experience in addition to the martial prowess to be considered a fit candidate to step into Sir Geoffrey's shoes. In the meantime, he was almost certain to fly off the handle when he found out, and Edwin had no intention of letting that happen just yet.

'All right,' said Turold, as he mounted. 'Now, if my lord should need to reach you before you come back, you'll be at Woodthorpe in Sherwood Forest? Sir Martin's father's manor?'

'Yes.'

'Good. I know where that is.'

Their way lay together for the first few miles, back through Gainsborough and then as far as the Great North Road, where they bid Turold farewell. Edwin gave him a significant look, to which he replied with a nod as he turned northwards while they went south.

Edwin was surprised at their slow pace, expecting to be hurried along by Sir Martin to make the journey of thirty or so miles in a single day. But they hadn't set off particularly early, Sir Martin having taken time to speak to Aelred about various matters, and even once they were on the way, he seemed in no haste at all. It was a hot day, to be sure, but Edwin suspected that they were stopping to rest and water the horses even more frequently than was actually necessary. They were obliged to sleep a night in a village by the highway – although 'sleep' wasn't exactly the right word for either of them.

The following morning, they turned off the main road and on to the local one that led them towards Edwinstowe and Woodthorpe. The sun beat down, and all of the agitation that Sir Martin had showed on the way to Rochford was back. Indeed, it was worse.

They would be there by the middle of the afternoon, and some of this needed working out before that happened. Edwin had to say something. 'Why don't you tell me about your brothers and sisters?'

'What?'

'Your younger brothers and sisters. I know there a few, because I've heard you mention them, but I don't know their names or how old they are.'

'*Half*-brothers and sisters,' came the reply. 'Same father, different mother.' Then, after a silence, 'To be honest, I couldn't tell you. You know I haven't been there for years. The eldest would be about twelve or thirteen now, I think? The first three are a boy, a girl and a boy, and after that I lose track. Another three or four after that? Or five?'

At least he'd opened his mouth. Perhaps if he kept talking and took his mind off his nerves, it would help? Plus, Edwin having at least some idea of what he was about to walk into would be useful. 'And your stepmother's name is…?'

'Jonilda.' Sir Martin certainly remembered that, but he almost spat the name out on to the road. Then, in a lower voice, 'Perhaps she did it.'

'What?'

'Maybe she killed my father. I wouldn't put it past her.'

Edwin pulled up. 'Stop that, right now.'

Sir Martin reined in likewise, and they faced each other on the road. 'Stop *what*?'

'I know you don't want to go home – or rather, to your father's manor, because I've never heard you call it "home", not once. And I know you don't like your stepmother. But slandering a woman's good name when you know nothing about her is a serious business, and you need to get that under control before you get there. If you accuse her without any evidence or proof, she will have a legal case against you, and I'm sure you don't want to get into all that. So, stop. Besides, think about it – how in the Lord's name would she benefit from your father's death? She's lady of the manor by right of her marriage. If and when he dies, it will go to you.'

'I don't know,' admitted Sir Martin, unable to come up with a proper answer. 'But she'll be up to something, you mark my words. She'll find a way to work against me so she can put her own brats forward.'

He was becoming illogical. Once again Edwin wished that Alys were here to help him deal with the situation, or that he could consult Sir Geoffrey. Was he better off trying to calm Sir Martin down, taking the heat out of his expressions, or would it be preferable to let him work out his rage here and now, before they got to the manor and whatever awaited them there?

Edwin set his horse in motion again. Perhaps it would be easier to talk if they were side by side and both looking at the road ahead, rather than facing off like this. 'Why don't you tell me what you know for sure about Jonilda,' he said, in what he hoped was a neutral tone. 'Then I'll know what to expect when I meet her. What does she look like? How old is she?'

Sir Martin shrugged and stared at Blanchart's ears.

'And she married your father after he was widowed. Sometime after, I assume, given the age gap between you and the others.'

Sir Martin looked away and said nothing.

This wasn't working. Edwin tried a different approach. 'There are two manors, I remember you saying. Next to each other. Your grandfathers held one each, and wanted to unite them by marrying the son of one to the daughter of the other.'

This proved to be a little safer, as it elicited a response. 'Yes. Woodthorpe – that's my father's, where we're going – and then Langley is just a mile further on. They share a church, like the one we saw at Rochford yesterday.'

'And what do they look like, these manors? Are they anything like Rochford? Bigger, smaller? Or is the land of a different type? What do they grow?'

Sir Martin shrugged. 'Not quite the same. And how should I know what they grow? I only lived there until I was seven, remember. After that my father sent me away so he could forget about me and have a new family.'

'That sounds unfair. He got you a place in the lord earl's household! That must have been such an honour.' And it really was, thought Edwin. Actually, how *did* the son of a provincial knight end up being taken on as a page and squire by Earl Warenne, whose other attendants were the sons of earls? He'd never really considered it before, but now he came to think of it, it was a bit odd.

A new idea struck him. 'So, wait. If your father was the heir to one manor and your mother the heiress to the other, then hers should have come to you as soon as she died, shouldn't it? Like Rochford came to Matilda, even though she needs someone to control it for her while she's little.'

'No.'

'Why not? Does your father still control it, in her name or yours? But you're twenty-one now, so surely–'

Sir Martin threw him an exasperated look. 'Because my grandfather is still alive. So, it won't come to me until he dies, and then it will pass directly from him to me because my mother, God rest her, never lived to be mistress of it. Now,' he added, after a pause long enough for him to calm Blanchart, who was beginning to dance, 'can we stop talking about it?'

He did seem to have calmed down a little, so Edwin let the matter drop.

Sometime after noon they reached the town of Edwinstowe, and Edwin was mildly amused to be riding through a place that bore his own name. He wondered if it had once been owned by a man called Edwin, or whether it was named after the old saint, like he was. One thing was for sure, though: they were now within the bounds of the royal forest. Edwin was careful not to stray from the road, or even to go near the edge of it, and if he so much as *saw* a deer, he'd look the other way.

In the middle of town they turned off to the left on to another road, which itself forked after a mile or so. By now the 'forest' was starting to look more like a forest, with open fields giving way to a sprinkling of trees and then a denser wood. The additional shade was certainly welcome, and they paused at the point where the way divided. Edwin took off his hat and used it to wipe the sweat from his forehead. It was a good thing Alys had packed him some spare shirts or he would stink to high heaven within a few days.

'Woodthorpe that way,' said Sir Martin, pointing off to the right. 'And the other road goes to Rufford Abbey.' Both led through areas filled with trees, the Woodthorpe road straight and the Rufford one going round a curve so Edwin couldn't see what lay beyond the first couple of dozen yards.

'An abbey?' he asked, with an interest that wasn't entirely feigned, to keep his friend talking. 'Is it as big as the one at Roche? Benedictine, or Cistercian?'

'Cistercian, I think,' came the reply. 'The ones who wear white.' And then, with a sudden burst of recollection. 'Abbot Geoffrey used to come to our house, sometimes, to talk to my father. And for a while I went there every day to be taught to read and write, but that didn't last long before I was sent away.' He paused. 'He was kind. I wonder if he's still there, and if he'd remember me. And it was funny that I should go from him to a knight who was also called Geoffrey.'

'I'm sure we can find out. But for now, we should get on. Your father's condition might be more urgent than you think, and we don't want to… leave it too late.'

Sir Martin was just agreeing and starting to turn Blanchart's head when they heard the sound of a group approaching from the direction of the abbey. Half a dozen men appeared around the curve of the road: three white-habited monks on mules, two lay brothers, in their brown overgarments, on foot, and one man in sober civilian dress on a horse.

The lead monk, who wore a pectoral cross, saw Edwin and Sir Martin apparently hesitating at the fork in the road. '*Benedicte*, good sirs. Are you in need of directions?'

Sir Martin did not immediately reply, so Edwin returned the greeting. 'Thank you, Brother – or Father? – but we're fine. We're heading for the manor of Woodthorpe.'

'As are we. And yes, it's Father, for I am the Abbot of Rufford.'

'No, you're not.'

Edwin winced, hoping that the words had merely slipped out and that Sir Martin hadn't meant to be quite so ungracious to a churchman they'd just met.

The abbot maintained his composure, even in the light of the startling appearance of the man who had so addressed him. 'I can assure you that I am, my son. My name is Thomas.'

'Where's Abbot Geoffrey?'

Comprehension dawned. 'Ah, you knew my predecessor. I'm afraid that Abbot Geoffrey went to God earlier this year, *requiescat in pace*. It was felt that none of the existing brethren at Rufford were yet of the experience to take over, so I was sent by the Order to become the abbot.'

Sir Martin turned his face away, and Edwin mentally cursed his poor friend's ill luck. Was *everyone* whom he remembered with affection going to end up dead?

'And might I ask,' continued Abbot Thomas, 'why you're riding for Woodthorpe? If you don't know already, I'm sorry to tell you that Sir Richard lies gravely ill.'

'Yes,' said Sir Martin, shortly. 'That's why we're going.'

Edwin felt that he ought to take some action before his friend's rudeness – again, from shock and nervousness, but the abbot wouldn't know that – got out of hand. 'And you're going there yourself, Father? Sir Richard will benefit greatly from your prayers if he's in any danger.'

'And from the earthly ministrations of our infirmarer, Brother Gregory.' He indicated one of the other two choir monks. 'Brother Gregory has attended Sir Richard every day since the… accident.'

'Accident?' broke out Sir Martin. 'What makes you say that? What happened?'

Abbot Thomas paused. 'Perhaps this conversation would be better held once we reach our destination, rather than on the road?'

'Yes,' rushed Edwin, before the knight could open his mouth again. 'Let's get on our way.' He threw his friend a glance that he hoped would be interpreted correctly. 'Shall we?'

They all set off, Sir Martin slightly ahead and Edwin's horse falling into step next to the abbot's mule.

'Is your friend an acquaintance of Sir Richard?' asked the abbot, conversationally. But he continued before Edwin could answer. 'That would explain… anyway, I fear Sir Richard is in dire need of prayers, for his time on earth looks likely to be short. And, of course, it's not only he who needs the Lord's help and support at this difficult time.'

'His wife and children–' began Edwin, as a precursor to explaining who Sir Martin was.

'Yes,' sighed the abbot. 'And particularly Lady Jonilda, who has a hard few years ahead of her. Their eldest son and heir Michael is, as you might know, only a boy, so when he inherits after Sir Richard's sad but inevitable death, she will need to act in his name for a number of years before he comes of age.'

Edwin swallowed and looked forward to Sir Martin, to see if he'd heard.

He had.

He stopped dead, then turned Blanchart round and paced back to the abbot.

The horse towered over the mule, and Sir Martin towered over the abbot, deliberately allowing himself to do so and with a furious expression on his face. '*I* am Sir Richard's eldest son and heir,' he snarled. 'And you would do well to remember it.'

Abbot Thomas registered shock, then astonishment, and his whole party halted in its tracks.

For a few moments Edwin was in terror that Sir Martin, in his current unstable emotional state, was about to resort to violence. He wasn't the only one, either – the one layman accompanying the abbot was looking at Sir Martin with some trepidation. As well he might, if his position was to protect the churchmen. There was a staff tied to his saddle, and he wore a short sword – and therefore probably knew how to use it – but he would be no match at all for the huge knight. And he evidently knew it.

Edwin moved to intervene again. 'You might not have known that, Father Abbot, if you haven't been at Rufford very long, as Sir Martin hasn't been able to visit his family for some time. But he certainly is Sir Richard's son, summoned here now by a letter from his father.'

The abbot turned to Sir Martin. 'Please accept my apologies. It was an honest mistake, I assure you.' He looked shaken.

Edwin moved towards his friend in an attempt to get them all moving again. The abbot murmured something to one of his party, but Edwin only caught the word 'complicated'.

There was no time to think about that now. The important thing was to get to Woodthorpe so Sir Martin could see his father before his condition deteriorated further. The dying man must have the consolation of seeing his son before he passed away.

'You see?' Edwin said under his breath to Sir Martin, as he turned once more in the correct direction. 'An honest mistake. I could see from his face that he was astonished when you told him – he didn't mean any insult to you. He really didn't know.'

'I can accept that,' replied the knight. 'But did he think the brat was my father's heir because he'd assumed it himself, or because it was what *she* told him? She's up to something, I tell you.'

He moved a little ahead, making it clear the conversation was over, and Edwin was forced to examine his own words and actions with a good dose of humility. He'd always considered himself so much clev-erer than Sir Martin, so much better able to see the truth of matters and to interpret what was happening, even when it involved people he'd never met. He'd dismissed his friend's fears as irrational, so sure that he, Edwin, must know better. But he must now seriously consider the possibility that he was wrong, and that Sir Martin had been right all along.

The arrival of so large a party at Woodthorpe could not go unnoticed, and by the time they'd passed the fields and cottages and reached the central yard, bordered on three sides by the manor house, a stable and a barn, a group was waiting outside ready to greet them.

Standing front and centre was a woman who, Edwin assumed, must be Sir Richard's wife, Jonilda. She was younger than he was expecting, and the part of her face visible between the neat headdress and wimple was puffy and swollen with weeping. She held herself erect, however, and her manner was one of dignity. She was flanked by two boys, one who looked to be about ten, and the other two or three years older, just in the first gangling stage of pubescent growth. A clutch of smaller children were behind, along with various household members and servants.

Sir Martin rode up to them, and there was briefly a sight that might have been amusing in other circumstances: all their mouths opened, and their heads simultaneously tipped further and further back as they looked in wonder at the approaching giant on his massive white horse. However, the moment was marred by the two youngest children bursting into tears.

The knight dismounted, ignoring his stepmother's curtsey and the bows that the two elder boys made after a prompt from her. 'My father?'

'He still lives, thank the Lord,' was Jonilda's reply. 'But…' her voice faltered.

'I'll go and see him now.' Sir Martin pushed his reins at the eldest boy and strode inside the house.

There was a moment of silence.

It was eventually broken by Jonilda. 'Father Abbot,' she said, attempting to keep her voice bright. 'How kind of you to come in person. Please, do come inside. Your mounts will be taken care of.' Then she turned to Edwin. 'Excuse me if I'm wrong, sir, but is your name by chance Edwin?'

'It is.' Edwin was in conflict with himself. All his instincts were to be polite and pleasant, to make up for Sir Martin's abruptness and because it was how he'd been brought up to behave, but he was at the same time uneasy and suspicious. She didn't *look* like a murderess or a villain, but he'd been fooled before, and he didn't know enough yet about what was going on to trust anyone.

'We've heard something of you, over the years.' She smiled. 'Please, do come in and take some refreshment.'

Edwin was glad to dismount after having spent the best part of the last week in the saddle; he was much better at riding than he used to be, but he still had his limits. The second boy came to take his reins, and Edwin smiled at him. The children were innocent in all of this, whatever happened. 'Please do take care of your brother's horse,' he said to the eldest, who was still nearby and looking rather overawed at the splendid beast in his charge.

Both boys moved off, together with the lay brothers leading the various mounts that had come from the abbey. Jonilda and the abbot led the way inside, followed by the two other choir monks and then the nurses and children.

The layman stood aside and gestured to Edwin to pass ahead of him, eyeing him curiously at the same time. 'Your name is Edwin, I think I heard?'

'Yes, of the household of my lord Earl Warenne.' As ever, it was too complicated to go into the exact specifics of his status and position, because Edwin still wasn't quite sure of that himself, even after several years. However, experience had taught him that this was adequate shorthand. 'Neither a knight nor a monk, if that was your next question.'

The man smiled. 'A description that could equally be applied to me. I'm Simon of Ollerton, the abbey bailiff.'

They passed through the door. 'A lay position? Oh yes, I suppose it is, even for a monastery.' If Rufford was a Cistercian foundation, like Roche, then it would function in the same way. The bailiff was in charge of law and order on all the abbey estates, which might run to dozens of scattered manors, so he needed to be able to ride about the countryside at will without needing to attend several church services a day.

Edwin looked around him as he entered, gaining his bearings. The frame of the manor house was of great wooden beams, dividing the space into four bays. The two central ones formed the main hall, with benches around the edges and an open hearth in the middle. To his left, separating off the end bay on that side, was a head-high screen that ran the width of the building. There were a couple of openings in it, through which he could see serving men moving back and forth. 'The pantry and buttery,' said Simon, seeing the direction of his gaze. 'And on that side the private parlour.' He pointed to their right, to the wall that partitioned off the final bay on that side. Jonilda and the abbot were just passing through the door in the middle of it, and Edwin caught a glimpse of some finer furniture. 'And I gather there are bedchambers above it,' concluded Simon, 'though of course I've never seen them. Kitchen in a separate building, and the latrines are outside in the yard round the back when you need them.'

Edwin looked about him for a while, smiling vaguely at anyone from the household who looked at him and gazing up at the smoke-blackened beams that Sir Martin must have known when he was a small child. Someone gave him some thirst-quenching weak ale, and he drank gratefully to wash the dust of the road out of his throat. He wasn't quite sure what to do with himself, to be honest, not having been specifically invited to follow into the parlour, so he sat down on one of the hall benches.

Simon took a seat next to him. 'Your news seems to have taken Father Abbot by surprise,' he said. 'He honestly had no idea that Sir Richard had an older son, and his plans were based on – he genuinely thought that young Michael was the heir. Your friend is from a previous marriage, I take it, for a man of his age can hardly be Lady Jonilda's child.'

'Yes.' Edwin was wary. He had no right to be talking about Sir Martin's private business, but he did need to find some balance between saying nothing and getting to know the people around here so he could discover more about what had been going on. 'Tell me,' he began, conversationally, 'what do you know about Sir Richard's accident? His illness?' He would use the same term as the abbot, for now. Bandying around the word *murder* tended to make people nervous and uncommunicative.

'Well, he was shot by an arrow. In the woods, while riding along the road we used today.'

'Shot?' That was a piece of news indeed, and a far cry from any thoughts of poisoning. 'A hunting incident?'

'Could have been, I suppose. Serlo says he didn't know of anyone out that day, but there might have been poachers, or noblemen passing through who didn't bother to tell him.'

'Serlo?'

'The local forester. He works for the sheriff, not Sir Richard or Master Christopher over at Langley, because this is all king's forest.'

'Ah, yes. So, anyone who wants to go out hunting near here has to be entitled to do so, in a royal forest, and is supposed to inform him of what they're doing?'

'That's about the sum of it, yes, although your very important men sometimes hunt without bothering to tell him, and of course he has to spend plenty of time looking out for poachers, too.'

Edwin would have to find out more about forest law. In the meantime, there were more practical matters. 'But tell me, if Sir Richard was shot with an arrow, how is he still alive? It must have been nearly a week ago now.'

'Brother Gregory will be able to tell you more about that.' Simon nodded at the two choir monks, who were seated in silence on a different bench.

The infirmarer heard his name. 'You called me?'

'Can you come and tell Edwin here a bit more about what's happened to Sir Richard?'

'Of course.' The monk made his way over, hands tucked in his sleeves, and accepted Edwin's invitation to sit. 'What would you like to know?'

'Sir Martin is a friend of mine. When he comes out from seeing his father, he'll want to know as much as he can. I thought it might be easier for you to communicate that to me so that I can tell him, even if you have to leave with your abbot before then.'

Brother Gregory inclined his head. 'I was summoned on the morning of the feast of St John the Baptist. Sir Richard had been riding the previous evening and was hit by a stray arrow that pierced his right side, under his ribs, or more likely just striking the last rib, which slowed it down enough not to be immediately fatal. He fell from his horse and was later taken up insensible and brought home.'

'With the arrow still in him?'

'Yes. It was fortunate that nobody tried to remove it by pulling before I arrived, or he would have bled to death.' The monk crossed himself before continuing. 'I examined the wound and determined that the arrow was of the broad, barbed kind. It could therefore not be either pulled back or pushed through safely – for fear of damaging his internal organs further – so I was obliged to offer Sir Richard a stark choice.'

'Which was?'

'If I made an incision to greatly increase the size of the wound and attempted to draw the arrow out with care, there was a very small chance that it might have saved his life. The greater probability was that this would cause copious bleeding and he would die within the hour. His second option was that I would break off only the shaft, to enable him to lie more comfortably, but leave the arrowhead inside him. Death would then be certain, but he would survive at least a week and probably a few days more, given that he was otherwise young and strong.'

'Christ,' came Simon's voice. 'I think I'd have picked the first one, one way or the other.'

'But Sir Richard chose the second,' said Edwin, his mind already at work.

'Yes. He wished to take the time to get his affairs in order, the more so, no doubt, because he was leaving the manor in the hands of a young b–' He pulled himself up short. 'But I should not speculate.'

'And this was already over a week ago.'

'Yes.' The monk spread his arms in a helpless gesture. 'His symptoms have progressed exactly as I explained to him. At first he was in pain but could still talk and take a little bread softened in broth. Then he became short of breath, experienced great sweating, and his jaw began to tighten so he could no longer eat.' The monk hesitated, then continued. 'If I had had the chance, I would have explained to your friend that when he sees his father now, it will look as though he is smiling, which can be disturbing – for it is not a smile but merely the stiffening of his face and the locking of his jaw.'

Edwin had heard of lockjaw, and he knew it was a terrible way to die. He crossed himself.

'I will go and see him again as soon as I am permitted,' continued Brother Gregory, 'but from now on there is little any of us can do, except to try to ease his last days and to pray.'

'How…' Edwin wasn't quite sure how to phrase the question. Best to be direct. 'How much longer will he live?'

'That is in God's hands, but it is my opinion that he will not see another Sunday.'

Today was Thursday. Edwin wondered if he might be permitted to see Sir Richard at some time this evening or tomorrow, before he became unable to communicate. Of course, the knight's own family had a much better right to be with him in these last hours and days, but Sir Richard himself had used the word 'murder', so he would surely want someone to know his suspicions about what had happened to him. He would want justice for himself and for his family, and Edwin would do his best to get it.

'What happened to the part of the arrow that you broke off?' Any physical evidence would be useful.

'I left it in the chamber. Whether or not it remains there, I couldn't say.'

The door to the private parlour swung open, making them all look up. It was Sir Martin, who hadn't stopped to exchange pleasantries with Abbot Thomas or Jonilda on his way. He didn't really pause as he strode through the hall, either, except to say curtly to Edwin, 'He wants to see you.'

'Who? Your father?'

'Who else? Through there and up the stairs.'

'Are you coming back in?'

'No. I'll leave you to it.' Sir Martin muttered something under his breath, which sounded to Edwin like 'I'm going to see my mother,' which couldn't possibly have been right, and then he stalked out.

Edwin rose and made his way to the parlour, where he hovered in the doorway, aware that Sir Martin wouldn't be the only one who was emotional at this point, and reluctant to cause further upset. 'If I may…?'

'Please, come in,' said Jonilda. 'Father Abbot and I have finished speaking, and he's kindly agreed to lead our family in prayers. You go up, and I'll fetch the children down so you and my husband can be undisturbed.' If she thought it odd that the dying Sir Richard should specifically ask to speak with a man he'd never met, she didn't show it.

Edwin followed her up a wooden staircase in the far corner of the parlour, and found himself in a sort of anteroom to the main chamber. It was evidently where the children slept, with palliasses on the floor and a few toys scattered about. Four children were sitting in one corner playing some kind of game, and when they stood to obey Jonilda's summons he could see them properly: two girls quite close in age, probably around eight and seven; a boy a couple of years younger; and a tot who looked perhaps a few months older than Edith and Matilda. Jonilda hurried them all down the stairs, nodding Edwin towards the door to the main bedchamber.

Once he was alone, Edwin peered into the room. It was dark, for the window shutter was closed; the only light was that of the late afternoon sun piercing the gaps around it and the lesser brightness from the doorway where he stood. There was a smell of sickness, of bodily fluids, of infection and despair.

A man lay on his back on the bed. He either heard or sensed that Edwin was there, and with aching slowness he turned his head. Despite the warning Edwin had received from Brother Gregory, it was still a shock to see the fixed rictus of a smile, and for a moment he wanted to draw back to leave the man to suffer in peace without needing to put up with the presence of a stranger. But Sir Richard managed to raise an arm a little way to beckon him in, so he obeyed.

There was a low stool next to the bed, and Edwin sat on it. 'Martin said you wanted to see me.' He corrected himself. '*Sir* Martin, that is. But you must have known that a long time. How proud you must be.'

Sir Richard moved his head in what might have been a nod. Then he made a valiant attempt to force his mouth open. 'You... Edwin?'

'Yes. I came with Sir Martin to bear him company, and because I was worried by your letter.' He hesitated, for the man was so ill, so near death. But perhaps it would give him peace in his last hours to discover the truth. 'You said in your letter that you'd been murdered. Do you think someone did this to you on purpose?'

Another nod. Again, Sir Richard opened his mouth, his neck as well as his jaw straining and stiff now that Edwin was close enough to see. Edwin waited for him to speak, but all that emerged from his mouth was a trail of dribble.

Edwin saw that there was a bowl and cloth on a table near the bed, and he wiped the sick man's mouth and chin. 'I want to help you as best I can,' he said, softly. 'But I don't want to cause you more pain by asking you to talk.'

'All right,' Sir Richard said. 'I'm all...' He couldn't keep his mouth open for any longer and let it snap shut again. Then he pointed to a jug and cup on the table next to the bowl.

'You want a drink? Is this it?' Edwin picked up the jug and sniffed it. There was no smell of herbs or anything he needed to worry about – it appeared to be no more than very well-watered wine. He poured a small measure into the cup, slid one arm behind Sir Richard's neck, and managed to get a little of it through the stiff lips. In moving to replace the cup on the table, he noticed the broken shaft of the arrow lying on the floor under the shuttered window. He picked it up and tucked it into the back of his belt before returning his full attention to the sick man.

'Th– thank.' Sir Richard lay still for a moment and then made a huge effort, forcing his jaw open. 'You...Martin...friend...help.' A pause. 'Help…them…all.'

His head fell back, but his hand grasped Edwin's sleeve with surprising force for a man so ill. 'Danger!'

Chapter Five

Edwin left the bedchamber and went downstairs, leaving Sir Richard in the care of Jonilda and Brother Gregory. The knight had managed to communicate a few words and phrases, but then he'd suffered an appalling spasm, his face setting into a rictus and his back arching so much that Edwin was terrified it would snap.

He'd shouted for help, and they'd arrived together with the abbot, who immediately began to intone the prayers for the dying. Jonilda fell to her knees by the bed and cried as she made ineffective attempts to comfort her husband, while Brother Geoffrey tried to ease the sick man's terrible stiff posture as much as he could.

'I'm afraid this still isn't the end,' he'd said, quietly, to Edwin. 'He might do this for two or three more days before he finally goes to God.'

'Is there nothing we can do? Nothing at all?'

'Once this spasm wears off, and there's a possibility of getting his mouth open again, I can give him a small amount of something towards the pain – but it will not take all of it away, and it will not prevent the progress of the condition.'

Edwin had looked down in sympathy at the agonised man. Thank the Lord that none of the children were here, at least, for the sight would terrify them. Which reminded him… 'I should go and find Sir Martin and tell him of this new development. And of course, I'll pray for Sir Richard.'

'Thank you.' Brother Gregory began to look in the bag that he had slung over one shoulder, extracting a couple of vials.

Edwin couldn't help wondering whether a very large dose of the monk's pain-deadening medication might not be the best idea, given that Sir Richard was certain to die anyway, but doing anything to hasten his end would be a mortal sin – even though it might cut his pain short – so it could not be attempted in case that was the effect. Every day of life was God's gift, and it needed to be treasured: that was what Edwin had always been taught, but in cases such as this, where life was no longer worth living and must shortly end anyway, he could not blame himself for having doubts.

When he reached the bottom of the stairs, the eldest boy was in the parlour. 'Mother told us not to come up,' he said. 'The noises… I sent the others outside.'

Edwin halted. 'That was both wise and kind.' He sifted through his memory for the abbot's words on the road. 'It's Michael, isn't it?'

The boy nodded, his face strained. He looked as though he was trying hard not to cry. 'He's going to die, isn't he?'

There was no point offering false hope. 'Yes, he is.'

'And–' there was a catch in his voice '–what will happen to us then?'

Edwin wished he knew the answer to that question. But much depended not only on Sir Martin, but also on who had killed Sir Richard and why – and whether Edwin could discover those two things. 'Your brother will look after you.'

'Will he?'

Edwin changed the subject. 'Can you tell me where your church is? I'd like to go and pray for your father.' That would also give him some time and quiet in which to mull over what he'd managed to glean from Sir Richard.

'It's about half a mile, in between here and Langley. If you go back to the road you arrived by, and then keep going onwards instead of back towards Edwinstowe, you'll come to it.' He paused. 'Shall I fetch your horse?'

'Thank you, but no, I'll walk. I could do with stretching my legs, and it won't be dark for another couple of hours, so I don't think I can get lost.'

'All right. If anyone asks, I'll say that's where you've gone.'

'Thank you,' said Edwin, again. The lad was trying so hard to be brave. He hoped it would stand him in good stead in the troubles that would shortly engulf the family once Sir Richard actually died.

Edwin made his way out into the hall, found his bag where he'd left it next to one of the benches, and tucked the broken arrow shaft away out of sight. There would be time to examine it properly later.

As he walked towards the church, he considered the few words that Sir Richard had been able to speak to him. After warning him of a danger that he was not able to specify, the sick man had said something about the woods, but it ended in a strange hiss as his mouth twisted and he started to dribble again. After some moments he'd made a huge effort and managed to enunciate '*trust Jonilda*' quite clearly. Then he'd begun a sentence with 'Don't let him take…' before the spasm had hit him and he could say no more as his body stiffened in agony.

It was those last words that occupied Edwin's mind as he walked. Who was 'he', and what shouldn't he be allowed to take?

Perhaps Sir Richard had been able to tell Sir Martin more. Edwin would ask him as soon as he got the chance, preferably out of earshot of anyone else.

That thought led to another as he reached the road. It was only *now* that the lockjaw was preventing Sir Richard from speaking clearly. But he'd been in that bed a week already, during which time he'd been attended by several different people, including his wife. Had he said anything more specific to any of them? If so, what had he told them? And if not, why not? Why would he wait all this time until Sir Martin arrived? Or, indeed, was it Edwin himself he'd been waiting for, having heard about his rather unusual previous experience? They'd all known who he was without him having to introduce himself.

The road lay mainly between open fields, though there was a part where the trees came right up to it, and he paused for a moment to enjoy their shade before continuing. He arrived at the church, a small, tranquil-looking place of some antiquity where the people of both manors had been baptised, married and buried for many generations. The churchyard around it was encircled by a low wall. Edwin opened the gate and made his way up the path, noting in passing that, oddly, one half of the enclosure was neat and well tended, while the other side was overgrown with long grass and weeds.

It was cool inside, and the first thing that caught Edwin's eye was a series of bright wall paintings depicting various saints. There was John the Baptist dressed in animal skins, St Peter with the keys to heaven, St Christopher carrying the Christ child, St Michael the archangel slaying the dragon, St Agnes with her lamb, the Annunciation…

Edwin was so busy gazing at the vivid life on the walls that he failed to notice the church's other occupant, and almost jumped out of his skin when Sir Martin's deep voice suddenly boomed out from right next to him. 'That's why the church is called All Saints.'

Once he'd recovered, Edwin was able to reply. 'I came to pray for your father. He had a nasty seizure of some kind, so I left him with your – with Jonilda and Brother Gregory. I thought the church would be empty, or I wouldn't have disturbed you just now.'

'I told you, didn't I? I came to visit my mother.' Sir Martin pointed to a small transept on the south side, where there were several recumbent effigies.

Edwin hesitated. 'May I?'

His friend nodded and led the way over. He stopped next to the only female figure, a simple yet elegant stone representation of a young woman whose face wore an expression of serene repose. A garland of roses, only a day or two old, lay on her breast.

Edwin stood for a moment. 'What was her name? I don't think you've ever said.'

'Rosceline. Born when the roses were in bloom, my father used to say, and married in the same season.' His voice took on a bitter edge. 'But with not enough years in between the two events.'

Sir Martin's father and mother had been only fifteen and fourteen respectively at the time of their marriage, Edwin knew that, and she had died in childbirth less than a year later. He felt a weight of sorrow for the loss that might have been avoided twenty-one years ago; grief for a girl who had once been young and happy, but who had now been dead much longer than she had ever been alive. He touched the edge of stone slab on which the effigy was lying, and bowed his head.

'It's funny,' continued the knight. 'Whenever I used to think of her, or dream of her, she was always made of stone, like this. Cold, grey stone. But when…' he held up his left arm. 'You know, when *this* happened, I could see her clearly and in colour for the first time in my life. She was real, and she was there with me.'

Edwin shivered as he remembered that dark day.

'Anyway,' continued Sir Martin, turning away and speaking a little too briskly, 'if you want to pray for my father, you should probably do it on the other side.' He pointed to the north transept, where there were more effigies and some smaller slabs laid in the floor. 'Woodthorpe on one side of the church, Langley on the other – that's how it's always been.' He gave a hollow laugh. 'I don't know what they'll do with me when my time comes – they'll have to put me in the middle. Or maybe I'll die overseas and save them the trouble.'

Edwin knelt down next to a flat inlaid slab carved simply with the name AMICE, and tried to pray. But it was difficult to know exactly what he was asking. That Sir Richard would live as long as possible, to put off the day of his family losing him forever? Or that death would come swiftly to spare him further agony? He settled for pleading that the Lord would do whatever He saw fit, but that everyone's pain should be minimised as much as possible and that, whenever Sir Richard's time came, his soul would pass quickly through purgatory and into heaven.

Sir Martin had returned to the figure of his mother, deep in his own thoughts as he stood and stared down at it, and both of them were startled by the sound of footsteps at the main door.

Edwin turned to see a man of middle age. He was dressed in a manner that indicated a decent status, but he was unkempt, his beard bushy and his clothes spotted and wrinkled. He carried a garland of roses. He took a couple of steps into the nave but then halted abruptly as soon as he noticed them.

Sir Martin took half a pace towards him, before speaking in a questioning, almost incredulous tone. 'Grandfather? Is that you?'

The man turned and left without speaking a word.

Edwin waited to see if Sir Martin was going to say anything, or whether he preferred not to talk about it.

There was a pause, and then he heard, in a bitter tone, 'Another one who can't bear to look at me.'

'That was your mother's father?'

'Yes. His name's Christopher. I haven't seen him at all since I was little – since I went away, in fact. Whenever I came back to visit, he was either away or too busy to come over and see me, and I was certainly never invited there. He blames me for killing his daughter, and he's right.'

This was all getting just as complicated as Edwin had feared. But he could leave grandfather Christopher for another day; there were more urgent matters. 'I have to tell you what your father said to me while I was with him. It wasn't much, but he did manage to get across that there was danger. And I think he means to you, or to Jonilda, or possibly the children, not just himself.'

'Jonilda? Danger *to* Jonilda? Not *from* her?'

'The one thing he did say clearly was that I should trust her.'

'Hmm.'

Edwin took a deep breath. 'Will you do something for me?'

'What?'

'When we get back to the house – and we should probably go now, before it gets dark – can you at least *try* to accept them all? The children, at any rate, even though you can't yet bring yourself to like or trust Jonilda. They're completely innocent in all of this, and they're scared. Sir Richard is their father too.'

There was a pause. 'All right. The children. I'll try not to frighten them any further.'

That was a start, at least, and Edwin felt some small measure of relief as they turned to leave the church.

'Oh – that explains something!'

'Sorry?'

Edwin pointed to a painting he hadn't noticed before, because it was directly over the main west door through which they'd entered. It depicted a man on horseback cutting his cloak in two and giving one half to a beggar. 'Saint Martin. I did wonder, once or twice, because your birthday is nowhere near Martinmas.'

'Yes, that's why they gave me my name. He's in the middle there, you see – neither on one side of the church nor the other.'

'Neither Woodthorpe nor Langley, but encompassing both.'

They made their way outside. As Edwin had noticed earlier, the church stood alone, with no presbytery nearby. 'Where does your priest live?'

'There isn't one, or at least there never used to be. The church only serves these two manors, so it doesn't bring in much money and it's not big enough for its own priest. If things are still the same now, then a priest just visits on Sundays and holy days, says Mass and goes away again.'

That went some way towards explaining the shabby churchyard, although Edwin still couldn't work out why only half of it should be that way. And it didn't say much for the spiritual and moral guidance of Woodthorpe or Langley if they didn't have a resident priest to look after them. The idea of Conisbrough without the reassuring form of Father Ignatius was almost unthinkable.

Edwin added this information to his list of matters to ponder as they made their way back along the road, a glorious setting sun lighting their way.

'Come, children, and make your greetings properly to your brother.' It was evening, and the family were gathered in the parlour after their meal. The abbey party had left, Brother Gregory promising to return in the morning, and Sir Richard was mercifully asleep. From the hall came the sounds of trestle tables being put away.

'Half–' began Sir Martin, before a look from Edwin gave him pause. 'Yes. And you can all meet my friend Edwin at the same time.' He sat up straight and made an effort to pay attention, though a smile still seemed to be beyond him.

The children stepped forward in age order as Jonilda introduced them. 'Michael, my eldest, and Gabriel.' The two bigger boys bowed.

'Then Constance and Eleanor,' – two curtseys, the first a little more polished than the second – 'and Jonny.' The smallest boy merely stared at them, sucking his fingers, until his sisters shepherded him away.

'And this,' concluded Jonilda, indicating the tot on her knee, 'is our little Adela.'

Edwin nodded at them all and smiled, but Sir Martin still did not. Instead he looked around in some puzzlement. 'There's one missing, isn't there? Another girl, in between these two in age.' he pointed at Michael and Gabriel. 'She's not married already, is she?'

There was a short silence.

'Your father did write to tell you,' Jonilda said, enunciating her words with care, 'when our dear Amice died, last year.'

Her pain was so palpable that it struck Edwin to the heart, as he thought of her loss and then immediately, with a stab, of his own children. He hadn't heard anything about this before. Sir Martin had never mentioned it – perhaps the letter had gone astray? But one glance now at his friend's mortified face told him that Sir Martin *had* known and that he'd forgotten about it, either momentarily or completely.

How he would react now was an important question, and one that might have a great bearing on the future. Edwin desperately hoped he would go about it the right way, but he couldn't say anything, couldn't give any hints or advice. Sir Martin had to work out for himself what kind of man he was going to be.

'I'm sorry,' he said, simply and with real contrition, and Edwin heaved a silent sigh of relief. 'Truly sorry. I did get Father's letter, and I have no excuse for forgetting such terrible news.' He glanced at Edwin. 'I don't have children of my own, but I have friends who do, and the idea of…' He shook his head.

All the children were now gazing at him mournfully, and being stared at by so many pairs of eyes brought back some of his usual brusqueness. 'Haven't you all got anything better to do?'

Jonilda clapped her hands. 'Yes. To bed, now, all of you. Connie, go and call the nurses in from the hall.' Then she seemed to hesitate and turned to Sir Martin. 'My husband lies in the main chamber, of course, and I stay in there with him, in case he needs anything during the night. It will be yours when… but for now, would you like the antechamber? I should have thought of it earlier, but I can move the children out of there while…'

'No,' replied Sir Martin, shortly, still evidently guilty and irritated with himself. 'No need for that. We can sleep down here, or in the hall. Let them stay where they are.'

She nodded gratefully. There was a general bustle, some being more willing to retire than others, but eventually the children were ushered up the stairs to bed. For a little while there was the sound of footsteps and floorboards creaking, and then silence.

Jonilda spoke to someone in the hall, and in due course, palliasses and blankets were brought into the parlour and made up. Once she'd checked that everything was ready, she turned to them. 'I'll retire now too, if you'll excuse me. He's been asleep for an hour or two, and that's as long as he's been able to manage recently. When he wakes the pain will return, so I'll go and make sure I have Brother Gregory's remedy placed ready.'

Edwin stood politely as she left the room, and then he heard her quiet footsteps above his head.

He and Sir Martin were now alone. The knight leaned back against the wall and stretched his legs out in front of him. He expelled a long breath. 'That was some day.'

Edwin nodded, wondering which of the many subjects on his mind to bring up first.

Sir Martin pre-empted him. 'So, my father told you there was danger?'

'Yes, but he wasn't able to give me any more details. Then he said "trust Jonilda", like I told you, and also "don't let him take…", and then he had to stop because he had that spasm.'

'Don't let him take?' repeated Sir Martin. 'Don't let who take what?'

'I don't know. But I'll try to find out. What did he say to you?'

'None of it was very clear. But he used the word "protect" a lot.'

'He must have meant that you should protect your family, surely. Your younger brothers and sisters.'

'*Half*–' Even in the poor light from the couple of tallow lamps that were still burning, Sir Martin could see the look on Edwin's face.

'They are to you,' said Edwin, softly, 'what Matilda is to me.'

'I… I never thought of that.' There was a moment's silence. 'And I shouldn't have forgotten about the girl. Amice. I do remember seeing her a few times when she was little. A pretty, happy little thing.'

'She was young and innocent, and I'm sure she'll be in God's grace now.'

'Perhaps Sir Geoffrey and Sir Roger will look after her, if they see her in heaven.' Sir Martin sighed. 'And my father will be there with her soon enough. But,' he added, sitting up a little straighter, 'we need to find out how this all happened. It doesn't seem to have been an accident, and something isn't right.'

'I agree. Tomorrow I think I should find out exactly where and how he was found, to see if that can give us any further information.'

'I'll come with you.'

Edwin shook his head. 'You'd be better staying here. Your father's health is deteriorating so badly that you might be called to his side at any moment, and your *family*,' he laid the slightest of emphasis on the word, 'will need you here. I'm sure a man can be spared to take me.'

'All right. And I can talk to a few people about the place while I'm here, to see what they know. And maybe see if I can speak to my fath–' he broke off and raised his hand to his face. A half-choked sob escaped him. 'Sorry.'

There were many other matters Edwin would like to discuss, questions he wanted to ask, which only Sir Martin or others close to Sir Richard could answer, but now was not the time. 'Let's turn in. Tomorrow will be a new day, and we can start to face things properly then.'

To Edwin's surprise, Sir Martin fell into a deep sleep almost immediately, and he eventually dozed off himself to the accompaniment of snores from beside him and muffled weeping from above.

'I can show you where,' said Michael.

Edwin looked at Jonilda for her permission. 'Yes,' she said. 'Why don't you take Michael and Gabriel with you? They know the surrounding area as well as anyone, and it will do them good to get away from…' her eyes slid upwards.

Sir Richard had experienced two more spasms that morning already, the second of them so severe that Sir Martin had to be called to hold him down, in case the straining and rigid form fell off the bed and he hurt himself even further. The children were cowed, the two elder girls crying while they tried to amuse the little ones, and Jonilda had dark circles under her eyes.

'Shall I fetch your horse?' asked Michael, already halfway out of the door.

'No, it would be better to walk,' said Edwin, watching the boy's face fall. 'I might want to look carefully at the ground.'

Sir Martin stepped outside with them. 'Be careful,' he rumbled down into Edwin's ear.

'I will,' Edwin replied. 'But I don't think I'm in any danger. There haven't been any attacks in the week since your father was shot, so I hardly think his assailant is still in the woods.' *And besides*, he thought to himself, *if there was another target, it wouldn't be me*. Nobody in their right mind would attack Sir Martin at close quarters, but even he was at risk from an arrow coming out of nowhere – indeed, more so than most people, as he was such an obvious target. This was the second, unspoken, reason why Edwin had wanted the knight to stay close to the house rather than coming to the woods. The yards and fields around the building offered a great deal of open space, with many people coming and going, so there was virtually nowhere a stranger could hide without being noticed. Or, indeed, an archer who wasn't necessarily a stranger, for Edwin was ruling nothing out as yet.

Edwin fetched the broken arrow shaft from his bag and followed Michael and Gabriel to the road that led through the manor, taking it in the direction of Edwinstowe and Rufford Abbey. Men and boys were at work in the fields, and some of them paused to watch their lord's sons walk past in the company of a man they didn't know.

One, carrying a staff, touched his hat and addressed Michael. 'Begging your pardon, but how is Sir Richard today?'

'He's no better.'

The boy's reply was curt, but only because he was upset, and the man's face softened. 'Well, God speed his rest and bless you and your brothers and sisters and your mother.' As he spoke, he looked curiously at Edwin.

'This is Dominic, our reeve,' explained Michael. 'And this is Edwin, a friend of my brother's.'

Edwin nodded by way of greeting.

'Farolf!' shouted the reeve, rather unexpectedly. 'Just because I'm talking, it's no excuse to try sneaking off!'

Edwin looked past him. Most of the men had already begun work again, their pause only momentary, but one shabby-looking fellow was sidling away. He now returned, a sulky look on his face, and muttered something about the reeve having eyes in the back of his head.

'Aye, and I need them, and all,' said Dominic, before turning back to Edwin. 'Your pardon. We saw you both arriving yesterday. I remember Martin from when we were littl'uns – we used to run wild and spend whole afternoons jumping in the hay barn whenever we could get away with it. Tell me, is it true he's a knight now? And he serves some great man?'

'He is and he does,' replied Edwin, watching the reeve's face break into a smile.

'Well, good for him. And he'll be a fine lord when…' he tailed off, looking at the boys. 'Anyway, must get back to work.' Dominic touched his hat again and returned to the men, poking the reluctant Farolf back into line with his staff.

They set off again. As he walked in the sunshine and got further from the house and its troubles, Michael relaxed a little and became more talkative, pointing out landmarks of interest in a voice that was just beginning to crack and waver between high and low, and asking a stream of questions about Sir Martin's fine horse.

Gabriel said nothing at all, until he suddenly announced, 'One thousand.'

Edwin paused. 'I beg your pardon?'

'One thousand paces. That's how far we've walked so far – I counted. And it's brought us exactly to the edge of the manor.' He pointed at the large boundary stone lying by the side of the road.

'That worked out neatly, then.'

Gabriel screwed up his face. 'But it's not always a thousand, not exactly. The last few times I've counted, it was between nine hundred and eighty-seven, and one thousand and ten. And yet the stone hasn't moved.'

Edwin was amused. 'Possibly that's because your paces are not always of identical length. The distance hasn't changed, but your unit of measurement is not uniform.'

'Of course!' Gabriel gave a little skip. 'Why didn't I think of that?'

'Always ask yourself – what's the most logical explanation? In this case, is it more likely that your pacing or the location of the stone is more consistent?' Gabriel nodded wisely, and they resumed their walk. 'So, you like counting, do you?' continued Edwin. 'And can you add up and take away, as well?'

'Of course. Much better than Michael can, and he's three years older than me.'

Michael immediately moved to reassert his seniority. 'Well, I can run faster than you, and ride and shoot better, too.'

Gabriel refused to be drawn. 'Who cares? I don't want to do any of those things anyway.'

'Tell me,' said Edwin, cutting off Michael before he could retort again, 'if I had sixty-five loaves of bread, and twenty-seven were eaten, how many would I have left?'

Gabriel looked at him in astonishment at being asked so simple a question. 'Thirty-eight, obviously.' His tone was derisive.

'Ah, I see that was too easy. All right, I have one pound, twelve shillings and sixpence. I spend seventeen shillings and fourpence–'

'Fifteen shillings and twopence,' rapped out Gabriel, before Edwin had even finished his question.

'And then I divide what is left equally with three friends?'

'You'd have three shillings, ninepence ha'penny each.'

Edwin was startled, and he began to ask Gabriel accounting questions of increasing complexity. By the time they'd gone another two hundred yards, he was forced to admit that for the first time in his life he'd come across someone who could reckon even as quickly as he could himself. He wondered whether baby Robert would inherit this skill as he grew older, and whether – if he and Alys were blessed with further sons – they would be as different from each other as Michael and Gabriel seemed to be.

'We're here,' announced Michael, who had swiftly descended into boredom and outpaced them, kicking at loose stones. He now stood in the middle of the road about a dozen yards ahead, and Edwin moved to catch up.

They were in the shade of a wooded area and could not be seen from the fields they'd left behind. 'This is the exact spot where your father was found?'

'Yes. He was lying on the floor like this.' Michael lay down flat on his back with his arms splayed. 'The men thought,' he said, from the ground, 'that he'd been hit by the arrow and then fell off his horse.'

'That would make sense.' This tied in with what Brother Gregory had already told Edwin, and he had no reason to doubt it. 'Which means that he didn't move after being wounded, so he was also exactly here when the arrow hit him. Now, you get up again, and you can both help me.'

'If I'd been here,' said Michael, belligerently, as he scrambled to his feet, 'I'd have found who did it and fought him.'

'But you can't do that now,' pointed out Gabriel, 'because he's not here any more and we don't know who he was.'

'No, we don't,' said Edwin. 'But we're going to try to find out a bit more about what happened.'

'How?' They both spoke in unison, something Edwin was already beginning to suspect didn't happen very often.

'By being logical. Now, do you know whether he was riding out from the manor, or back to it?'

'Back,' said Michael. 'He'd been at the abbey.'

'Good. So, he would have been facing in this direction.' Edwin turned round. 'And he was shot on his right side, so the arrow must have come from down there, not up that way.' To his right, the ground sloped away, while to his left there was a slight rise; this fitted with the knowledge that the arrow had come up under Sir Richard's ribs, not down into his torso from above. 'The shooter was to his right, and lower down.'

Michael came to stand next to Edwin. 'But how will we know how far away he was?'

Gabriel looked thoughtful. 'An arrow has to come in a straight line. So he must have been somewhere where there are no trees in between where he was and where Father was.'

'Correct,' replied Edwin. 'Well done. Now,' he turned to Michael, 'if you need to shoot an arrow a long way, how do you aim?'

Michael mimed shooting up into the air at a raised angle.

'But if our assailant had done that, the arrow would have been falling down when it hit your father. But it wasn't.'

'Which means,' said Gabriel, frowning, 'that whoever shot the arrow must have been close enough so that he didn't have to aim upwards?'

'Exactly. Now, Michael, how far away would you say that would be?'

'Depends on what sort of bow he had, and how powerful it was. Father's bow will shoot a lot further than mine.'

'Hmm.' Edwin looked about him. 'All right, we'll do a test. Gabriel, you climb up on to my back and pretend you're riding a horse.

You won't be quite high enough, but it will have to do. Michael, you pick a path over in that direction and find somewhere where you've got a clear line of sight up to Gabriel. And don't forget, our bowman was aiming at quite a small, moving target, so he'd have to be close enough to be confident of not missing, as well as being able to shoot straight. He'd only have one shot, because if your father heard or saw an arrow passing close to him, he'd ride off quickly.'

Gabriel clambered up, and Edwin stood watching as Michael picked his way through the undergrowth. He paused a couple of times, looking back, but each time there was a tree trunk or branch in his eyeline.

He moved another half a dozen paces and then appeared to get a few inches shorter as he stepped into a hollow. There he paused and looked back, miming again the shooting of an arrow. 'Somewhere around here, I think.'

Edwin put Gabriel down, and they both went to join Michael. 'Careful now,' he cautioned. 'We need to look closely, and not trample over everything.'

They all crouched. 'What are we looking for?' asked Gabriel.

'Any sign that a man might have stood here for some while.'

'Like that?' Despite the recent warm weather, the bottom of this shaded hollow was still damp, and Michael pointed to what were unmistakeably footprints.

'Exactly like that,' said Edwin, satisfied. 'I think we've hit on just the place, so well done.'

'But there are so many prints,' said Michael. 'I don't understand – was there more than one man here?'

Edwin opened his mouth to reply, but was forestalled by Gabriel, who held up a hand. 'No,' he said. He looked up at Edwin. 'What is more logical? That many men were here, or that it was one man who moved around and made lots of prints?'

'Very good.'

'So,' continued Michael, 'it was like hunting. If you're after deer, you stand very quietly, and you might be in one place for a long time until you see one.' His face was puzzled. 'So, someone was out to shoot deer and his arrow hit Father by mistake?'

Edwin shook his head. He didn't really want to break it to them, but eventually they would have to know. 'I think it's unlikely that anyone could mistake a man on horseback, in clear sight on the road, for a deer. Or that he wouldn't have seen your father in his eyeline even if he was shooting at a deer on the other side of the road.'

Michael nodded, though he still didn't look like he'd quite grasped the implications.

Gabriel was quicker. 'Which means that whoever shot Father must have done it on purpose.' His face took on a horrified expression. 'Why would anyone want to do that? I don't understand.'

'Neither do I,' said Edwin, 'Not yet. But I'll work as hard as I can to find the answer to that question.'

He stood up while the two boys remained crouching, looking at the muddied footprints. The only useful piece of information that could be gleaned from them was that the assailant was a man with feet that were around average size, which didn't help much – Edwin could hardly imagine that a woman or child could have shot the fatal arrow.

'Stop right where you are,' came a sudden voice from behind him. 'Move your hands away from your body and drop any knife you might be holding. Don't even think about taking a step, or I'll shoot you dead where you stand.'

Chapter Six

Slowly, Edwin held his arms out to his sides. 'I mean you no harm!' he called out. 'I'm going to turn round so that I can see you, but I will make no other move.'

His main concern was protecting the boys. Should he tell them to remain hidden, in the hope that this man, whoever he was, wouldn't see them? Or would that make it worse if he did spot them and realised that Edwin had deceived him?

Edwin inched his way round so that he faced the man. He was standing at the edge of the road, quite difficult to see in the dappled light due to the subdued natural colour of his clothes, but what *was* obvious was that he was holding a bow, and that there was an arrow already nocked on the string. He looked competent and would be able to draw and loose before Edwin had moved two yards, so Edwin made very sure to stand completely still.

'Who are you?' he called, hoping to get some kind of conversation going that would last long enough for him to work out what to do.

'I'll ask the questions,' came the reply. 'Who are *you*? And what are you doing in these woods, off the road?'

'Serlo!' Michael called out, and he and Gabriel both erupted out of the undergrowth.

Edwin couldn't avoid letting out a yelp, but on hearing and seeing them, the man lowered his bow. 'Michael, Gabriel. What in the Lord's name are you doing there? I could have killed you.'

Edwin couldn't help wondering if Serlo was generally in the habit of shooting before he'd checked who he was aiming at. But that line of thinking could wait; for now he needed to focus on the immediate situation. As he and the boys made their way back to the road, he recalled where he'd heard the name – this was the forester, the official who patrolled on behalf of the sheriff and the king, owing no allegiance to any of the local landowners.

'You know you're not supposed to stray from the road once you're off your own manor lands,' began Serlo to the boys, in a hectoring tone, as soon as they reached him. 'Show me your hands.'

They both obligingly held out their hands, turning them over so he could see front and back.

'All right,' said Serlo, grudgingly. He noticed Edwin's puzzlement. 'Not from round here, are you? Being caught with bloody hands is an offence against forest law even if there's no deer to be seen.'

'I can explain what we were doing,' said Edwin. 'Michael and Gabriel were just following my instructions.'

'Oho, your instructions, was it? Giving orders to the sons of the lord of the manor? And just who do you think you are?'

Edwin very rarely pulled rank, because he didn't like it, and he preferred to be respected for what he did rather than who he worked for. But sometimes it was the quickest way to deal with another man's truculence, and the fact that this fellow's first reaction on seeing him had been to threaten to shoot him dead did not exactly endear him. 'My name is Edwin of Conisbrough,' he snapped, 'and I'm a member of the personal household of Earl William de Warenne. The king's cousin,' he added, for good measure. 'I've been sent here to enquire into the circumstances of Sir Richard's death, and I expect full co-operation from everyone I meet, including you.'

Serlo's eyes widened as he took in this level of eminence. 'Of course, sir, of course. And I work for the law, too, so I can – but wait… Sir Richard's *death*? Is he…?'

'He was still alive when we left the house this morning, but I'm afraid his remaining life can be measured only in days, if not hours.' Edwin heard a sniff from where Gabriel stood beside him, and saw Michael reach out to put a comforting, albeit shaking, hand on his younger brother's shoulder. He was glad now that they were already aware of the criminal possibilities, because it meant they wouldn't be quite so shocked by what he said next. 'I have reason to believe that what happened to Sir Richard wasn't an accident.'

Edwin watched carefully as Serlo's face assumed an expression of shock. But was his seeming surprise because this was a new idea to him, or was it that he was terrified he'd be caught? A forester, who knew the woods better than anyone, who had every excuse to be out there at any time of day or night – and who carried a bow.

But then again, said the dry, rational part of Edwin's mind, what possible reason could Serlo have for wanting to harm Sir Richard? Some old words of his own father's came back to Edwin: *Think not just of who and how, but also why*. And until he could find that crucial *why*, and some kind of proof against anybody, his suspicions were just that.

'I'll have to inform the sheriff,' said Serlo, uncertainly.

Edwin dredged the depths of his memory. Nottinghamshire didn't have its own sheriff; it was all rolled up into one position, High Sheriff of Nottinghamshire, Derbyshire and the Royal Forests. A man with such wide-ranging responsibilities would have little time for the plausibly accidental death of one minor lord, but he would probably send a deputy just to show that he was doing his duty. Edwin felt sure he could deal with such a man, if he arrived; the two of them might even be able to collaborate.

Looking at the forester, with a quiver of arrows hanging at his side, gave Edwin an idea, and he pulled the broken arrow shaft from his belt. 'Can you tell me anything about this? Who it might have belonged to, who might have made it? Is it distinctive in any way?'

Serlo took it from him. 'Is this…?'

'Just answer the question, please.'

The forester examined the fletching, much keener to help now he had an idea of Edwin's status, and interested in a subject he knew well. But then he shook his head. 'You won't find out much from this, I'm afraid,' he said. 'It's from the fletcher over in Edwinstowe – his standard fare. He turns them out by the dozen.'

'How can you tell?'

Serlo began a lecture on the precise way in which the local fletcher cut the nock in the end of the arrow, the type of glue he used and his manner of winding thread around the feathers to keep them in the right place. 'You'll find arrows exactly like this in every sheaf for miles around,' he concluded. 'The only real difference is if someone's mended his own. Look.' He extracted an arrow from his quiver and pointed. 'See? A nick got taken out of the cock feather here, but I wasn't going to go all the way back just for a repair, and I didn't want to lose the whole arrow, so I cut out the damaged part, made a replacement by snipping a bit out of a spare feather, and fixed it in.'

Edwin looked: the repair had been so well done that it was almost invisible, but when he examined it closely he could see that there was a small difference in the shade of the new piece of feather, and an extra thread had been wound round it to keep it in place.

Serlo returned the broken shaft of the arrow that had hit Sir Richard. 'There's nothing like that on here, nothing to make it different. The only thing I could say is it's neither ancient nor brand new, but it could have been made any time more than a few weeks ago, in the last two or three years. And, like I say, he turns them out by the dozen.'

So there was no point in travelling to see this fletcher, thought Edwin, in disappointment, to see if he could identify the man to whom he had sold this particular arrow.

'What sort of head did it have?' asked Serlo.

'A broadhead, Brother Gregory said.'

The forester nodded. 'Most of them are, round here. If you're from an earl's household, you've probably seen a lot of bodkins – the long, thin heads. But they're for war, for shooting at men wearing mail, and we don't have a lot of call for that round here.'

'We've got some bodkins in our stores,' volunteered Michael.

'Well, I suppose that's in case you ever need to defend your manor. Most of us just use our arrows for shooting at animals, so broadheads are better.'

'But I thought that was against forest law?' asked Edwin.

Serlo was about to make a curt retort, probably about Edwin's ignorance, but he managed to swallow it. 'No local man can shoot in these woods – the venison here is for the king and for any of the great men of the land passing through, although even they have to alert a forester to what they're doing. But on his own manor a man may shoot game or give his tenants permission to do so.'

'Dominic's teaching us,' interjected Gabriel. 'Michael and me. Father lets him go out with a bow because he can trust him to hunt game on the manor for our table and not keep any back for himself. He brings it to the kitchen.'

'I've bagged a few rabbits and hares myself,' added Michael. 'We're allowed, especially when the crops are young, because otherwise they can dig up the seedlings and eat them.'

'He's better than me.' Gabriel sounded completely unconcerned by this fact as he turned to his brother. 'You got that duck a while ago, remember? Even though it was flying. And we ate it for our dinner the next day.'

Michael puffed out his chest.

'So long as you and the quarry are both inside your own boundary,' Serlo couldn't help repeating. 'And not one pace outside it.'

Before any reply could be made, a steady rhythm of hoofbeats could be heard, and they all looked along the road. Simon, the abbey's bailiff, came into view, and he reined in when he saw the group. 'Is everything all right?'

'He says what happened to Sir Richard wasn't an accident.' Serlo was eager to give the big news as he jerked his thumb at Edwin. 'And he's someone quite important,' he added, in a rasping whisper that Edwin could hear perfectly. 'Best stay on the right side of him.'

The bailiff nodded slowly. 'I did wonder, when you were asking questions yesterday. So, if Sir Richard dies…'

'It will be murder,' confirmed Edwin. He was all too aware of the boys still standing next to him, who should be spared the worst of all this, if possible. 'But perhaps here and now is not the time to discuss the matter. We'll return to Woodthorpe – is that where you're heading?'

'No, but I need to pass through both Woodthorpe and Langley to get to where I'm going.'

'Well, perhaps we can travel part of the way together.' Edwin looked around to say farewell to Serlo, only to find that the forester had vanished.

'Indeed.' Simon dismounted to lead his horse.

'You're on your way to a manor owned by the abbey?' asked Edwin, thinking it would be better for the boys if he avoided the subjects of death and murder until he could discuss them out of their earshot.

'Yes. All of this area is king's forest, as you know, but only the woods are under direct control. The manors within the forest are each under their own lord's jurisdiction – although in fact all those for ten miles around belong to the abbey, except for Woodthorpe and Langley.'

'You must spend a great deal of time on horseback.'

'That's true. Though I must admit – shockingly for an abbey man, I know – that I prefer that to the endless church services.'

Edwin saw Michael attempting to suppress a smirk. 'Do you live at the abbey?'

'Not in the abbey itself, no, though my cottage is on abbey land.'

Edwin walked on in silence for some moments. All the manors for ten miles around belonged to the abbey, except for the two he was most concerned with. An island of independence in a sea of Church jurisdiction. Might this be relevant? And he had questions about exactly what was, and was not, permissible in different places. 'I must learn more about forest law,' he said, eventually.

'There's some parchments in the parlour at home,' broke in Gabriel. 'Can I read them with you?'

'It would certainly be very useful if you could show them to me,' replied Edwin, 'so I can–' He broke off as he became aware of a rustling sound from the nearby undergrowth that didn't sound completely natural.

Simon had heard it too, and now paused with one hand on his sword. 'Nothing to worry about, I'm sure,' he said, for the benefit of the boys. 'Just a deer or a hare.' He exchanged a glance with Edwin, and then untied his staff from where it lay along the horse's flank and passed it over. It was more a badge of office than anything else, like the reeve's, but it would do as a weapon in an emergency. *Although only if we're attacked in person*, thought Edwin. *It won't be much use in fending off an arrow.*

They set off again, at a slightly faster pace.

It wasn't long before they were safely out of the woods and back to the manor boundary in bright sunlight, much to Edwin's relief. The workers were all going about their business in peace, the only difference from earlier being that the reeve had moved along one field to organise another group of men.

They halted. 'Another time, when we've leisure,' said Simon to Michael, 'I'll come out with you while you ride one of your father's horses. The practice will do you good, and we can go for a good gallop.'

'Really?'

'You have my word, if your lady mother will allow it. And I'm sure she will – you're old enough not to be babied. I'd be willing to wager your big brother didn't get where he is today by being a milksop.'

Seeing how this cheered the boy, Edwin added, 'and at some point today, Sir Martin will either want to ride, or at least to check on Blanchart, his own horse. If you ask nicely, he might let you watch or even groom him yourself.'

'That would be wonderful,' breathed Michael. 'I've never even *seen* a horse as fine as that before.' His face fell. 'But I don't suppose he'll let me.'

'We'll see. Now, off you go, both of you. I'll catch you up in a few moments.'

'I'll look out the parchments!' cried Gabriel, excitedly, as they ran off towards the house.

They would be safe now, thought Edwin. Or as safe as they might be, given the present circumstances.

He turned to Simon and handed back the staff. 'A deer or a hare?'

'Or a forester or a poacher,' came the reply. 'But in any case, it might be wise if you and they didn't go out into the woods without an escort. Especially if your suspicions about what happened to Sir Richard are true.'

'I'll go back to the house now. But when you return to the abbey later, perhaps you'd be kind enough to tell Abbot Thomas that Sir Richard's time is short.'

'I think he was already planning to visit this afternoon,' said Simon, 'or so Brother Gregory said when I saw him first thing. But yes, of course, I'll pass that message on.' He hesitated. 'And… my best wishes to Sir Richard and Lady Jonilda. This can't be easy for anyone. I'll call in myself later, to see if there's anything at all I can do.'

Simon nodded and rode off, leaving Edwin to make his way back to the house. There, the strain was evident. Unhappy people went about their business as quietly as possible, those outside stopping every so often to cast fearful glances up at the shuttered window, while those inside looked in trepidation at the parlour door.

Sir Martin was just making his way down the stairs as Edwin entered the parlour. He put a finger to his lips, then pointed upwards and whispered, 'He's asleep. And he was completely beyond speech even when he was awake.'

'Sleep is the best thing for him,' breathed Edwin. 'At least he can't feel the pain.' He glanced over at Michael and Gabriel, in the far corner of the room and seemingly frozen in Sir Martin's presence. 'Listen,' he said, still keeping his voice very low. 'Gabriel needs to show me some parchments about various things, but we can do that very quietly, and I can ask him some questions at the same time. You could do the same with Michael, if you took him with you to the stable. Get him talking about horses, and then slip in some other questions to see if he knows anything about what's been going on recently?'

He felt his friend tense at the very idea of being alone with one of his relatives, especially the one who might be considered the nearest thing to a rival, but he didn't issue an outright negative, and Edwin hoped he wouldn't see through the ruse. If a family reunion were to be brought about, it needed to be done one step at a time.

After some moments Sir Martin's bunched muscles relaxed a little. 'All right. It'll get him out from under your feet, at least, and it'll be useful to see if he knows anything. He's old enough to be in league with his mother, you know.'

He cleared his throat and addressed the boys. 'If Father or anyone else needs me, I'll be in the stable.' Then, to Michael, 'Perhaps you'd better come and show me where everything's kept.' He walked out without waiting for a reply.

Edwin grabbed Michael's arm as he was passing. 'He's not as terrifying as he looks,' he whispered. 'Just talk about horses and you'll be fine.'

Once he and Gabriel were alone in the room, the boy went over to a kist in the corner and began to pull out handfuls of parchment. 'Careful!' cautioned Edwin, remembering to keep his voice low. 'They'll be filed in order.'

Gabriel looked down at the sheaf he was holding and then peered into the kist. 'I'm not sure they are.'

Edwin went over, looked at the mess of manuscripts and sighed. 'Oh well. We can sort them out as we go.' Between them they moved a table over to the window, in order to catch the best of the light, and began.

To start with, Edwin sorted the parchments into rough categories. Anything that resembled a private letter he put to one side without opening; that was not his business. The rest was a confused muddle of financial accounts, official proclamations that had been sent to Sir Richard or his father, and various historical documents relating to the manor. Anything more than twenty years old went straight back into the kist – in a rather neater pile than it had been to start with – and eventually Edwin was left with a manageable stack.

The financial documents he passed over cursorily, seeing nothing suspicious or particularly interesting, but then his eye was caught by the marriage settlement between Sir Richard and Jonilda. It was dated to the year 1207 and it noted that Jonilda brought a dowry of cash, rather than land, to the union. The agreement specified that Sir Richard's son from his first marriage would remain his heir, and that any children of Jonilda's would only inherit if Martin pre-deceased his father without leaving an heir of his own body, or if he died later without children. Provision was then made for an income to support Jonilda for the rest of her life if Sir Richard should die before her. And that provision was…

Edwin sat back. He didn't know the manor's precise financial situation, but it appeared prosperous, which made it surprising that the amount allocated to Jonilda was relatively small – barely enough to sustain her in any kind of comfort, even if she didn't also have six children to feed and clothe. If she was aware of this settlement, which she surely must be, then it completely destroyed any motive for her to kill Sir Richard: her own prosperity and economic security depended on him remaining alive so that she continued as lady of the manor, whereas his death would cast her into penury. Even discounting her obvious fondness for him, she had every reason to want to keep her husband alive; and, indeed, if she were going to kill anyone she would be much better off getting rid of Sir Martin.

She would be much better off getting rid of Sir Martin…

'You've been looking at that one a long time,' noted Gabriel. 'Is it about the forest law?'

'Er, no,' said Edwin, coming back to himself and wondering if he would ever reach a point in life where he wasn't suspecting anyone and everyone of murder. He couldn't help it. *And who else would gain if Sir Martin were dead?* asked the inconvenient part of his mind. Why, Michael, of course. And he must be a pretty good shot with his bow and arrows if he could hit moving hares and ducks at any kind of distance.

He had to stop this, or he'd be suspecting the tiny children and their nurses next. Edwin forced himself to stop looking at the marriage settlement and to keep his voice neutral. 'This one needs to go with the finances,' he said, putting it down and then immediately laying two sets of accounts for the sale of surplus grain on top of it. 'Here, look at these,' he added, to change the subject. 'They're dated two years apart. What can you tell me of the percentage increase in the price of wheat, year on year?'

It was some while later that Edwin found what he was looking for, and the two of them pored over several legal documents of different dates, Edwin pausing after every couple of lines to explain and translate the Latin. Gabriel picked it up very quickly, soon recognising common words and phrases, and Edwin wondered if any thought had ever been given to sending him to the abbey for a more rigorous education than he seemed to be getting at home.

Forest law was complex, and the earlier penalties for any transgressions were severe indeed: death or mutilation, in most cases. Edwin remembered what Sir Martin had said about how the local people would view the loss of his hand. But here was a large document dated from 1217, only four years ago, that seemed to supersede the earlier ones. It proclaimed itself a copy of 'the Charter of the Forest' and had been given by the young king early in his reign, along with the Great Charter, something Edwin knew of already.

Under these new terms, the punishments for taking venison were much reduced – fines and imprisonment – and there were all sorts of other concessions allowing free men to dig ponds and construct mills and buildings on their own land even if that land was in a royal forest. Edwin skimmed over the parts about common pasture and terms such as *pannage*, *estover* and *agistment*, thinking that he'd already gained what was most pertinent in the document and wondering if anyone except himself had ever read it in detail since it had arrived on the manor. If Sir Richard was anything like Sir Martin in character, his eyes would have glazed over long since. Plus, of course, because he was a resident lord who ran the manor himself, he had no steward who could take care of such matters for him.

A line on a different subject caught Edwin's attention:

> Whatsoever archbishop, bishops, earl or baron, coming to us at our commandment, passing by our forest, it shall be lawful for him to take and kill one or two of our deer, by view of our forester, if he be present; or else he shall cause to blow a horn for him, that he seem not to steal our deer.

Edwin drummed his fingers on the table. This made sense of something Serlo had said earlier, which Edwin hadn't quite grasped at the time. Had any nobleman or high-ranking churchman been in the woods on the day Sir Richard was shot? That would alter the situation quite drastically, not to mention making his own investigation much more complicated.

But no, wait, what was it Brother Gregory had said? 'I was summoned on the morning of the feast of Saint John the Baptist.' That had been the day after the incident, which meant that Sir Richard had been shot before the hart-hunting season began. And if Edwin knew one thing about noblemen, it was that they took hunting – and hunting rules – very seriously indeed. Random noblemen passing through the area could therefore be ruled out, and the culprit must be someone who was not in the woods for legal hunting.

There was a sudden burst of noise from the room above them. Furniture moving, Jonilda and Brother Gregory's voices raised in alarm, and a horrible kind of screeching sound, as though someone was trying to cry out in pain through a mouth that was clamped shut.

Edwin looked at Gabriel's ashen face. 'Why don't you run to the stable,' he suggested, 'and ask Sir Martin to come back. Tell him he's needed because your father is having another spasm. And… make sure your younger brother and sisters are well out of earshot.'

Gabriel nodded. 'The nurses took them down to look for frogs in the pond earlier. I'll make sure they stay there.'

It wasn't long before Sir Martin came racing in, hotly pursued by Michael, who began to follow him up the stairs.

The knight stopped. 'You stay down here.'

'No. I'm coming up with you.'

'What? You do as you're told.'

Michael shook his head, stubbornly. 'He's my father too.'

Sir Martin was on the verge of a retort when another strangled scream sounded, stopping him in his tracks, and Michael was able to shoot past him and disappear. Sir Martin swore and then gestured to Edwin. 'You'd better come.'

'Quickly! I can't hold him much longer!' Brother Gregory's desperate voice was the first thing Edwin heard as he got to the top, and he entered the chamber in time to see Sir Martin flinging himself forward to prevent his father's agonised, straining form falling out of the bed. The monk was trying to hold him in place and say prayers at the same time, while Jonilda wiped at her husband's head with a cool cloth, helpless and hopeless in the face of his profuse sweating and agony.

It was evident to Edwin that Michael had had no idea of what he was letting himself in for. He stood frozen in horror at the side of the room, unable to look away from his father's bulging eyes and fixed, rigid smile, the sight of which was almost worse than anything. Edwin moved to stand by the boy, murmuring words, any words, into his ear in a futile attempt at comfort.

Please, Lord, let it be over soon. For all their sakes. Edwin made no pretence at wanting to prolong the sanctity of Sir Richard's life; it was far too late for that. The coming of death was the only mercy the Lord could show him now.

But such a blessing was not swift to arrive, and the spasm seemed to go on and on, the sick man's stiff body arching with the strain as everyone else in the room cried and exclaimed and knew not what they said, powerless in the face of such cruel and unjustified punishment.

And then, finally, there came one last muffled scream and a loud, sickening crack.

Sir Richard dropped back on to the bed, and he did not move again.

The only sound in the room now was of panting and sobbing. Edwin held Michael tightly while Brother Gregory checked for breathing and put his ear to Sir Richard's heart.

Eventually the monk lifted his head and shook it. 'It's over. *Requiescat in pace.*' He crossed himself and began to intone the prayers for the dead.

Sir Martin and Jonilda stared at each other over the body as they knelt on either side of the bed, their faces desperate and streaming with tears, neither of them able to say a word.

Jonilda was the first to break away. She sat back, and then, realising she still had the cloth in her hand, wiped away some of the sweat that bathed Sir Richard's lifeless face. She attempted to close his eyes but could not.

That awful, fixed grin seemed to mock them all.

Brother Gregory finished his prayers and drew the sheet up over Sir Richard's face. He looked at Jonilda. 'His children and servants will want to come and pay their respects, and it is perhaps better that they don't see…'

Jonilda nodded, sniffing and swallowing her tears. 'Yes.' Then her demeanour changed as she glanced at Sir Martin, still kneeling by the bedside. A chill seemed to come over her. 'But none of that is up to me, is it?' She stood, smoothing her skirts and mustering her dignity, and addressed him directly. 'We await your orders, my lord.'

She curtseyed deeply and made her way out of the room, stopping only once to lean on the doorpost as she sought to stop her knees from collapsing under her.

Chapter Seven

Brother Gregory straightened the sheet that covered the body and then began to collect up his vials and pack them away. When he was satisfied that all was as it should be, he stood in respectful silence at the foot of the bed for a few moments before addressing the remaining three in the room. 'I'll leave you alone. As soon as Father Abbot arrives, I'll give him the news and ask him to pray.'

There was silence for a few moments after he'd left, and then Michael let out a muffled sob into the front of Edwin's tunic.

Sir Martin, still kneeling, slowly raised his head to glare at the two of them. 'Get. Out.'

His tone was so chilling that even Edwin didn't dare make any reply, and he steered Michael out of the room and down the stairs. By the time they reached the parlour the boy was shaking badly, so Edwin sat him down and then took the blankets off his temporary bed in the corner to wrap them around Michael's body as tightly as he could. 'You stay there,' he said, gently. 'I'll try to find your mother, or see if Brother Gregory might be able to help.'

Edwin went out into the hall. There was no sign of Jonilda, but the infirmarer was there, greeting the newly arrived abbot. Standing with the two monks was Simon, along with a well-dressed man whom Edwin did not recognise. Judging by the way the other members of the household were all staring at him as they stood about in subdued, whispering huddles, he was equally unknown to them.

Although he had no real authority here, Edwin felt that he was the best-placed person to represent Sir Martin until the knight was a little more himself, especially with Jonilda absent, so he made his way over to the group and explained the situation.

Brother Gregory, with his abbot's permission, went to see Michael, while the abbot himself hesitated. 'I should find the widow, who will be in need of spiritual comfort, but it is also of the utmost importance that prayers should be said over Sir Richard's body.'

'I'll see if I can find Lady Jonilda,' volunteered Simon, 'as I'm not the right man to say the prayers. Don't worry, I won't disturb her if she'd rather be alone, but I can at least check that she isn't lying insensible from grief anywhere, in need of medical attention.'

This was agreed, and Simon departed. Belatedly, the abbot introduced Edwin to the stranger, who seemed most displeased at having been left until last. 'Eustace of Lowdham, deputy sheriff.'

Edwin blinked. 'How did you get here so quickly?'

'I beg your pardon?'

'It was only a matter of hours ago that I was speaking to a forester, who said he would alert the sheriff to the situation here.'

'I was already on my way here after I heard of Sir Richard's accident. Is that the situation you speak of?'

'Yes, though I'm not sure it was an accident.' Edwin outlined his principal suspicion – that is, that the arrow had been loosed with the intention of killing Sir Richard, and that Sir Richard himself had thought so – but without naming any possible culprit, given that as yet he had no idea of that himself.

'Hmm,' said Eustace. 'Well, I have only your word for that. If it *is* so then I'll need to investigate further, though the obvious perpetrator, of course, is the heir. Probably wanted to get his hands on the manor rather sooner than anyone intended.'

'I hardly think–'

'What you think is neither here nor there. I will see the body now, and I will speak with this heir. An estranged son, I understand, from an earlier marriage. How has he been supporting himself if he hasn't been living on the manor at Sir Richard's expense? Garrison service somewhere? Trade? Is he an apprentice?'

'I really should explain–'

Again, Edwin was waved away. 'You!' Eustace snapped his fingers and pointed to the nearest serving man. 'Summon this heir and bring him here to me.'

The servant looked at Edwin, who merely shrugged. The deputy sheriff had asked for it; it was only fair to let him have it.

Eustace ordered a table to be set up for him at one side of the hall. He was waiting for this to be done and, as it happened, looking directly at the open parlour door when the shadow fell across it. Edwin watched, in some satisfaction, the changes in his expression as Sir Martin ducked under the lintel, slowly drew his huge, burly frame upright, and cast his eye around the room in fury. 'Who,' he growled, the deep voice rumbling like thunder, 'has thought fit to "summon" me?'

Edwin tried not to smirk. 'This is Eustace of Lowdham, the deputy sheriff. Eustace, I have the honour to introduce Sir Martin du Bois, a knight in the personal household of Earl William de Warenne.'

Sir Martin moved closer, deliberately allowing himself to loom over the other in the menacing manner he normally tried to avoid. 'Tell me, Eustace of Lowdham, what do you have to say that can justify dragging me away from my father's body at such a time?'

It probably wasn't fair, but Edwin had taken an instant dislike to the man and his high-handed manner of intruding on a grief-stricken household. 'I believe Eustace wishes to confirm that you had nothing to do with your father's death, given that you're the main beneficiary.'

Sir Martin threw a glare at Eustace that by rights should have killed him stone dead. 'I can give you the personal testimony of Earl Warenne and of the heirs to the earldoms of Arundel and Salisbury that I was with them at Conisbrough Castle on the day my father was shot. Is that good enough?' He paused and then held up his left arm so Eustace could get a good look at the metal hand. 'Besides, I couldn't shoot a bow if I tried.' He leaned his face down closer to Eustace's. 'So, if that's all, I'll go back to praying for my father's soul.'

Sir Martin returned to the parlour, and Edwin just about resisted the urge to applaud.

Eustace stood with his mouth open.

'In answer to your next two questions,' said Edwin, before the other could speak, 'a battle wound gained in the earl's service, and an inch over six and a half feet. Now, if you'll excuse me, I need to check on Michael.'

Brother Gregory was sitting with the well-wrapped Michael, giving him small occasional sips of what smelled like wine, and Edwin was pleased to see that the boy's teeth had stopped chattering and that there was a little more colour in his cheeks. He sat with them until Sir Martin came downstairs again, accompanied by the abbot.

The knight seemed marginally more himself now that the immediate shock had worn off. 'Thank you, Father,' he was saying. 'We can manage now, and I'll send a man to bring the priest here for the burial. Tomorrow, if possible, or if not then on Sunday when he'll be here anyway.'

'Very well. We'll keep Sir Richard and all of you in our prayers, and I'll return in due course to see how you're all managing.'

'Really, Father, there's no need.'

'It's no trouble, my son – indeed it's my Christian duty. But for now, farewell. Brother Gregory, if you're ready?'

The infirmarer followed him out of the room.

Sir Martin gestured to Edwin to join him. 'There's a lot to do.' He glared over at Michael. 'Not least having a word with that boy about disobeying orders, but that will wait.' Then, after a pause, 'Where's Jonilda?'

'I don't know. She went straight outside after she left us earlier. Simon – the abbey bailiff – said he'd find her just to see she hadn't swooned or anything, but he hasn't come back to fetch Brother Gregory, so I assume it's just that she wants some time to herself.'

There was the merest hesitation. 'Best leave her to it, then. If she's not back by nightfall we'll send someone after her.' Sir Martin squared his shoulders. 'But for now, duty.'

Edwin hated to say it, but… 'I don't think the smaller children know yet. I sent Gabriel to make sure they stayed away. And then there's your grandfather over at Langley–'

'What about him?' Sir Martin's voice was sharp.

'Well, he'll have to be informed, won't he? As the lord of the neighbouring manor, and also as family?'

Sir Martin rubbed his chin. 'I can't… there's so much to do here.'

Edwin took pity on him. 'How about if I act as messenger, while you deal with things here? If you keep your attention on practical matters, it might help.'

'Yes. Good idea.'

He didn't move.

Edwin laid a hand on his friend's arm. 'This is difficult,' he said, quietly, 'but you can get through it. You've done difficult things before, and I have faith in you.'

Sir Martin's eyes bored into him for a moment, and then he nodded. 'Right.' He walked out of the parlour and into the hall, and within a short space of time Edwin could hear him giving authoritative instructions – for the priest to be contacted, for a coffin to be made, for the evening meal to go ahead as planned, and for the hall to be set up afterwards to receive the body, so that the manor's inhabitants could pay their respects.

Edwin slipped out into the afternoon sunshine.

First things first: he asked directions to the pond and went to find the children. As it happened, they and their nurses were already on their way back. Gabriel looked pensive, as did Constance and Eleanor, who were old enough to have some idea of what was going on, but Jonny and Adela were skipping, giggling and making frog noises at each other. Edwin's heart broke for them.

Gabriel stopped as soon as he saw Edwin, and the remaining colour drained out of his face. 'Father?'

Edwin crouched down so that he could speak to all of them, and explained as gently as he could that their father had gone to God, but that he would be happy in heaven and that their mother and Sir Martin would make sure they were all looked after.

It was Constance who broke the stunned silence. 'Does that mean he'll come here to live with us?'

It was best to be honest. 'I'm not quite sure, but I don't think he'll be here all the time. He has other duties as well, and other places to be.'

'Then how will he look after us?'

Gabriel chimed in, rubbing his eyes with his fist. 'And who will run the manor?'

'I don't know exactly how it will work, but that's not for any of you to worry about. The adults will deal with everything.'

Neither of them looked convinced.

'Now,' continued Edwin, looking at the two nurses as well as the children. 'You should all go back to the house, so your mother and brother know where you are. Try to be as quiet as you can, and those of you old enough to know your prayers can say them for your father.'

'Are you coming too?' Gabriel plucked at Edwin's sleeve.

'Not just yet. I have to go and tell your reeve, so that he can tell everyone else on the manor, and then I have to make a visit to Langley.'

Gabriel was horrified. 'You're not going there? On your own?'

Edwin was confused. 'Shouldn't I?'

'We're not allowed.' Gabriel leaned forward to whisper. 'The lord there is very bad-tempered, and he'll shout at us if we go, that's what Mother always says. We see him on the other side of the church on Sundays, but he never speaks to us, just walks straight out afterwards.'

'Don't worry about me.' Edwin was puzzled, but he guessed he would soon find out, one way or the other, what sort of a reaction he would get when he arrived unannounced. 'You take care of the others, now, and also be nice to Michael when you get back.'

'He stayed, didn't he? And saw…'

'Don't think about it,' said Edwin. 'Just make sure you all stay together and don't let any of the little ones wander off. Your mother is upset, and it will be some comfort to her to have you all about her. All right?'

Gabriel nodded manfully, and Edwin watched them all set off again.

A couple of enquiries brought him to the reeve, who was in a field planted with strips of wheat. A few words sufficed to pass on the news to him and to the surrounding men, who all removed their hats and paused for a moment before getting straight back to work. The crops didn't care who lived and who died.

Just as Edwin was leaving, Dominic called out to him. 'If you've been round and about on the manor this afternoon, I don't suppose you've seen Farolf anywhere? The one you heard me shout at this morning?'

'No, I haven't, I'm afraid.'

'He's gone missing again. What he chooses to do on his own workdays is his own concern, but Fridays is for working on the manor strips, and he's not pulling his weight.'

'If I see him, I'll tell him to come back to you.'

'Thank you. Though he's good at hiding himself when there's work needs to be done.' Dominic's face darkened. 'And if he's poaching and he's caught, he won't like the consequences. I know we turn a blind eye when he catches the odd hare here on the manor, but the forest is different – it's the king's land.'

Edwin was reminded of the rustling sound he'd heard in the woods earlier, but he had no reason to suspect that had been Farolf. He therefore said nothing, although he did wonder, as he walked on, at how casually the reeve spoke of turning a blind eye to the man poaching on the manor. That couldn't be normal, surely.

As he was aware, the boundary between Woodthorpe and Langley was the church. Its strange half-and-half graveyard, one side well tended while the other was unkempt, now made sense: each lord must be responsible for his own side, and one was more punctilious about it than the other.

Similar scenes of slovenliness met him as he crossed the boundary and observed the fields and hedges on either side of the road. It wasn't a scene of devastation, by any means; crops were growing and men were at work, but there was an air of things not being supervised properly, of routine maintenance not being done, of a general lack of care. Fences were leaning or had broken spars, and the drainage ditches were so choked with weeds that Edwin doubted they'd be fit for purpose.

The road was a public one, so Edwin had every right to walk down it, but the sight of a stranger was enough to make the labourers stop and stare, and he felt obscurely uncomfortable until they'd gone back to work.

When he reached the house, it looked identical in plan to the one at Woodthorpe, although the thatch was bare in places and the plaster patchy, exposing the wood beneath. He waited outside for a moment, to see if anyone would come out to greet him, but when nobody did, he poked his head through the open door and called out. A serving man eventually emerged from the pantry and agreed that his master was in the house, pointing to the open parlour door.

Feeling obscurely like a trespasser, Edwin went to knock. Inside the room, someone was sitting with his back to the door, staring out of the open window. From what Edwin could make out, it was the same man he had seen in the church.

Despite the rapping of his knuckles being perfectly audible, he had to repeat it and clear his throat loudly before there was any reaction.

'Who is it?' The man didn't turn round.

'Are you Master Christopher? I'm a friend of your grandson, Sir Martin.'

'He sent you here?' He half-turned.

'Yes. May I come in?'

'Do.' Christopher stood up and looked about him, unsuccessfully, for a second chair.

'It's all right, sir, I can stand.'

'What does he want?'

'I'm here with bad news, I'm afraid – I'm sorry to have to tell you that Sir Richard died this afternoon.'

There was a long-drawn-out sigh. 'At last.'

'Yes, he's been suffering for over a week, I understand.'

'No, I meant – at last, he'll be with dear Rosceline again.' The older man collapsed back into his chair.

There was no reason Edwin should pretend not to know what he meant. 'Your daughter. Sir Martin's mother.'

'Yes. I killed her, you know. It's been twenty-one years and eighty-two days, and the burden of my guilt never gets any lighter.'

Edwin took a couple of steps towards him. 'As I understand it, she died in childbirth.'

'Yes, but who arranged her marriage so that she was with child in the first place? Me. And it killed her. The light of my life.'

This was not the conversation Edwin had expected to have, but there seemed little else to do except continue. 'You had good intentions.'

'Oh yes. Good intentions. And you know which road is paved with them, don't you?'

Edwin made no reply.

Christopher rubbed both hands down his face. 'We were friends. We owned adjoining manors. I had a daughter and he a son, and they liked each other – it seemed obvious. They were to marry and have a happy brood of children who would fill both houses with laughter. And then...' he gestured at the empty, dusty room.

'Surely it was God's will...'

Christopher grunted. 'If His will was to cut off the life of a bright, beautiful girl before it had hardly begun, then I don't pretend to understand it.' He shook his head. 'She should be a matron by now, with half a dozen children at least – and still young enough to be having more.' Then, after a pause, 'Still, at least her husband will be with her now. And... Martin will come back now he's lord of the manor?'

'I–'

'I know he won't want to see me, of course. He's never known his mother, and that's all my fault. It's no wonder he blames me.'

A number of things now became clearer in Edwin's mind. Christopher's apparent bad temper when he saw Sir Richard's children, whom he felt should have been Rosceline's, not those of a second wife. The flowers on the effigy in the church, and the lack of care and interest about other, more mundane matters.

Once again, Edwin felt that he should tread very carefully, because this was his friend's private business, not his own. But... 'In all the years I've known him,' he ventured, 'I have *never* heard Sir Martin blame you for his mother's death.' No need to add that he'd actually never mentioned his grandfather at all, to the extent that Edwin hadn't even known of his existence until a few days ago. 'If anything, he blames himself.'

That brought some life back into Christopher. 'But that's ridiculous! He was a baby – how can he possibly blame himself for being born?'

Edwin shrugged. 'Nevertheless.'

There was silence for a while. 'Perhaps, if he's going to be living at Woodthorpe from now on, we might meet. Sometime. If he wants to.'

'Perhaps.' Edwin wasn't going to get into the complexity of Sir Martin owning more than one manor and needing to be in attendance on the earl.

After a few moments' silence, Edwin recalled that he was speaking to a man who had lived in the area all his life, and he should take the opportunity to gain what information he could. 'Tell me,' he began, 'do you know anything of a man called Eustace of Lowdham? The deputy sheriff?'

'Oh, he's here, is he? What can he want? It's not time to make the shire payment yet, though I wouldn't put it past him to find another reason to demand money.'

'He's been around here before, then? On financial business?'

'Yes. The sheriff is supposed to deal with all the accounts himself, but he leaves it all to Eustace, and it's well known he collects a lot more from us than he hands over to the exchequer.' Christopher began to look marginally more alert. 'You tell Martin to beware of him, and not be fooled.'

Hmm… A man of few scruples, then, and one who was out for what he could get. Edwin wondered if Eustace had been falsifying the shire accounts, or possibly taking or offering bribes – and if so, whether Sir Richard had found out. Had Eustace been in the area longer than he claimed? He'd certainly arrived much more promptly than might have been expected.

By now the sun was beginning to set, casting slanting rays over the bare floor and illuminating dancing motes of dust. 'I'd better get back,' said Edwin. 'Before it gets too dark to find my way. And to see what help I can be to Sir Martin and Jonil–' he noticed Christopher beginning to wince. 'And everyone else.' He paused. 'I can send word about the day and time of the funeral, if you'd like to attend?'

'Only if he wants me to.'

'I'll ask.'

Christopher went so far as to accompany Edwin to the main door. 'I'll think on what you've said.'

Edwin paused, remembering the other thing he'd meant to ask before he got sidetracked into the unexpected, yet perhaps welcome, conversation about Sir Martin's mother. 'I have another question, if I may.'

'Go on.' Christopher's voice was a little wary.

'These manors are nice, prosperous places, but they're a far cry from the world of castles and earls. Do you know how it came about that Sir Martin was taken on by Earl Warenne as a page and squire? I just can't see how it could have happened.'

Christopher seemed relieved at the choice of subject. 'Ah, that. When Martin was six, his father was called up to serve in the king's army – the old king, John, this was – to travel over the sea to Poitou. He'd lost some lands there to the French king, and he wanted to get them back. They were all at a siege somewhere when Richard saved Earl Warenne's life.'

'How?'

'As I understand it, the earl was standing with his back to the castle while he gave some orders, and he wasn't wearing his helm, or he had his coif down – something that exposed his head and neck, anyway. Richard saw a crossbow bolt heading towards him from the castle ramparts and pushed him out of the way.'

'But Sir Martin couldn't have been there.' Edwin didn't quite make the connection.

'No. But the earl promised Richard a reward and said he could name it. He was probably expecting to be asked for money, or a horse and armour, or maybe to give Richard a position. But Richard said he wanted nothing for himself, but he had a fine son that he wanted the best for, and would the earl consider giving him a position in his household instead.'

'Ah. And the lord earl felt he had to go along with it, because he'd already given his word.' That made sense. Edwin remembered when the earl had once asked *him* to name a reward, and he'd requested something unexpected.

'Yes. There was an official letter about it, with the earl's seal and everything, saying to send the boy to him as soon as he turned seven. So young Martin got lucky with being given the position in the first place, but you can be sure he wouldn't have kept it if he hadn't done well. These great men have no qualms about getting rid of anyone who doesn't suit them.'

Again, Edwin knew that all too well. He wondered if any of this could possibly have any bearing on Sir Richard's death, but he couldn't immediately see a link.

'He's served the earl well all these years, so I've heard, but I'll be glad to see him home again.' Christopher patted Edwin on the back almost cheerfully and went back inside.

Edwin walked through the Langley lands feeling relatively pleased with himself for starting a conversation that might lead to a reconciliation between Sir Martin and his grandfather. But as he passed the church in the dwindling light, another thought struck him. The direct result of Sir Richard's death was that Sir Martin inherited the manor. Edwin knew that he did not intend to spend much of his time there, but to anyone else the natural assumption would be that he would move back to run it in person. Christopher, a lonely man with no close family except for Sir Martin, had seemed pleased at this expectation. And his first reaction to hearing of Sir Richard's death was joy that he should be reunited with his first wife, not sorrow at his passing. So recent events had, in fact, worked in his favour. But how much influence had he exerted on the course of those events? Did he, in fact, have a motive for murder?

'He resents me for taking his mother's place,' said Jonilda. 'Of course he does. But does he think I had any choice in the matter?'

She and Edwin were sitting alone in the parlour. It was dim, only a single lamp lit to give the barest minimum of light while hiding the ravages of her swollen, tear-streaked face. The children were in bed upstairs and Sir Martin was in the hall, where his father's body now lay on a trestle table, decently covered to avoid any shock to onlookers. Good wax candles were lit in there, giving a steady illumination, and members of the household were gathering to pay their respects. In here the window was open to the cool night breeze, and on the air came the distant hammering sound of a coffin being constructed.

The evening had not started as peacefully as this. When Edwin returned from Langley it had been to find Sir Martin berating Michael for having disobeyed his orders earlier, with Jonilda trying to calm him but only making things worse, and Edwin had been obliged to step in before the situation became too heated. Thankfully, the sheriff's deputy had by that time already departed, to be accommodated at the abbey instead of expecting to be put up at Woodthorpe, but Edwin had no doubt he'd be back in the morning. And then it had been a tense evening meal, nobody managing to swallow more than a few mouthfuls of their fish, and various children bursting into tears at semi-regular intervals.

'Your marriage was arranged for you, I take it.' Not everyone was as lucky as Edwin and Alys had been, able to choose their life partner for themselves.

'Yes.' Jonilda stared into the light and into the past. 'I was sixteen. My father was a saddle-maker, and I wanted to marry the draper's son. But Sir Richard was known to be a widower, and when he called into the shop a number of times about a new saddle he wanted, my father saw his chance. He was in trade, of course, not a member of the gentry, but he was financially well off, and Sir Richard needed money to equip himself to go to France with the king's army. He looked at me and thought I was pretty enough; and he already had a son and heir from a woman of better blood. So it was all arranged, my father advanced him what he needed, and when he got back from France we were married.'

'You didn't object?'

'How could I? My mother and father kept telling me what a God-given opportunity it was, how girls like me wouldn't normally ever become lady of the manor, and what a wonderful future I would have. And once my father had laid out the money, there was certainly no going back; he wanted his side of the bargain. It was all arranged between the men, some kind of document drawn up, and that was that.'

'But...' Edwin looked about him at the pleasant parlour, and then, meaningfully, upwards at the floorboards of the room the children were in. 'You accustomed yourself to it? You don't need to tell me that you were fond of Sir Richard – I could see it.'

'Once I knew it was inevitable, I did my duty. I married Sir Richard and became his wife. And it wasn't long before I found I was with child, and I thought – well, I can either spend my years being resentful for the life I could have had, or I can make the most of this one. I did come to love him over the years, especially as our family grew larger. And I'd do anything for our children.'

She looked pensive. *Anything*, thought Edwin. *Do you really mean that?*

'But now,' she continued, oblivious to his thoughts, 'I'm almost as powerless as I was back then, when I was a young girl. This manor and everything in it belongs to Sir Martin, and my children and I have no claim on it at all. If he doesn't take pity on us, I don't know what we'll do, except possibly move back to Edwinstowe and try to get the boys apprenticed. Even now I'm a guest in what has been my own home, and once dear Richard is in the ground...' she dissolved into tears.

'He'll provide for you.' Edwin tried to sound reassuring. 'He looks intimidating, but...'

Jonilda shook her head. 'It's not just that. It's not his size, or his rank. It's that he thinks I've schemed and connived to take his mother's place. She'd been dead more than six years when Richard and I married, and I never even met her, poor soul. And then, of course, Martin – Sir Martin – was sent away to take up his place in the earl's household very soon after we married. But that was nothing to do with me, I assure you. I liked him. He was a lovely little boy, and I hoped that I could help – not to *replace* his mother, not like that – but to show him some of the love he'd never really had. He was lonely, and I wanted to look after him.'

Edwin felt his eyes beginning to sting. He was three years older than Sir Martin. He'd long been friends with the squire of his own age who was the next one up in the earl's household, and he well remembered the arrival of the tight-lipped, self-contained younger boy. They'd both tried to be kind to him, as had the late Sir Roger – who at that time had been the earl's senior squire – but the new page didn't seem to want or need their efforts. Always independent and determined, getting on with his tasks, training, taking his hits, riding, falling off his horse, getting back on again, hardly ever speaking. It was only in the last few years, since the incident that brought Edwin closer into the earl's household, that he'd ever heard Sir Martin utter more than about three words at once.

Jonilda sighed. 'After that he only came back very occasionally, and I always seemed to have a new baby… there were just a couple of times when he seemed to be softening towards Michael, and our dear Amice–' she gulped. Then she shook her head, unable to continue.

'Why don't you get some sleep?' suggested Edwin. 'Or at least some rest, even if you can't sleep after everything that's happened today.'

She nodded and got to her feet, then stopped. 'But the bedchamber isn't mine any longer, and…'

'It will be difficult for you to go up there, I know, with the memories of Sir Richard. But I know Sir Martin, and I know he'll be happy to stay sleeping down here for the time being. So, you go on up. I'll be sure to tell him, don't worry. And if you can't bring yourself to use the bed, you can at least be near your children.'

She wiped away a tear and nodded. 'Poor dears. They might wake in the night, and they'll need me.'

Edwin stood to let her pass, and she paused again. 'Thank you. Thank you for listening, and for understanding.'

She left, and Edwin sat in silence. Before he could retreat into his own thoughts, however, he heard a sound from the room's entrance.

Because of the candlelight in the hall, the doorway was clearly illuminated, and Edwin was just in time to see the unmistakable shadow turning away. Something about the way Sir Martin was moving, or some instinct of Edwin's own, told him that his friend had overheard everything that had passed.

Chapter Eight

'Edwin. Are you awake?'

'Yes.'

There was a pause. Then, 'Edwin, what's going on? I don't… with everything that's happened in the last week, I just don't know what's happening. I feel like I'm going mad, or I'm in some kind of dream and I can't wake up.'

'It's been a lot to take in.'

'Ten days ago, all I owned was a horse and a sword, and my only duty was following orders. And now I'm betrothed to be married and I'm the lord of two manors. With more than a hundred lives in my care, men, women and children. I just… I don't think I can.'

Edwin shifted on his palliasse so he was leaning up on one elbow, facing Sir Martin, although the parlour was so dark they couldn't actually see each other. 'You're going to be better at it than you think.'

'Am I? How?'

'Well, the fact that your first thought about the manors was the people who live on them – rather than, say, the income they might bring you – is a good sign.'

Sir Martin digested that for a moment. 'I suppose so. But the responsibility! And…'

'What?'

'It's just – I don't know how to say it. How can I be in both of these places at once *and* remain in the lord earl's service?' He paused. 'I certainly know which of those I'd rather be doing.'

'Nobody imagines that you'll be everywhere at once. Think of the lord earl. He owns castles and manors all over the kingdom, and he travels between them and leaves other men in charge. Neither he nor anybody else will expect you to know all the details of every grain harvest or how many rows of peas have been sown. And think of Sir Geoffrey: he served the earl all his life and only went home for a few weeks every year.'

There was a longer silence, and Edwin realised that he'd used the wrong word.

'That's the other thing,' came Sir Martin's voice, slowly. 'This isn't home. It was strange, when we spent those couple of days at Rochford – I felt as though that could have been, even though I was only seeing it for the first time. I could… *see* myself there. With Matilda, later on, and with you and Alys visiting, or even maybe… but here? This isn't home, and this isn't my family. You are.'

Edwin shook his head, pointless as that was in the dark. 'They *are* your family. We all are, in different ways. But Jonilda and the children – they're in need of your particular protection just at the moment.'

A noise came from the other palliasse that Edwin couldn't immediately identify. 'I still wouldn't put it past her–'

'I think that's wrong,' said Edwin, firmly, but wondering how far he actually believed it himself. 'I know you were shocked, on the road here, when the abbot didn't know about you and thought Michael was to inherit, but I think that was just his own assumption – he hasn't been here very long, don't forget. I can't imagine that she told him that, for it would be foolish, not to mention easily disproved, as soon as you turned up.'

'Yes, but–'

'And,' continued Edwin, 'I haven't had the chance yet to tell you what I found out from looking at those documents earlier.' He outlined Jonilda's financial settlement. 'So, you see, her best interests would be served by your father remaining alive as long as possible.' He forced himself to thrust the other thought, the one that had so disturbed him earlier, to the side.

Sir Martin took some time to ponder that – so long that Edwin nearly dozed off. But then the deep voice came again. 'Well, if it wasn't her, then who? You're convinced, aren't you, that it wasn't an accident?'

'I am. I just don't see how it could have happened by chance, even allowing for extreme ill luck. No – someone hid in that hollow and then loosed his arrow at your father deliberately.'

'But *why*? I just don't understand. He was a good lord to the people here – I've heard them say so, this evening. And, like that what's-his-name said, the only one who benefits is me. Everyone else is worse off.'

'That's what I'm going to find out, I swear. You can't leave to go back to Conisbrough until this is sorted out – it might be dangerous.' Edwin sighed. 'And neither can I.'

'It's not fair of me to drag you away from your own family for so long. I know you miss them.'

'I do.' Edwin paused, wondering how far he might step. 'But you're the other way round: you've got your family around you, and you're ignoring them. Honestly–' He continued in a rush, before Sir Martin could interrupt him, '–you don't know how lucky you are. Make the most of them while you're here.'

'How?'

'Like I said before, in the church – the children are frightened, and they don't know what the future holds. A few kind words of reassurance from you would go a long way towards helping them. And the older ones are half scared of you and half desperately trying to impress you. Michael would worship you as a hero if you gave him the chance.'

That was definitely a snort. 'Him? He wouldn't even do as he was told, earlier.'

'Because he was doing what he saw as his duty. I can think of someone else who disobeyed an order, a while back, in order to do what was right.'

'That was diff–'

'In fact,' concluded Edwin, 'Michael reminds me an awful lot of you.'

This time the silence was so long that he really did fall asleep.

Edwin reached into the kist and drew out a sheaf of letters. As before, he didn't open any of them, but instead turned them towards the late-morning light so he could examine the seals. He soon found the one he was looking for: an impression of the chequered shield of Warenne.

To start with, Edwin wondered why the hand was not that of Father Ignatius. The missive had been written before Brother William joined the earl's household as a dedicated clerk, back when the already over-worked parish priest had been obliged to add scribing for the earl to all his other duties. But, of course, he soon realised his mistake – the document had been drawn up in Poitou, not Conisbrough, so the earl must have commandeered one of the clergymen in the king's army to write it for him.

Edwin ran his eye over the lines of Latin. In recognition of the great service rendered to him by Sir Richard du Bois, Earl Warenne agreed to take into his service as a page Martin, the son and heir of the said Sir Richard, who should be delivered to him at the castle of Conisbrough the following Easter when he reached the age of seven years. As Edwin had expected, the earl had been cautious with his further promises, and everything subsequent was conditional: *if* Martin rendered satisfactory service, he would in due course be promoted to squire, and *if* he met the requirements, he would later be dubbed a knight.

That ought to have been it, but there were still a number of lines of text below that, before the list of witnesses. Edwin peered more closely. The penmanship was probably not the anonymous clerk's best effort, the document no doubt squeezed in among many others he had to write that day under less-than-ideal circumstances, and it took Edwin some moments to read it properly. Then he read it again and sat back.

Well, this certainly put a different complexion on things.

He glanced over to where Sir Martin was sitting. He'd already been out for an early morning ride – alone, against Edwin's advice – and after dinner he intended to accompany his father's body to the church. The priest had not yet arrived, so the funeral would not take place until this evening or tomorrow morning, but the church was the coolest suitable location in the area and a much better place for the coffin in the interim than the hall, which was warm even with all the doors and windows open. Dinner would be ready shortly, and Sir Martin had been persuaded to sit down for a while instead of striding about the place impatiently.

The four middle children were all seated with Jonilda at the table, learning their letters by means of a psalter and an alphabet etched on a flat piece of wood. Gabriel was bored, unsurprisingly given the intellectual level of the work, while Constance and Eleanor concentrated hard, and Jonny had to be continually recalled to his task as his attention wandered.

Michael was out in the stable, but little Adela was in the room. Edwin watched her complacently, wondering what Edith and Matilda would be doing at home at this moment. They, of course, always had each other, while she was on her own, and she soon got bored of the game she was playing in the corner with her doll. Casting about for some other source of entertainment, her gaze fell on Sir Martin, and Edwin watched in amusement as she gradually sidled closer to him.

Eventually her staring caught the knight's attention. 'What?' he asked, curtly, though his tone wasn't belligerent.

'Did you lose your hand?'

Edwin winced at the directness of small children as Adela pointed. Fortunately, Sir Martin was wearing the hand-shaped replacement today, which was less frightening than either of the others, but it was still quite clearly made of metal rather than flesh and blood.

Strangely – or not? – Sir Martin was not in the least offended or angry at the question. Perhaps he was also thinking of Matilda and Edith. So he merely replied, 'Yes, I suppose I did.'

Adela regarded him gravely, her little brow creasing as she frowned in thought. Then she took hold of his huge right hand with both of her tiny ones and made a comically unsuccessful attempt to heave him up out of his seat, leaning backwards and straining with all her might to absolutely no effect.

'What now?'

'I'll help you look for it.'

On the other side of the room, the lesson was still going on. In the hall, tables and benches were being set up with a clatter. Nobody except for Edwin, therefore, heard the exchange or saw the change in Sir Martin's expression as he stared at the little girl for a few moments. His face softened, then he swept her up into a giant hug that made her squeak with pleasure before settling her on his knee. 'That's a very kind thought, thank you. But I don't think we'll find it.'

'Why not?'

'Well,' he began, and Edwin hoped he wasn't about to say anything too gory. But he merely told her a tale of how he'd lost it a long time ago – 'when you were just a tiny baby!' – and in a place many miles from here. So it was too late to search for it now, but look, he had this new one in its place, and could she count how many fingers there were on it? And was that the same as her own hand, even though hers was so much smaller?

Jonny soon became aware of the attention being given to his little sister, and before long he slid down off his stool and wandered over to try for his share of it. And it wasn't long after that that he was perched astride Sir Martin's shin, pretending to ride it like a horse as the knight bounced his leg up and down and both the children giggled.

Edwin smiled. Perhaps he'd been looking at things the wrong way round when he'd encouraged a family reunion, and it was better to start from the bottom up rather than the top down.

Then his eye strayed over to Jonilda, who had paused the lesson and was gazing at Sir Martin, Jonny and Adela. Edwin would like to say that she, too, was appreciating the sight, but on her face was the saddest smile he'd ever seen. Indeed, she looked on the verge of tears.

It wasn't long after dinner that the abbot arrived, accompanied by Simon and Eustace, the latter two deep in conversation. No Brother Gregory today, of course, for his services were no longer required now that Sir Richard was in his coffin, and the infirmarer no doubt had sick brothers to tend to back at the abbey.

'Oh, what does he want *now*?' growled Sir Martin, though Edwin couldn't immediately work out which of the men he was referring to.

He did, however, recognise an early warning sign when he heard it. 'Why don't you take your father's body to the church, as planned?' he suggested. 'And take Michael and Gabriel with you, as well as the men to help lift the coffin once you get there.'

'And you'll get rid of them for me?' Sir Martin nodded his head towards the group.

'I'll talk to them, yes. There might be more to find out.'

Despite the sad purpose, Michael and Gabriel were pleased and proud to be called to take their place on either side of Sir Martin as they walked behind the cart, and Edwin watched the procession make its way slowly towards the road.

By the time he reached the newly arrived group, the abbot was already walking off with Jonilda, the two of them engaged in earnest conversation. The most likely explanation for this was that Jonilda found herself in need of spiritual comfort, but Edwin – despite all his protestations to Sir Martin in the night, and the indubitable proof he had of her financial circumstances – still couldn't help feeling a twinge of suspicion.

He noticed that Simon was also staring after them, but before Edwin could formulate a tactful question Eustace was speaking to him. Or, rather, not so much speaking as issuing orders. 'Given that you seem to be the new lord's deputy here, however unorthodox that is, I will address myself to you. I will need a table set up for my enquiries – either in the hall or perhaps out here – and then I wish to speak to all members of the household. In descending order, would probably be the best. After that I will decide whether Sir Richard's death was an accident, or whether we need to continue with any sort of further investigation.'

Edwin frowned. 'Shouldn't that be done by summoning a jury?'

Eustace attempted to stare him down, which didn't work. '*I'll* say when or whether we need to summon a jury,' was his eventual reply, and Edwin noted that the bluster didn't contain an actual answer to his question. He was wary of taking the point further, though, in case this was some other facet of forest law of which he was unaware, but he promised himself that he'd spend more time with the manor documents later, in case he'd missed anything. In the meantime, he was quite happy for Eustace to be pinned down here, as it meant that he himself would be able to move around at will in the knowledge that the sheriff's deputy wouldn't bother him. He therefore made some mild suggestions to the serving men, who did everything required.

When Edwin had the chance to turn back to Simon, it was to find the other about to remount his horse. 'I'm only on my way through,' he explained. 'Thought it would be useful to stay by Father Abbot's side through the woods, but he'll be all right now. I'll call in on my way back to see if he's still here.'

'You don't think he's in any danger, surely?'

'Who knows, if there are outlaws or footpads about?'

Edwin didn't think that footpads or outlaws, if they'd attacked Sir Richard, would have let the horse get away or left the body without stripping it, but he let that pass for now. The greater caution everyone showed, the better. But... 'Can I ask you something?'

'Of course.' Instead of mounting, Simon took his reins and began to lead the horse towards the road, Edwin walking next to him.

'Do you have any idea why the abbot is calling here so often? And why it should have shocked him so much to hear of Sir Martin's existence?'

'I...' began Simon, before tailing off.

Of course, he wouldn't want to say anything negative about his abbot. Although the fact that it appeared there *was* something negative was, in itself, illuminating.

Edwin changed the subject a little. 'Do you know where he was before he came here? I think he said he'd been appointed abbot from elsewhere, not elected from among the brothers at Rufford?'

Simon seemed relieved. 'Yes, he was at Stoneleigh, in Warwickshire.'

'And... do you know anything of his reputation while he was there? He was promoted to an abbacy here because of his superior piety, presumably?'

A faint noise of what might have been scorn was quickly stifled. 'More for his organisational capabilities, I think.'

'And… perhaps also his financial acumen?'

Simon looked at him sharply. 'If you already knew, why are you asking?'

Several things were beginning to make sense. 'While at Stoneleigh, he was no doubt responsible for increasing the abbey's income.'

There was no denial.

'And possibly some of this income was raised because Abbot Thomas successfully arranged to increase the abbey's landholdings. Taking over local manors if they fell vacant, for example, or if the owner was happy to sell them.'

There was silence for a few moments before a reply that sounded reluctant. 'I shouldn't say it, really. Because I work for the abbey, for my lord abbot, for the Church. But… sometimes I think the Church can be a little too acquisitive.'

Edwin had to agree. Not all clergymen were like Father Ignatius, happy to carry out their duties to their parishioners while living simply and humbly among them. Then again, that was probably *why* he was a parish priest. 'A little more prayer and service, a little less attention to building work and the current price of wool?' he murmured, more to keep Simon talking than anything else.

'Yes.' Simon gestured at the fields and buildings around him. 'I'm not saying that this place wouldn't be well run under the abbey, or that its people wouldn't be well fed and looked after. They are in other places. But the atmosphere here has always been different to the manors I have to look after. Here there's life, and family: a husband and wife and children in the manor house–' He brought himself up short. 'Your pardon. That was a thoughtless thing to say under the circumstances.'

'Perfectly understandable.' Edwin sighed. 'But I know what you mean. The running of the manor must be a little more impersonal if it's under the jurisdiction of the abbey.'

'That's exactly it,' replied Simon. 'Impersonal. And I would be sorry to see Woodthorpe go the same way. It deserves to stay under family guardianship.'

They had reached the road, and he mounted. 'But all this is between you and me, I hope, and will not be repeated to my lord abbot? I need to keep this position.'

'Of course,' said Edwin, and he meant it. He certainly wanted to save this new knowledge for himself until he had found the time to think it over properly.

Thinking was how he could most profitably occupy himself at present. Better to sit and contemplate matters for a while, attempting to make at least some sense of the tangled threads, before he spoke to anyone else. But to do that he needed peace and quiet, to remain undisturbed for some while. The bustle of the house and its hall and parlour would be no good, and besides, Eustace was still sitting outside, now interviewing the reeve and with a couple more men already lined up behind. Edwin wondered again about Eustace's reasons for being here – was it really only because he'd heard a report of Sir Richard being shot?

The barn caught Edwin's eye. The hay harvest was safely gathered here, just as it had been at Conisbrough and Rochford, so there would not be a constant stream of traffic in and out, no crowd of men and carts and horses. There he might find the peace he was seeking.

The door was ajar, in this fine dry weather, so he pushed at it and slipped in. A good harvest, indeed: the whole of the ground floor was stacked with hay, as was the loft that made a second storey in the back half of the building. A ladder was helpfully already leaning against the upper floor, so Edwin climbed it, thinking with a brief smile of the generations of children who had no doubt clambered up with the sole intention of leaping down into the deep piles of soft hay underneath.

He made his way through the mounds to the barn's far wall and then sat with his back to it, taking a moment to enjoy the quiet, the scent of the hay and the winter safety it represented.

Now, *think*...

Sir Richard's death had not been an accident. That was a point of certainty in Edwin's mind. Which meant that somebody had shot him on purpose, and Edwin needed to find out who and why. These were not separate questions, but rather different facets of the same one.

The person who benefitted most from Sir Richard's death was his son and heir, Sir Martin; but he could not possibly have either committed the murder or ordered it. Edwin also ruled out outlaws, footpads or an attack by a random stranger. Either of the former would have robbed as well as killed, and if a madman was on the loose there would have been more attacks, not just the one. No, this was targeted. But by whom?

Those who could not have loosed the arrow themselves included Jonilda and Abbot Thomas, although as either of them might conceivably have ordered someone else to do it, they could not yet be discounted as culprits. Other than the monks, any able-bodied man or older boy would have been able to nock an arrow and draw the string, though a certain amount of skill and experience would be necessary in order to be confident of hitting the target.

That meant, approximately, that the archer had to be more skilled than Edwin, though not necessarily by a great margin. He would have backed himself to hit a static target at the distance he'd measured out in the woods, on a good day, but not a moving one, which the assailant – the murderer – obviously had. Plus, as the additional thought occurred to Edwin, the shooter would need the nerves to keep his aim steady when he knew he was about to attempt cold-blooded murder. Edwin had shot a man in the heat of battle, once, but that had been instinctive and done to save another's life; it was a very different matter from standing, waiting, aiming carefully and then killing in such a way. No, whoever the archer was, he was not to be trifled with.

So, who had a bow? Virtually everyone, unfortunately. And even those who didn't own one would be able to find one to use, when there were so many about the place. Serlo, the forester, certainly had a bow and was not afraid to use it. Had he mistaken Sir Richard for a poacher? Surely not, especially given that he was riding a horse. Or did he shoot Sir Richard on purpose? It couldn't be ruled out, but why would he do such a thing?

Farolf, the man suspected of being a poacher, might well have been in the woods with a bow. He could hardly have mistaken Sir Richard for a deer or hare, and must have recognised him, but had he shot his lord because Sir Richard had seen him breaking the law? Had he panicked, loosed an arrow and then run off? That at least would explain why Sir Richard had not been robbed nor his horse stolen.

There were certainly other able-bodied men around. Did Dominic the reeve or Simon the abbey bailiff have anything to hide? And what about Christopher, the lonely grandfather who seemed so glad at the prospect of Sir Martin returning to the area to succeed his father? Or – Edwin hesitated even to think it – what about Michael? Either on his own behalf or at his mother's behest? But neither of them could possibly have wanted to kill Sir Richard, as it would leave them worse off… unless, of course, something also happened to Sir Martin.

Which brought Edwin all the way back to the *why* part of the question.

All right. Try a different thread, now. Consider for a moment that the murder might not have been rooted in the inheritance of the manor, even though that seemed the most obvious idea. Had Sir Richard upset anyone personally? His wife and children all loved him, and their affection seemed so genuine that Edwin was loath to believe he'd been any sort of secret tyrant. Similarly, Sir Richard's tenants respected him; nobody had needed their arms twisted before deciding to file past his body to pay their respects, and Edwin had not seen or heard anything except sorrow at his passing.

The nature of his death, then, more than a week after sustaining the injury. Had he actually been only slightly injured, and then worse had been done to him after he was brought home? Dirt or poison introduced to the wound? But that could only have been done by either Jonilda or Brother Gregory, and an infirmarer, sworn to care for the sick – and a monk, at that – would never do such a thing. Besides, Edwin knew only too well that even a superficial arrow wound could get infected and lead to eventual death, despite anyone's best efforts, never mind a large broadhead being embedded in the body and the internal organs. No, Sir Richard's death had surely been caused by the original injury from the arrow shot at him in the woods.

Why had he been in the woods, and who knew he would be riding there on that day? At the time of his death, Sir Richard had been on his way back from the abbey. Had he and Abbot Thomas argued about something? Was the abbot perhaps attempting to put pressure on him to sell his lands? But then why kill him? He couldn't negotiate with a dead man, and Sir Martin would be an even tougher prospect.

Oh, wait.

The abbot had been genuinely surprised to learn of Sir Martin's existence. So, with Sir Richard out of the way, he would have thought that he would be dealing with a woman and a boy, both of little experience in the world and additionally feeling vulnerable and bereaved. Had he ordered Sir Richard's murder so that he could browbeat the young heir – as he thought of Michael – and his mother into accepting an offer on the manor?

'Don't let him take–' had been the half-sentence that Sir Richard had managed to communicate to Edwin. Had he meant 'Don't let the abbot take the manor away from my family'? It certainly seemed plausible.

Could it be that simple? Edwin suspected not, and his next thought confirmed it as he berated himself for his idiocy. If this had been the case, and Sir Richard had known it, why had he not said anything about it during the week he lay ill but still able to speak? He could easily have made it known that his wish was for the abbey *not* to have the manor, come what may. And he could also have revealed what that long-ago letter from the earl contained, something he had evidently not done. So why had he waited an entire week, until he was so taken by the lockjaw that he could hardly speak? Why had he been so keen to have Sir Martin come to his side before he dropped any hint?

That last might not be related to the murder. Of course, as he lay on his deathbed, Sir Richard's thoughts had turned to his heir, the beloved son he hadn't seen for so long, and for whom he had given up the chance of advancement of his own. That was perfectly natural and might have nothing to do with the murder. But then *why*...

Edwin's head was beginning to go round in circles with that part of the question. Perhaps it would be better to put *why* to one side for now and concentrate on who might have been in the woods at the time Sir Richard was shot. He might be able to take several names off his list simply by looking at this from a practical point of view. Be logical, as he had told Gabriel.

'… Father Abbot?'

The proximity of Jonilda's voice made Edwin jump. Had she entered the hay barn? But no, the sound had come from behind him. He looked down to his left to see that a couple of the wooden boards that made up the barn's wall were loose. He was, of course, ten feet off the ground up here, so either nobody had noticed or fixing them hadn't been a priority because it was too high for rats and mice to get in.

Eavesdropping was not something Edwin liked or approved of, and had their conversation been any sort of sacramental confession he would have stopped his ears until he was sure they were gone. But Jonilda and the abbot were simply walking along together and were passing the outside of the barn, chatting as they went. They didn't stop, so he was not party to their whole conversation, catching only the part of it that wafted up to him as they went by.

'I don't think it is, unfortunately,' was the abbot's reply to whatever Jonilda had asked him.

'But surely, an allowance could be made for the circumstances? Have pity, I beg you. I don't have…'

And then they passed out of earshot.

Edwin sat for a while, wondering what they might have meant. But what he'd overheard was so short and so general that he wasn't sure he could make anything of it. Jonilda had asked the abbot some kind of question, he had returned a negative, and she had asked him to reconsider. Had he been trying to exert influence to gain the manor? No, that couldn't be it, for it was she who had asked and he who had declined. Was she wanting to sell it to him, even though they both knew that she had no right to do so? But that didn't make sense, either.

In truth, they could have been talking about anything, and for once Edwin was sorry that he hadn't put greater effort into overhearing. *An allowance could be made for the circumstances…* that must refer to

Sir Richard's death, surely. But why did she need an allowance, and why did she need it from the abbot? Whatever it was, it must be important to her. *Have pity, I beg you* – those were not words spoken lightly.

Edwin tried to settle back into his thoughts, but he couldn't, especially when noise began to intrude. He ignored it as best he could for a few moments, and then realised that it wasn't simply a background hum of normal manor work – what he could hear was sounds of alarm. He made his way back to the ladder, successfully avoided the childish temptation to jump, and climbed down safely.

Outside he was met with a sight that stopped him in his tracks as fear gripped his heart. The cart that had conveyed Sir Richard's body to the church had returned, and was now empty, as expected. But two of the three manor men who had gone with it were struggling to lead and control the obviously agitated horse, while the third was being supported by Sir Martin – and there was red blood on both of them. Simon was also there, on foot and leading his own horse, upon which Michael was mounted with Gabriel perched behind him.

Edwin ran forward, along with others who had seen the party.

Sir Martin's voice was agitated. 'We need to see to him first.' He indicated the man he was supporting. Edwin looked them both over and was at least partly relieved to see that all the visible blood belonged to the other, and that it was coming only from his hand. He did look pale from the shock, though, which was no doubt why Sir Martin was half-carrying him. 'Quickly!' bellowed the knight. 'Brother Gregory's not here, is he? The wound needs cleaning out properly – wine or something, or salves, before it gets infected. And for God's sake don't just tie it up with a wet rag.'

Abbot Thomas, Jonilda, Eustace and Dominic all hurried over to join the group, followed by various other workers who were nearby. Jonilda was at first frantic with worry about her sons, but Simon assured her they were fine, and that he'd just put them on his horse in case he needed them to flee from the area at speed.

'But why would you need to flee?' Edwin got the question out before anyone else could.

'Because,' said Sir Martin, grimly, passing the injured man over to willing arms, 'someone has just shot an arrow at us.'

Chapter Nine

There were exclamations of horror from all round.

'We must pursue the culprit!' cried Eustace. 'Indeed,' he added, somewhat accusingly, 'why did you not do so?'

'We did,' replied Sir Martin, curtly. Or, at least, *he* did.' He indicated Simon, who was helping Michael and Gabriel down from the horse.

'They were on their way back,' explained Simon, his uneven tone giving away how rattled he was. 'Off you go, now, boys, and get inside.' He watched them depart and then turned to Edwin and Eustace. 'Then an arrow out of nowhere. Between here and the church, where the woods come close to the road. I rode for where I thought it had come from, but I couldn't see or hear anyone, and then the trees got too thick for riding at speed, and I was worried about him falling on that uneven ground.' He patted his horse's neck. 'So, I thought it better to return to the road to escort the others back. I put the boys in the saddle so they could get away quickly if it turned out there was another shooter.'

'I heard the buzzing of the arrow just in time,' said Sir Martin, 'and shouted to everyone to get down. The boys ducked, but he–' he pointed at the wounded man now being taken into the house, 'flung his arm up over his head and it caught him on his hand.' He looked around. 'I'm sorry, I don't even know his name, not yet – I must learn – but he needs taking care of, do you hear?'

Jonilda was still hovering, and now she spoke, her voice also indicating shock. 'The children's nurses will be with him by now, but I'll go and tend to him personally. We have a herb garden and I've always got salves ready made up for when the children scrape themselves.' Her voice wobbled further as she thanked Simon for his care for her sons, before turning away.

So sweet, so caring, so innocent-seeming. But Edwin couldn't shake the idea from his head as he watched her depart: *She would be better off getting rid of Sir Martin*. But to risk her own sons at the same time? Surely not. And who could have loosed the arrow on her behalf, if it was not Michael himself?

'If I may, my lord,' interjected the reeve, 'his name's Bernulf, and I'll go and tell his wife, so she can come and tend him. It's not fit for Lady Jonilda to have to do it herself.'

Sir Martin stared at him. 'Dominic? Is that you?'

The reeve was delighted to have been recognised. 'Aye, my lord, it is, after all these years.'

'Why, it's so good to see – but yes, do that now, and we can catch up later. And tell Bernulf's wife she may have whatever salves and medicines she needs from the house.'

Edwin heard all of this only distantly, because the thoughts in his head were moving so quickly. First things first. 'Have you got the arrow?'

One of the men who had been leading the horse reached into the cart and handed it to him. The head, smeared lightly with blood, was of the triangular, broadhead type, and Edwin shuddered at the thought of Bernulf's lucky escape. Lucky, that was, if he avoided infection, but he was going to be well cared-for, and his situation was much more hopeful than it would have been if the arrow had lodged in his body anywhere.

Sir Martin moved to stand by him. 'Anything? Just looks like a normal arrow to me.'

'Yes,' sighed Edwin. 'From the fletcher at Edwinstowe, no doubt, who turns out sheaves of identical ones by the dozen.'

'How did you–? Never mind.'

Edwin looked at it more closely. 'Except,' he said, slowly, 'for this repair to the fletching.'

'Does that mean something?'

'It might.' In fact it certainly *did*, for Edwin had seen this exact arrow before. But he needed to think over the implications of that before he said anything about it to Sir Martin. 'Were you able to see how the arrow flew at you? I mean, did it come straight across, or was it coming down from a height? And can you make any guess as to which of you it was aimed at?'

'It was heading flat, definitely.'

'So, loosed from close range.'

'Yes.'

'And as to the target?'

Sir Martin rubbed his chin. 'Difficult to say, and of course it depends on how good a shot he was. But it was coming in relatively high, so it's probably a fair assumption that it was aimed at me.' He paused. 'I knew it was a mistake not bringing my armour with me. But I didn't think I'd need to, when we left Conisbrough – we were only going on a short visit to Rochford!'

While this conversation was going on, the abbot had been conferring with Simon. 'If there is no immediate need of me here, I will return to the abbey. I left Brother Prior to say the service of Sext, earlier, and I should not be absent for Nones as well.' He inclined his head to Sir Martin. 'If I can be of any assistance to you, I will be happy to offer it. And do send your injured man to the abbey to ask for Brother Gregory if necessary.' Then he addressed Eustace, who was still standing by. 'Will you return with us to the guest house?'

'No,' came the abrupt reply. 'I haven't yet finished my business here. I'll be in no danger riding back on my own later – nobody would dare harm the king's deputy sheriff.'

Why was Eustace so confident? Was he really so sure that his position would spare him, or did he know something about who the shooter was, and why that man wouldn't aim at him? He worked for the sheriff, and so did Serlo…

That was a thought to keep for later. 'Are you going to add this new incident to your enquiries?' asked Edwin, conversationally, as they watched the abbot's mule being brought out from the stable and saw him depart with Simon.

Eustace made a 'pshaw' sound. 'Of course not. A minor injury to a peasant? Who cares? Not worth my time or anyone else's.'

'But the two things might be link–' began Edwin, before realising he was speaking to Eustace's departing back.

Sir Martin was just beginning to give orders that the horse and cart should be dealt with when all six of the children emerged from the house. Most of them looked hesitant, especially as they gave Eustace a wide berth, but Michael strode confidently up to Sir Martin. 'He's been bullying the little ones.'

'Who has?'

'Him.' Michael pointed back at Eustace, just disappearing through the main door. 'While we were at the church and not here to look out for them.'

'He wanted to talk to the *children*?' Sir Martin looked from them to Edwin.

'I did hear him say he wanted to talk to the household in descending order,' said Edwin, with a pang of guilt, 'but I thought he meant Jonilda and the officials, not the children. I'm sorry, if I'd known I would have stopped him, or at least stayed nearby.'

Michael addressed Constance and Eleanor. 'Tell him.'

Eleanor shrank back from Sir Martin, but Constance's indignation overcame her trepidation. 'He shouted at us,' she declared, hotly. 'He said we were all brats who were hardly worth talking to, but we must know more than we were letting on, and we'd be in trouble if we didn't tell him. I was cross, but he made Ellie and Jonny cry.'

'He did *what*?' Sir Martin's voice was low and even, but it had taken on a dangerous edge.

Michael was nodding. 'Connie came to tell me about it as soon as we came in, and I wanted to come out and say to Eustace that he shouldn't act like that to children, but Gabriel said we'd better tell you first.'

'You were both right. Right to tell me, and right to know that someone needs to have words with him.' Sir Martin's gaze swept all of them. 'Leave it with me.'

He stalked off, and Edwin mentally started counting as he saw his friend duck through the doorway. He hadn't got to five when the bellowing started, although thankfully he couldn't hear anything that sounded like physical violence.

'Told you,' said Gabriel to the others. 'Told you he'd be on our side, this once at least.'

Edwin was just starting to wonder what he was going to do now he'd apparently been left in charge of six children while their mother and nurses were engaged with the injured man, when yet another commotion started.

This time it coalesced into the figure of Serlo, who was pulling along with him another man who was restrained, his hands tied together in front of him. They were surrounded by a crowd of shouting and gesticulating manor people, women and children as well as men.

As they came closer, Edwin could see that the man under restraint was Farolf, and that the most vociferous among those who were pleading with or shouting at Serlo was Dominic, the reeve. 'Best run and tell your brother,' he said under his breath to Michael, who hared off.

Serlo managed to make it unharmed into the manor yard with his captive still in tow. 'The sheriff's man is here,' he called to Edwin. 'I know he is. Well, he'll be able to see that I've done my duty!'

Edwin opened his mouth, but he was cut off by a roar. 'What in the name of God's blood is going on *now*?' He turned to see Sir Martin bursting out of the house, with Eustace just behind him.

Serlo had little attention or deference to spare for the lord of the manor now that a representative of the sheriff – his ultimate employer – was before him. 'I've caught a poacher, sir.'

Eustace stopped. 'Oh. I thought something important had happened.' He seemed completely uninterested, even bored. 'So what?'

'Well…' began Serlo, clearly nonplussed.

'Was he in the woods just now?' broke in Edwin. 'Whereabouts?'

Serlo attempted to address himself to Eustace again. 'Caught red-handed, sir. Look!' He seized Farolf's tied wrists and held the hands up long enough for Edwin and all the other onlookers to see that they were smeared in blood.

This caught Eustace's attention, and he turned back. Now he had a malicious gleam in his eye that Edwin didn't like. 'Well, I think that gives us the culprit for this morning's arrow.'

'Don't be ridiculous,' shot back Edwin, before anyone else could open their mouths.

'Sorry, who are you, again?' Eustace was now taking on an air of mocking superiority.

'It doesn't matter who I am. Your accusation is plainly false.'

'The blood on his hands…?'

'Is the very reason why it can't have been him. Why would he have blood on his hands, if he was shooting an arrow from a distance? The only blood was on Bernulf, from where the arrow hit him. It wouldn't have gone anywhere near the shooter.'

There was a murmur of agreement from the onlookers, and a matching rumble from Sir Martin.

'Was he carrying a bow when you caught him?' Edwin asked Serlo.

The forester looked from Eustace to Edwin. 'No, sir, only a snare.'

Edwin noted that Serlo did not have his own bow with him; he was using both his hands to restrain his captive.

'Well,' Eustace continued. 'Perhaps he didn't loose the arrow, then. But he's certainly been poaching, and caught with bloodied hands in the king's forest, so he'll need to be punished. Forthwith.'

Farolf had not seemed able to keep up with most of the conversation so far, but he certainly understood that. He began to struggle. 'No! Please, no! You can't–'

Dominic stepped forward. 'Please, sir, of your mercy. You don't understand. He's–'

Eustace cut him off with a wave of his arm. 'I don't need to understand, and nor do I care. Examples must be made, lest men start to believe they can poach in the king's forest with impunity.'

That's odd, thought Edwin. It was almost the opposite of what Eustace had said only a few moments ago. What was he up to?

The reeve now turned to Sir Martin. 'Please, my lord. You know what the punishment is.' His eyes slid to the knight's missing hand.

All the colour had drained from Sir Martin's face.

Edwin waited for Eustace to correct the misapprehension, noting that Serlo was also looking at him expectantly. He was the sheriff's deputy and must know the current law.

'I can't,' began Sir Martin. 'I won't condemn anyone to...'

'My lord,' continued Dominic in a desperate whisper. 'I know you can't go against the law, or you'll get in trouble yourself. But surely there must be some way...'

Edwin looked from the dazed Sir Martin to the pleading Dominic, the confused Serlo, the terrified Farolf and the seemingly amused Eustace. He saw the frightened faces of the men, women and children who were looking on in horror.

Enough was enough. 'Stop this, now.'

All eyes turned to him. Sir Martin's were alight with hope at the thought that Edwin might be able to pull him out of the terrible hole he was in, and Eustace's glowed with fury.

'You know perfectly well,' said Edwin to Eustace, coolly, 'that the law has changed, and the loss of a hand is no longer the punishment for poaching in the king's forest.'

There was a general intake of breath.

'Gabriel, would you please go to the kist in the parlour and bring out the charter we were looking at? The big one about forest law, with the seal attached?'

While the boy was gone, Edwin addressed Eustace. 'We have the proof, but you don't need it, do you? You knew already.'

Eustace smiled. 'Have I said one word about cutting this man's hand off? All I said was that he needed to be punished. It's these parochials who don't know the law.'

'But you were going to stand by and let it happen! You were going to let Sir Martin...'

Belatedly, realisation dawned. 'You were going to let Sir Martin commit what would have been a crime in itself, mutilating a man with no cause,' Edwin continued, incredulously. 'And all because he just took you to task for bullying the children and you felt humiliated.' Edwin found it hard to disguise his disgust. 'Is this all a *game* to you? People's lives? Farolf here was going to lose his hand and maybe even his life, just so you could get back at Sir Martin?'

The murmur from the people around him took on a different tone, and Edwin saw Sir Martin reflexively reach for the place his sword hilt would have been, had he been wearing it.

Eustace felt the change of atmosphere, and his eyes narrowed. The amused expression vanished. 'Very well. I leave you to dispense justice to this man. Oh, put that away, boy! I know what the law is.' He made a shooing motion at Gabriel, who had arrived with the charter.

'You keep a civil tongue in your head when you talk to him,' growled Sir Martin, who now appeared to be recovering his wits a little. 'Edwin, read out what it says, so we all know and there's plenty of witnesses.'

Edwin read out and then translated the relevant passage. Serlo nodded, with a look of relief, which Edwin might have interpreted in two ways. Maybe he'd only been doing his job and hadn't meant to cause so much trouble; but it was also possible that he was mightily thankful to have got away with something much more serious. And where were his bow and quiver?

Something else Edwin didn't understand just at this moment was the palpable relief that swept through the manor's inhabitants. If Farolf was a habitual poacher and shirker, why did they all care so much?

He looked at Eustace again, expecting him to back down and make an excuse to leave; however, he seemed rather to be puffing himself up, and Edwin realised he'd misjudged the man's pride in himself and the resultant malice that might produce. He might be ruthless if he had ambitions of his own. Maybe he was even after the top job, that of high sheriff? He evidently did some of the work for it already; Christopher had said that it was Eustace, not the sheriff, who made the county's accounts to the exchequer. Ah, wait…

'I will be leaving now,' Eustace announced, 'but only temporarily. My enquiries have led me to believe that Sir Richard was murdered, and that the main beneficiary was his son and heir, Sir Martin. I will therefore be summoning a jury to try him for murder or the causing or ordering of murder.'

Edwin just about managed to thrust an arm out in front of Sir Martin, which was enough to prevent the start of a lunge forward. But he hadn't counted on Michael, who was already hotly disputing Eustace's accusation and getting dangerously close to laying a hand on him.

Fortunately, Eustace merely laughed in the boy's face. 'Now, have my horse fetched, and remember, I work for the sheriff and the king.'

The reminder, or the threat, was enough, and he was allowed to depart in peace. He might have been markedly less sanguine, however, if he'd known just how clearly Edwin could now see through him.

There was silence among the crowd for a few moments after the sound of hoofbeats had died away, before Sir Martin shook his head to clear it and remembered – without Edwin needing to prompt him – that he was in charge.

'Back to work, then, all of you,' he said to the throng. 'But be assured that Farolf will be dealt with according to the new law, not the old one.' Then, under his breath to Dominic, 'Stay a moment, if you would, so I can talk to you,' and then again with a raised voice, to Serlo, 'You can leave him here. I give you my word he won't be allowed to escape.' He paused. 'You have my thanks for doing your duty and bringing this matter to my attention.'

Serlo bowed and left. Edwin desperately wanted to talk to him, but he also needed to stay here until things were calmer, so he was forced to watch the forester walk away.

A small group now emerged from the house: Jonilda, with Bernulf and a woman who was presumably his wife.

Sir Martin took a few paces towards them in concern. 'Your hand?'

'Cleaned and properly bandaged,' said Jonilda, when the man looked reluctant to speak. 'I think it will heal nicely.'

'It's Sunday tomorrow, my lord,' said Bernulf, barely daring to look Sir Martin in the face. 'We don't work in the fields then. But I'll be fit to take my place with the other men on Monday, I swear.'

Sir Martin blinked. Then he laid a large and heavy hand on Bernulf's shoulder. 'That's not why I was asking,' he said. 'You work for me, and that makes you my responsibility. You had no blame in what happened, and my concern is that you're healthy and whole, not that you can wield a spade on Monday.'

Bernulf and his wife both seemed overcome, and they stuttered out their thanks while other manor people surrounded them and bore them away. Edwin was pleased to see that Sir Martin was the subject of many smiles and much goodwill.

The knight didn't notice that himself, having already turned to the two men who were still standing by with the horse and cart. He pointed at Farolf. 'Take him to the stable with you and make sure he stays there.' Then he addressed the poacher directly. '*Don't* make this any worse for yourself by attempting to escape, do you hear me? Or I won't be so sympathetic next time.'

Farolf nodded and gabbled out some incoherent thanks, and Sir Martin told the others to release him from his restraints. He rubbed at his wrists; the cord used to tie him had been very thin, and it had cut into him as he struggled. Edwin took it and nodded to himself as he examined it.

Sir Martin turned to Dominic. 'Now. Tell me – tell *us* –' his glance encompassed Edwin – 'what we don't know about this. Even I can see that there's something going on, and that nobody wanted him punished.'

The three men sat down on a bench set against the outside wall of the manor house.

'I did try to explain to that sheriff's man,' began Dominic. 'We all know that he slips off poaching sometimes. Small game, I mean – he'd never take a deer.'

'Then why cover for him? Why excuse him?'

'It was on your father's orders, my lord.'

Edwin straightened in surprise and saw his friend do likewise. 'How so?'

'Farolf's wife is dead, my lord, and he's been left with three sons. Big lads, now, but two of them are cripples and the other one's an idiot.' Dominic took off his hat and used it to rub sweat from his brow.

'None of them can work, and he just can't labour enough or grow enough to feed them all. They've no mother, and of course none of the single women want to marry him and take all that on. So, it's four hungry mouths and only one worker.'

'And my father knew of this?'

'Yes, my lord. He did what he could to help, and he made us understand we could turn a blind eye to the odd hare from the manor itself – they don't get much to eat, those boys, and a bit of meat does them good. But he *did* warn him only to stay on the manor and not go into the forest, because his word wasn't law there and Farolf would get into trouble.'

'And yet Farolf risked his life or the loss of a hand – or so he thought, at least – by going into the woods anyway?'

'He'd do anything for those boys, my lord, including risking his life to feed them. That's what he was doing, I'm sure of it. He wasn't going to sell the meat on and make a profit. He was just looking out for his family.'

Sir Martin was silent for a moment. Then he leaned across Dominic to address Edwin. 'You know this law. When it says "imprisonment", does it say where?'

Edwin ran his mind back over the lines of text. 'No.'

'So, we could "imprison" him on the manor for a year?'

'I would say so, yes.'

'Good.' After a pause, Sir Martin nodded, more to himself than to the others. He addressed Dominic. 'So, this is what we'll do. Go to him now, and say I'll make a bargain with him. As long as he stays on the manor for the whole of the next year – not setting one foot outside of it, mind – I'll pay his surety afterwards so he doesn't have to go into exile. And as long as he keeps strictly to that, the manor will provide food and shelter for him and his children regardless of the fact that he can't shoulder enough work for four.' There was another pause. 'And if anyone else here thinks that I'm showing favouritism, tell them it's our Christian duty to look after the sick, which I'm sure is what a priest would tell them, if we had one.'

Dominic stood. 'Thank you, my lord. And there won't be any trouble about it on the manor, you have my word. We're all just glad that our new lord is set fair to continue the good ways of the old one.' He replaced his hat and whistled to himself as he made his way over to the stable.

Edwin leaned back, stuck his feet out in front of him and smiled.

'What?'

Edwin squinted at his friend in the bright afternoon sunlight. 'What do you mean, "what"?'

'Aren't you going to say something clever?'

'No.'

'No?'

'Don't need to. You've done that yourself.'

Sir Martin said nothing, but Edwin could tell that he was more relaxed than he'd been at any time since he'd arrived here, despite the fact that it was not two hours since someone had tried to kill him, and that he was under official suspicion for murdering his father.

The lord earl – and many others, Eustace probably included in that number – saw individual manors as little things, as mere units of economic resource that provided them with the income they wanted. Edwin, meanwhile, saw them as places full of people. Real people, all trying to live their lives as best they could in the situation in which God had placed them.

He felt a deep and comforting sense of contentment to know which of those viewpoints Sir Martin had chosen.

Edwin couldn't think of any better way to attempt to find Serlo than walking along the road through the woods and shouting his name, but fortunately this worked.

The forester was making himself much more obvious than usual, crashing through undergrowth and swearing under his breath. 'What do you want?' he called out, before noticing who it was. 'Oh, sorry, sir, didn't realise it was you. That poacher been dealt with, has he?'

'Sir Martin is following the law, yes – the new law.'

Serlo seemed distracted as he looked around him. 'Wasn't my place to speak out over the deputy sheriff, but I would've said something if it'd really come to the point of chopping his hand off, I swear I would.'

'I'm glad to hear it.' Edwin paused. 'I'm going to step off the road to come closer to you.'

'That's fine. I know who you are, and you've got no bow or snare.'

'And neither do you, I see.'

Serlo's puzzlement increased. 'I left them just here.'

'Your bow? And your quiver?'

'Aye. When I saw the poacher I nocked an arrow and told him to stand still. Once I had him I had to tie his hands, so he couldn't wipe the blood off before I could show it to anyone. I had no rope, so I used my bowstring, and I left my bow here, along with the quiver, 'cos that's an awkward thing to carry if you don't need it.'

'Are you sure it was just here?'

Serlo gave him a scathing look. 'I am, sir. I know every tree in these woods. But what I'm wondering is, why is the bow still here but the quiver isn't?' He reached behind a trunk and brandished what Edwin momentarily took to be a staff, but was in fact a bow stave, bare and straight.

'Here,' said Edwin, passing over the string he'd taken when Farolf was released. 'You'll want that back.' Serlo's tale accorded so far with Edwin's own observation, but was there more?

He looked about him. By his judgement, they were about a quarter of a mile away from where the arrow had been shot at Sir Martin. 'And it was exactly here that you apprehended Farolf?'

'Aye.'

If Serlo was lying, and he'd been in the part of the woods near the church from where the shot had been loosed, then his claim to have 'lost' his quiver here was extraordinarily convenient. But he clearly *had* caught Farolf and could not have been in two places at once. Unless they'd both been a quarter of a mile away – but then why was Serlo's bow here? And Edwin had seen the string tied around Farolf's wrists himself. They could hardly be colluding with each other; Farolf had been genuinely terrified that he was about to lose a hand and would surely have shouted out anything he knew in an attempt to save himself.

All of this continued to puzzle Edwin through the afternoon and during the family meal. By the later part of the evening, his mind was still full of disconnected thoughts and he couldn't concentrate on them all at once, so he reached for his portable chess set in order to give himself something else to do while the nagging questions sat at the back of his mind.

He would have to play against himself, but he was used to that and it was no hardship. Indeed, he felt it improved his game. He did set the pieces up rather more slowly than usual, thinking with sadness of Sir Geoffrey, but eventually he got going and was able to focus his mind properly.

He didn't know how long it had been, but the game was moving into its final stages when he became aware that Gabriel was standing by him, silently observing. 'How long have you been there?'

'Since that piece was there.' Gabriel pointed to the black king, which Edwin had castled some moves ago. 'What are you doing?'

'Have you never seen a chess set before?'

Gabriel shook his head. Edwin, assuming that a boy who could add up as fast as he could might also have the sort of mind that excelled at chess, began to explain to him the basics of the game and how each piece moved.

'And you play it by yourself, do you? Being both sides at once?'

'No, normally there are two players, one taking black and the other white, and they play against each other, like a war or a battle. But if you're in a place where you're the only person who knows how to play, you can act for both sides at once. It makes the gameplay different, because you know what's in your opponent's mind, but it's an interesting challenge nonetheless.'

Gabriel hovered, but seemed reluctant to ask his next question.

'Yes, you can, if you like,' said Edwin. 'The end of this game was going to be predictable, so it's no matter to stop it now and reset the pieces.'

He did so, and began a very slow game during which he advised Gabriel on what to do, encouraged him to think several moves ahead instead of focusing on the present, and delighted in his quick mind.

Given that Edwin was effectively playing against himself again, the game went on for longer than it might otherwise have done, and by the time they'd finished he was aware of the lateness of the hour. 'Not now,' he said, in reply to Gabriel's enthusiastic request for another. 'But we can play again tomorrow, if you'd like.'

The offer was eagerly accepted. Gabriel picked up some pieces, but instead of putting them back in the bag, he began arranging them in different combinations on the board.

'What are you doing?'

'This is Father,' said the boy, pointing to the white king he'd placed in the middle. 'And Mother,' he added, indicating the white queen.

'And these are you and your brothers and sisters?' hazarded Edwin, looking at the seven white pawns that were lined up in a careful row, each just touching the next.

'Yes.' Gabriel picked up the one that was second in the line. 'But I need to move Amice away.' He gazed at the pawn, turning it round gently in his fingers before putting it down off to one side of the leather board. 'I miss her. Michael says not to think about it too much, but she was nice, and kind, and she loved us all.' He sighed.

'There's nothing wrong with that,' said Edwin, in a low voice. 'You and Michael are different people, and you deal with things in different ways. It doesn't mean either of you is right or wrong, and of course it's a good thing that you loved your sister.'

There was a silence. As Edwin looked at the pieces, another idea came into his mind. 'Will you help me with something?'

Gabriel came out of his reverie. 'Yes, of course. What?'

'I don't want to upset you by talking of your father's death, and of what happened this afternoon, but it strikes me that we could use these pieces to think logically.'

'And that might help us to find out what happened? And who did it?'

'Yes. But if you don't want to, then that's fine.'

Gabriel thought for a moment. 'I can help.'

'Thank you. Any time you want to stop, you just say. All right?'

'Yes.' Gabriel looked at the board. 'What do we need to do?'

Edwin picked up the white king. 'This is your father. On the afternoon that he was shot, he was riding through the woods.' He placed the piece towards one edge of the board. 'But none of the rest of you were there.'

'No.' Gabriel moved the queen and the six remaining pawns to the other side. 'We were at home.'

'Can you remember exactly what each of you was doing? Or, at least, yourself, Michael and your mother? Were you all in the house?'

Fortunately, Gabriel didn't pick up on the exact reason why Edwin might be focusing on his eldest brother and mother. His hand hesitated over the pieces and his brow furrowed in concentration. 'We'd all been outside, down at the pond. Then we came back to the house. Mother was there; she'd been talking about meals with the cook. Then Jonny and Adela went upstairs with the nurses for a sleep.' He pushed two pawns to one side. 'Connie and Ellie wanted to play at skipping. I remember that because Amice used to skip with them, and they hadn't done it since she… So, anyway, they stayed just outside the house and did that.' Two more pawns were moved, leaving the final two with the queen.

'And…?'

'I went out again because I wanted to watch the hay being stacked in the barn. I thought it would be fun to count how much there was and work out how many days it would last for.' He moved another pawn. 'I was there for a while, right up until Father's horse came in without him. Then when the shouting started I went back to the house, and everyone else was there.'

Edwin said nothing for a few moments.

'Did I do all that right?' Gabriel's voice was anxious.

'Yes, of course you did.' Edwin made an effort to move his thoughts on. 'Now. That's what you *know* happened; let's think about what *might* have happened elsewhere, and with other people.'

'By being logical?'

'Yes. Now, let's start with Abbot Thomas.' Edwin picked up the black bishop.

'Shouldn't he be white? Like his robe?'

'Good thought, but let's use black for people who aren't in your family so we don't get mixed up. He must have been at the abbey, because that's where your father had come from.' He set the piece down on the far side of the white king. 'So, let's pick some random others… say Simon the abbey bailiff, Serlo the forester, Dominic the reeve, Farolf and Master Christopher from Langley.' He picked a black knight for the first, on the basis that Simon often rode a horse, then three pawns and a rook.

Gabriel confidently chose one pawn and placed it next to the white one that represented himself. 'Dominic was at the barn all afternoon, overseeing the hay. I know that because I saw him.'

'Good! Well done. Now, what about the others?'

Gabriel hesitated. 'Master Christopher must have been at Langley.' He moved the rook to the far side of the table.

'But you can't be sure?'

'No.' Gabriel paused. 'But it is logical; he hardly ever leaves it.'

'All right.'

'I didn't see Serlo that day, but he's often in the forest. And Farolf could have been anywhere.' After some hesitation, the other two pawns went over near the white king.

That just left the black knight, and neither of them had the faintest idea where to put that. For now, Edwin placed it with the bishop.

'You've got two missing,' said Gabriel. 'Actually, three.'

'Go on.'

Gabriel picked up the second black knight and one of the white ones. 'This is that horrible sheriff's man who was here earlier, and *this* is our brother.'

'And the third?'

'Why, you, of course.' Gabriel's hand hovered over the remaining black pieces, and to Edwin's amusement he picked up the king. 'Well, we've used both knights, and you're not a castle or a bishop.'

'Fair enough. But why do you need them? None of us was anywhere near here on the day your father was shot.'

'No. In fact you were so far away that I'd have to put these pieces at the other end of the room. But you said you wanted to talk about today as well, and you were all here today.'

He really was sharp. 'Yes, that's right. So, our proposal for now is that both arrows were shot by the same man, so I want to see who might have been in the right place at both times.' Edwin looked at the board.

'Michael and I were on the road with our brother.' Gabriel moved the white knight and pawns.

'Yes. And Simon was with you, because he chased the shooter, and Eustace, Dominic and I were all here at the manor.' Edwin also placed his pieces.

Gabriel was frowning. 'Well…'

'And your mother was talking to the abbot, also here.' The black bishop moved to stand next to the white queen. 'Which leaves Christopher, Serlo and Farolf.'

'But we know that Serlo and Farolf were both in the woods.' Gabriel pointed to where two black pawns already stood, not needing to move them. 'And we don't know where Master Christopher was, but again, probably at Langley.' Another non-moving piece.

Edwin stared and stared, trying to make some sense of what he was seeing, and sure that there was something just out of his reach that he was missing. Serlo and Farolf had both been in the woods together at some point, but where, exactly? And what made everything even more frustrating was that those with the best opportunity to shoot the arrows had the least reason to do so, while those who gained by Sir Richard's death – or Sir Martin's – could be discounted from having shot either or both. It was a puzzle much harder than any game of chess.

'Have we helped?' Gabriel looked as bewildered as Edwin felt.

'I'm not sure yet. But we certainly haven't *not* helped, if you know what I mean. No information is ever wasted.' Edwin looked up and noted again how late it was. 'You'd better go to bed.'

'Before I go, can I ask you some questions?'

'Yes.' Edwin was interested to find out what was on his mind.

'If our brother – Sir Martin, that is – had been killed by that arrow today, what would have happened?'

Edwin stopped himself from giving the obvious answer until he'd run through in his mind the earl's letter of many years ago, which he realised he had still not told Sir Martin about. But there was nothing there that would affect... 'Then Michael would inherit the manor here. I don't know what would happen to Langley in due course, because I don't know what other heirs Christopher might have.'

'But how could Michael run the whole manor? He's thirteen!'

'Well, he would need an adult to act for him. Like the king has.'

'The king?' Gabriel picked up the chess piece he had used to represent Edwin.

'Yes. The real king, I mean. He's only thirteen as well, so he has people to help him rule. It's called a regency.'

'Hmm.' Gabriel turned the piece in his hand. 'And what if–'

Edwin noticed the anxious pause. 'What if what? It's all right, this is between us, and I'm sure nothing you can say is going to shock me.'

Gabriel took a deep breath. 'That man said he was going to have our brother tried for murder. We know he didn't do it, but what if he's horrible enough to have him found guilty?'

Edwin correctly worked his way through all the hes and hims. 'That's a very interesting thought. Of course, if your brother were found guilty – and he won't be,' added Edwin, hastily, 'and to be honest, I don't even think it will get as far as a trial, or at least not if I can help it. But *if* that were to happen, he would be execu– he would certainly not be allowed to inherit the manor. But I'd have to check to see whether such a serious crime would mean that the rest of his family was debarred as well.'

'So, we'd *all* lose the manor? And have to go somewhere else?'

'Not necessarily. And remember, that's not going to happen. But theoretically, yes, it might cause a situation where someone else could put in a legal claim.' Edwin wondered at his mind being so full that this possibility had not yet occurred to him. 'Do you know, you're a very useful fellow to have around,' he said, watching the cheering effect that the compliment had. 'Truly. But now it really is time for bed.'

Obediently, Gabriel slipped off the stool. 'Can I help you again tomorrow?'

'I'm sure we can find you something to do. Good night.'

After Gabriel had gone, Edwin turned back to the board.

Sir Martin, who had apparently been in the room all this time without Edwin really noticing, came over to sit by him and gestured at the scattered pieces. 'I didn't like to interrupt. Does all of this… mean something?'

'I'm not sure yet,' said Edwin, the same reply he'd given Gabriel earlier. But some patterns were beginning to form. 'Why don't you go to bed too? This lamp won't last long, but I'll just sit here until it goes out.'

In the dim, flickering light, Edwin stared and stared at the chess pieces. If he tried hard enough he might be able to work out exactly where each person had been at the relevant times, but he would never be able to see into their hearts or minds, and the inanimate and crudely carved figures wouldn't help him with that.

Just as the light guttered, he put out his hand to sweep the pieces back into the pouch. Most of them went away immediately, but he hesitated over the last four. The pawns representing Serlo and Farolf were still in the woods, and he stared for a while, but then some instinct made him pick them up and stow them in the pouch.

That left only the white queen and the black bishop, standing close together and seeming to watch Edwin's every move.

Chapter Ten

It was not much past dawn on Sunday morning, but the whole household was already organised and prepared to walk to church for Mass and then Sir Richard's funeral. A grim-faced Sir Martin and a weeping Jonilda had each courteously attempted to cede first place in the procession to the other, and Edwin was pleased to see that a compromise had been reached whereby they would walk side by side. Michael and Gabriel followed next, with Constance and Eleanor between them, and then the two nurses with Jonny and Adela. Edwin would have been happy to bring up the rear behind the rest of the manor inhabitants, but he found himself just behind the children and beside the reeve. Dominic's manner was both sad and restless, and several times he seemed on the verge of saying something to Edwin, before deciding that it wouldn't be right while everyone else was pacing in sombre silence.

Edwin's senses were alert as they walked, but they reached the church without mishap and filed in to stand on the Woodthorpe side, well away from the deep hole that had already been dug in the north transept. The people of Langley also entered, with Christopher taking his place last. Neither he nor Sir Martin looked at each other.

The Mass was short, the visiting priest seeming keen to gabble through it as quickly as possible. At the sound of *Ite, missa est*, everyone from Langley began to drift out, but Edwin managed to catch Christopher's eye and indicate that he should stay. He didn't have Sir Martin's specific permission for this, which is what Christopher had wanted, because he had deliberately not brought up the subject in case Sir Martin said no. It was Edwin's opinion that a more natural-seeming encounter might be preferable, and he was determined to engineer a proper conversation between them if he could.

The burial service was at least conducted with a little more solemnity and decorum, the priest speaking the words at the proper pace. As the coffin was lowered Edwin took the opportunity for a surreptitious glance at as many faces as he could, but they were all showing great sorrow and this told him nothing except that Sir Richard had been well loved. Even Christopher, standing back at a respectful distance with his hat in his hands and his head bowed, was grieving. And yet somebody, somewhere, had killed Sir Richard – had murdered the man who was a respected lord, a loving husband and a doting father. A particularly generous father, as Edwin was going to have to explain to Sir Martin before too much longer.

Who could possibly have wanted to do such a thing? Edwin didn't mind admitting to himself that he was still at a complete loss, and his silent prayers were pleas for divine assistance in the matter as well as supplications for the dead man's soul.

Once the service was complete, Edwin prevaricated for a while, playing for time and aiming to keep both Sir Martin and Christopher inside the church while everyone else made their mournful way out. He successfully drew their attention to his interest in the wall paintings, including a smaller one near the altar that he hadn't spotted last time. It was the four evangelists, each depicted with a copy of his own gospel and his particular symbol: the divine man of St Matthew, the lion of St Mark, the ox of St Luke and the eagle of St John.

By the time he'd finished murmuring a few comments he could see that the church was empty other than their three selves, and Sir Martin and Christopher had fallen silent and were staring at each other. Good.

'I'll leave you to talk,' Edwin said, quietly, and stepped back. He remained inside the church for a few moments, standing at a slight distance from them and concentrating his gaze on the painting. He had no intention of eavesdropping, but he did want to make sure they'd at least started speaking before he left, so they wouldn't just nod at each other and depart to go their separate ways in silence.

But then he found his attention really caught by the image in front of him. Something – just the small seed of an idea – was beginning to form in his mind. Or, rather, he was reminded of something. But what was it? *Think.* Who had said the words that were now hovering just outside his consciousness, and why were they important? Edwin stared and stared at the divine man, willing the thought to become clearer. Yes, that was it! And it did make sense... But no, the evidence he already had in hand meant that it was physically impossible.

Edwin sighed at his own inability to untangle the threads of the puzzle. He came back to himself and became aware that the two other men were now in earnest conversation, so he slipped out of the church, hoping that matters might resolve themselves into a more recognisable pattern if he just left the new thought at the back of his mind to stew in its own juice.

Most of those who had attended the burial were already on their way back to the manor, but Dominic was standing just outside the church door.

'If you're waiting for Sir Martin,' Edwin said, 'I think he'll be some little while.'

'Actually, sir, it was you I was looking for.'

'Me? How can I help? And please, there's no need to call me sir. Just Edwin will do.'

They turned and began to walk in the direction of Woodthorpe as the reeve spoke again. 'You seem to know all about what's going on with the law. How can we stop that son of a– that sheriff's man from making his wicked accusations against our lord?' There was a real undercurrent of anger in his tone.

'It's ridiculous, I know, and I'm sure it won't even get to the stage of being put before a jury, but I think I might have an idea of why he did it.'

'A jury? You'd not find a single man around these parts who'd convict Sir Martin, not for his own sake nor for his father's, neither.'

'His actions since he's been here certainly seem to have made him popular.'

'It's not just that.' Dominic shook his head. 'I know he only lived here for a short while when he was younger, but anyone who remembers that time, who knew him as a boy, will know he's as honest as the day is long.'

Edwin smiled. 'He certainly is that. There's no guile in him at all – what you see is what you get.'

'Why, once we got in trouble for something when we were young 'uns – I even forget what it was now, just some mischief or other, but I remember his reaction. There's lots of high-born boys, no doubt, would be happy to see common lads take all the blame, but no, he said straight out, "it was all my idea and my fault, and if you must punish someone then it's me and not Dominic".'

Edwin nodded. 'That sounds exactly like him, even now.'

'And he took his beating, and never a cross word about it to me ever after. I tell you,' repeated the reeve, 'I'll stand by him in front of any jury, and so will the other men. Even if the jury's all knights and other lords, which I suppose it would be. I'm not afraid to stand up for what's right.'

'I can see why you and he have always got on well.' By this time, they had reached the place where the woods approached close to the road, and Edwin halted. 'This must be about where they were when the arrow was loosed at them.'

Dominic nodded. 'Aye, I'd say so. Plenty of cover from those trees.'

'I just want to look for something,' began Edwin, moving off the road.

'Here, don't you go down there on your own,' said Dominic, anxiously. 'My lord won't want anything happening to you.' He followed.

'The arrow came fairly flat, he said,' noted Edwin, as he began scrambling through brush. 'So, the archer can't have been all that far away.' He repeated the sort of exercise he'd carried out with Michael and Gabriel in the other part of the woods, until he found what he was looking for. And not just footprints or broken twigs this time, but proper evidence. 'Here,' he called to Dominic. 'Come and witness this for me, before I touch it.'

As the reeve approached, Edwin pointed down into the undergrowth. 'There.'

'It's a bow!' Dominic reached out towards it.

'Wait.'

The reeve's outstretched arm stopped. 'What?'

'Look carefully before we move it, so we can give proper testimony. What do you notice?'

Dominic frowned. 'It's still strung. That's not going to do it much good.'

'Which, I believe, means that whoever used it then discarded it in a hurry before running off. Do you agree?'

The reeve nodded. 'Sounds right. If you had time then you'd unstring it and put it away properly, not just throw it down like that.' He paused. 'But didn't they say that bailiff from the abbey chased into the woods as soon as the arrow came? Him coming down fast on horseback would scare your archer, wouldn't it?' He pointed to where a couple of hoof-prints were visible on a damp patch of ground.

'Yes,' said Edwin, bending to pick up the bow. He held it out. 'You're probably going to tell me that there's nothing particularly distinctive about it, aren't you?'

The other's expression told him that he was right. 'If you had your own bow, and you'd used it for years, you'd be able to pick it out, but recognising someone else's is difficult, unless there's some obvious flaw or nick in it. This is a yew bow with a hemp string just like all the others, until someone claims it as his.'

'Yes,' said Edwin, pushing some undergrowth aside with his foot in quest of what he suspected would be there. It was.

Dominic peered down. 'A quiver. Well, makes sense, I suppose.'

The weaving was beginning to take shape in Edwin's mind. 'A quiver is an awkward thing to carry, if you don't need to,' he said, almost to himself.

'I'm not sure I understand you.'

'It's all right. Just working something out, that's all. Now, we'll take these back with us. I suspect that we will soon find the owner of the quiver, but I doubt very much if anyone will claim the bow.'

'Why not…? Oh, of course. Anyone who says it's his would be as good as saying he loosed the arrow.'

'Correct.'

'Although I suppose we could look for a man who's *missing* his bow?'

'We could,' sighed Edwin. 'Though, knowing my luck at the moment, we'll find that this is just one from the manor stocks.'

'The manor does own some, yes.'

'Well then.'

They made their way back to the road, and parted once they reached the manor buildings, Edwin promising he would do everything he could to stop the accusations against Sir Martin reaching a formal stage. They were, of course, ludicrous, and Edwin had no idea how Eustace thought they might stand up in the face of the scepticism that would surely be shown by a jury of local knights and manor lords, to say nothing of daring the wrath of Earl Warenne. Edwin thought to himself of all the many times he'd wished his lord could control his temper better, whereas now he'd be quite happy to see an enraged earl descending upon them, and Eustace in particular. Ambitious men took risks, but they had no right to cast accusations at the innocent.

Sending a message to the earl would remain a last resort, Edwin was determined. For now, his next task was to visit the abbey. Abbot Thomas would be busy on a Sunday, of course, but that couldn't be helped, and Edwin didn't want to leave it another day. He stowed the bow and the quiver of arrows in the barn to keep them separate from any of the manor stocks for now, and then decided to set off straight away.

It was a couple of miles to Rufford, he knew, so he would go on horseback to save time. He was aware that he still hadn't told Sir Martin the all-important information from the letter, and that he'd want to return well before the end of the day. But his business at the abbey shouldn't take that long, and hopefully by mid-afternoon Sir Martin and his grandfather would have engaged in a long and conciliating conversation.

Edwin reached the abbey without a problem, returning to the junction where he and Sir Martin had first met the abbot and then turning right before riding another mile. The stone buildings were easily recognisable from a distance, and Edwin was admitted into the precinct once he'd explained his business to the ancient monk who was the gate porter.

He was first directed to the abbot's house. As he waited for Abbot Thomas to finish the private devotions in which he apparently engaged between the many church services, Edwin paced up and down in an antechamber. He knew what information he wanted, but was unsure about the best way to obtain it. Direct questioning might work for some matters, but for others he would have to be a little more roundabout.

He was still considering his options as the door opened.

The room was, as he'd expected, austere, with whitewashed walls adorned only by a crucifix.

Abbot Thomas was sitting behind a table, and greeted him without rising. 'You've come to speak of matters at Woodthorpe, I take it.'

'Yes, Father. And to ask you a few other questions on related matters.'

The abbot raised his eyebrows. 'Related matters?'

'Yes. I have to ask, though you are of course free not to answer if you so choose.'

Abbot Thomas stared at him steadily, and Edwin knew he'd have to be on his guard: a man did not rise to such an eminent position in the Church unless he was very intelligent.

'Father,' began Edwin. 'As abbot, it's correct, isn't it, that you're responsible for everything about the abbey – its finances as well as its people?'

'This is not a secret, my son – it's the same in every abbey, of our Order and others.'

Had he relaxed slightly at this easy question? 'So, it's in your best interests – and your Order's – to make the place prosperous?'

'Yes.' The abbot's brow furrowed. 'But why–'

'Is that why you wanted to add Woodthorpe to your possessions?'

A brief moment of surprise was succeeded by a neutral expression. 'What gives you the idea that this was my design?'

'Nearly all of the manors round here are under abbey jurisdiction,' continued Edwin. 'When you knew Sir Richard was dying, it might have seemed straightforward for you to negotiate with–' he wouldn't say *bully*, not yet '–the child you thought was the heir and his mother, who is unversed in many of the ways of the world, to see if they would sell the place to you.'

There was a flicker in the abbot's eye, so brief that Edwin might not have noticed if he hadn't been looking for it. 'There would be little point in doing so, when it was not Michael who was due to inherit the manor.'

'But you didn't know that: your surprise, when you met Sir Martin on the road that first time, was completely genuine.'

The abbot changed direction. 'Even if young Michael *had* been the heir, it would be cruel of me indeed to attempt to deprive him and his mother, and his brothers and sisters, of their home. Where would they go?'

'You could have got round that. Persuaded them that running the place would be far too difficult for them, that it would be in the best interests of all the manor people if they were to sell up to you. From what I've seen, concern for others would have weighed heavily on them. And you could have promised them a simpler life and accommodation in return, given that you must have corro–'

Edwin stopped in mid-word as the answer to a completely different question crashed in on him. *Of course*. He knew now why the abbot had been speaking so earnestly to Jonilda recently, even after Sir Richard's death and after he knew that the manor was Sir Martin's. But he wasn't going to give that knowledge away, not just yet.

'I find your questions increasingly impertinent.' The abbot was seeking to take advantage of Edwin's pause, perhaps thinking it was due to uncertainty. 'As you say, I have every right not to answer them any further.' He began to reach for a small bell that sat on the table.

'Just two more, if you please, Father, and both directly related to the crime of Sir Richard's murder, which I'm sure you're as eager to see solved as I am.'

The abbot's hand hovered and then withdrew. 'Very well.'

'Sir Richard's last words to me, delivered when he was in agony from the lockjaw and couldn't make himself properly understood, were "don't let him take–". If he wasn't talking about you and the manor, what you think he might have been referring to?'

There was a pause, and Edwin noted an expression of puzzlement on the other's face that seemed sincere. 'I… I honestly don't know,' Abbot Thomas replied. 'Don't let who take what?'

'When I find that out,' said Edwin, drily, 'I think everything will be a great deal clearer.'

'And your other question? I think you said you had two more?'

'Yes.' If Edwin's burgeoning suspicions were correct, he knew what the answer was going to be, but he had to phrase the question neutrally, so as not to put words in the abbot's mouth. 'When Sir Richard came to see you, on the afternoon he was shot, what did he talk to you about?'

'I beg your pardon?'

'I believe you heard me.'

'No, I mean, why do you think that I spoke to Sir Richard on the afternoon he was attacked? I did no such thing.'

'Everyone at the manor is agreed that he was returning from the abbey when he was shot. So the natural assumption would be that he came to see you.'

Abbot Thomas was shaking his head in what again seemed to Edwin to be honest surprise. 'I assure you he did not.' He thought for a moment. 'I did see him, I think, praying in the church in the late part of the afternoon, or the early evening… yes, it would have been just after Vespers. But I didn't speak to him, nor was he seeking me.'

'Then whom else might he have been seeking? Sir Richard must have been at the abbey for some while by Vespers, and he can't have come only to pray; he could have done that in the local church.'

There was the hint of a shrug. 'I can ask the brethren, of course, though I think my best guess would be Brother Gregory? His medical advice is often in demand locally, sought by lay people as well as our community here.'

That was interesting. Perhaps Sir Richard had been aware of some medical condition, and then Brother Gregory had confirmed that it was serious and Sir Richard had retired to pray about it before he went home? 'Might I have your permission to speak to him while I'm here?'

'Yes, you may. He will be in the infirmary, or possibly in his herb garden at this time of day and in this weather. I will give orders for you to be taken to him.' Abbot Thomas picked up the bell and rang it.

The monk who glided in silently listened to his abbot's instructions and then gestured to Edwin to follow him. He spoke no word either on the way or when they reached the herb garden, where Brother Gregory was on his knees pulling out weeds.

Edwin hailed the infirmarer and explained that he had the abbot's permission to speak. 'I wanted to ask you a question.'

Brother Gregory dusted his hands and stood up. 'Of course. What would you like to know?'

Now, how best to phrase this so as not to make his questions leading ones? Edwin didn't want to state his theory and ask the infirmarer simply to confirm it – a general approach would be best, to see if he would volunteer the information himself. Name no names. 'On the eve of the feast of Saint John the Baptist, you had a visitor.'

'Yes, I did.'

'Who needed your help – your medical help.'

Brother Gregory nodded, his face sad. 'Recovering from the death of his daughter is a very lengthy process. Prayers always help, of course, but so did the sleeping draught.'

That wasn't what Edwin had expected to hear. But, of course, why shouldn't Sir Richard, a loving father, still be grieving? Edwin thought of Gabriel's face in the candlelight as he'd held the pawn from the chess set, and of the word 'Amice' carved deeply into the stone floor of the church. A sleeping draught, though? How did that fit into…

Brother Gregory shook his head. 'So many years. You'd think the pain might have dimmed, but it hasn't, so when he came to me–'

Edwin's mind crashed into a stone wall. 'What?'

The infirmarer looked puzzled. 'Surely you know the story of Sir Richard's first wife. Your friend's mother?'

'Wait. Are you telling me that on the day before the feast of Saint John the Baptist – that is, the day that Sir Richard was shot – you had a visit from Master Christopher of Langley?'

'I thought that's what you were asking me?'

Edwin took a few paces away, and then turned back. 'You gave him a sleeping draught?'

'Yes. It's made of–'

Edwin held up a hand. 'Please, just tell me – how strong was this draught?'

'Only enough to help him off to sleep, as long as he took it in the right quantity.'

Oh, dear Lord. 'And how much did you give him?'

'Enough for a week. I didn't want him to take it for longer than that, because if taken too regularly the patient finds that he can't go to sleep without it.'

Edwin closed his eyes, wondering how to phrase this without seeming to blame or accuse Brother Gregory, who had only been trying to help. 'So,' he began, 'a week's-worth would be seven doses. Tell me, what would be the effect if a sevenfold dose were to be taken all at once?'

Brother Gregory looked shocked. 'Nobody would do that – it would be extremely foolish. No, my instructions were clearly only to take a small nightly dose, because having too much at once could prove fatal–'

Edwin didn't hear anything further, because he was already running for the stable.

Edwin was still not a competent enough rider to risk a full gallop, but the road was a good one so he went along at the fastest canter he could manage. Back towards Woodthorpe, and then straight through it, hoping against hope that he was going to be in time. How long was it since he'd left Christopher and Sir Martin together in the church? And how long had they stayed there in conversation?

As soon as he reached the church he threw himself off the horse's back, just about remembering to tie the reins to the lychgate before he sprinted inside.

The building was empty.

Edwin tried to calm himself sufficiently to look in every nook and cranny, just in case, but there was definitely nobody there. So, it was back out to remount and then to fly to Langley as quickly as he could.

He reached the manor house, dismounted and tossed the reins to the nearest, rather surprised, serving man, and dashed inside. He didn't stop in the hall but went straight for the parlour door and crashed it open, his breath by now coming in gasps.

Inside, Christopher and Sir Martin were sitting chatting with every appearance of amity.

Each of them held a drink in his hand.

Edwin launched himself forwards even as he shouted, 'Stop!'

They were sitting far enough apart that he couldn't dash the vessels from both hands at the same time, so he aimed for the dangerous one… the one being held by Christopher.

Sir Martin exclaimed in surprise as he saw his grandfather's wine splattered on the floor amid broken pottery – though he did obey Edwin's instruction to put his own cup down. He stood up. 'What's going on?'

Edwin turned to Christopher, his shoulders and chest heaving as much from relief as with the effort of getting here so quickly. 'Where is it? Was it all in there, or was there some left?'

He could see at a glance that Christopher knew exactly what he was talking about, but it was Sir Martin who spoke. 'I said, what's going on? Edwin, explain, please.'

'Do you want to tell him, or shall I?'

Christopher shook his head and looked at the floor, so Edwin continued. 'A couple of weeks ago–' there was no need to complicate things by noting the exact day '–Christopher went to the abbey to consult Brother Gregory. He came away with a sleeping draught. It was a week's worth if he took a small amount each night, as he was meant to, but drinking the whole lot at once would put him in a sleep from which he would never wake.'

Sir Martin gasped. 'Is this true?'

His grandfather nodded without speaking.

'But *why*?'

After waiting for a response that didn't come, Edwin continued, more gently. 'I should have noted how deep your despair was, when I came here the first time. You still blame yourself for your daughter's death, even after twenty-one years. You've kept going because of the sense of duty you feel towards the people who depend on you, although you can't find the energy to do it as well as you used to.'

Sir Martin broke in. 'Edwin, what are you saying? That…?'

'Let him continue,' mumbled Christopher, getting to his feet and squaring his shoulders. 'He's correct so far.'

It was a difficult subject, but now he'd started Edwin thought he'd better go on. It was surely preferable to have it all out in the open. 'You went to Brother Gregory. Of course, you couldn't explain the real reason you wanted the draught or he wouldn't have given it to you, but you made sure you came away with enough of it to do the job.' He paused.

Christopher shrugged. 'Keep going.'

'You were perhaps going to kill yourself that very night, but the news of Sir Richard's accident, or incident, stopped you. Again, it was your sense of duty: there was going to be enough trouble on the manors for a while, and you didn't want to add to it.'

'Yes,' came the dull reply. 'My life is all duty. There is no enjoyment, no pleasure, no real *point* to it, but I keep going, day after day, year after year, because others need me.'

'And then you discovered that your grandson was on his way here. That you would be able to see him for yourself, perhaps to judge how well he would run things once you were gone.'

Christopher looked at Sir Martin for the first time. 'I was taken by surprise, the other day, when I ran into you in the church. Really, I only wanted to see you from a distance… I wanted to see if I could trace anything of Rosceline in you, and watch how you conducted yourself, but I knew you wouldn't want to speak to me.'

'What?' Sir Martin's voice was incredulous.

Now that they were addressing each other and the immediate danger was over, Edwin took a surreptitious step backwards.

'You blame me for your mother's death.' Christopher's voice held two decades of agony. 'And you're right to do so.'

'No! Of course I don't. It was me being born that killed her, so if anything it's my fault.'

Christopher took a swift pace forward. He couldn't reach Sir Martin's shoulders, so instead gripped both of his arms just above the elbow. 'It wasn't your fault. Do you hear me? You were a newborn babe. *It was not your fault*,' he repeated, doing his best to shake his grandson.

Sir Martin now had tears running down his cheeks, but he didn't break Christopher's grip on his arms to reach up and wipe them away. 'She… such a loss for both of us,' he whispered, hoarsely.

There was a moment of silence, and Edwin risked speaking again, his voice soft. 'If Rosceline were here now, what do you think she'd say? To both of you?'

Christopher was also crying. 'She would make the best of things and seek to make everyone happy. Because that's what she did. She was the sunshine in all our lives. You were deprived of that from the time you took your first breath, and I'm sorry.'

'She came to me, you know.' Sir Martin's voice was still hoarse. 'When I thought I was going to die.'

Christopher looked down at the false hand. 'When that happened?'

'Yes.' There was a pause. 'I don't remember much about it all, except for that. She was there to look after me. And… one other thing: when I was lying there afterwards, the monk who saved my life said to me, "If you don't want to feel hated, Martin, you have to stop hating yourself." I can still hear his voice. It's good advice, advice I've tried to live up to, and now I'm giving it to you.'

Christopher shook his head.

'So,' continued Sir Martin, 'we have to forgive each other, and we have to forgive ourselves. Look at me.'

His tone was so compelling that the older man obeyed.

'You bear no blame for my mother's death, but if you feel that you do, and you need absolution, then I forgive you. Do you hear me? I forgive you, absolutely and completely.'

Christopher's shoulders were shaking. 'And I say again, *you* bear no guilt, and you never have. But if you need to hear it, then I forgive you too. And I know that dearest Rosceline would do the same.'

'For both of us.' Sir Martin freed his arms from the grip and engulfed his grandfather in a fierce embrace, shedding tears on to his head while Christopher soaked the front of his tunic.

Edwin had by now backed away almost to the door, but he paused when Sir Martin broke off, rubbed his sleeve across his eyes, and asked, 'But what of this sleeping draught? Why now? You… you were disappointed in what you saw in me?'

'No!' Christopher's voice held real shock. 'No, quite the opposite – I knew that Langley would be safe in your ha– safe in your care. And I could finally lay down my burden.' He pointed at the shards of the cup, and the liquid stains on the floor rushes. 'I'd seen and heard of what you'd already done in the short time since you'd been here, and then our conversation this morning assured me. When I invited you back here, it was to comfort me in my last hours. You would be the last person I saw before I fell into my sleep, and I could rest in peace. You weren't to know anything about it; I would start to doze, you would leave, and then I would… go. All you would hear later was that I had died quietly in my sleep. You wouldn't suspect a thing.'

Edwin shuddered, but he refrained from pointing out that others might certainly suspect something. That Sir Martin had lost his father and inherited a manor because of Sir Richard's death – or so everyone thought – was one thing, and even that had already led to suspicions. For his grandfather to die in the same week, leaving him a second and neighbouring property, would simply add fuel to the fire.

Edwin also forbore from mentioning that the torments of hell that would await a suicide were much worse than anything he might be enduring on earth. Thank the Lord he'd arrived here on time; Christopher's soul had been saved, as well as his life.

The emotion of the occasion was getting too much for Sir Martin. He didn't know how to deal with it, and he was beginning to resort to belligerence and a raised voice. 'No!' he cried. 'I… I bring death wherever I go, and I can't – I *will not* – bring it here as well.' He jabbed his finger towards Christopher's chest. 'You can't die, not yet. I've only just met you, I want to know you better, so we can look at all this together and work together.' He gulped and almost wailed. 'You're my family!'

He pulled Christopher into another embrace, and this time Edwin took the opportunity to slip out.

It was some while later when the two of them set off back for Woodthorpe, walking while Sir Martin led Edwin's horse. The knight pointed at the churchyard as they passed it. 'We've already given orders that the Langley half should be tidied up and looked after properly. And he's going to tell me more about the manor and its people soon.'

'That's a good first step.'

Edwin slowed his pace, ostensibly to look over the low wall towards the church, but in reality trying to work out how he was going to break the news to his friend. 'I have something to tell you.'

Sir Martin caught the seriousness of his tone. 'What?' he asked, warily.

'It's about the inheritance of Woodthorpe.'

'What about it?'

His poor friend didn't need any more shocks today, but Edwin had been keeping the knowledge to himself for too long already. 'Why don't we sit down?'

Sir Martin tied the horse up where it could graze for a while and then settled himself on the wall next to Edwin. 'Whatever it is, don't sit there dithering. Just tell me straight out.'

'When I was going through the manor documents, I found the original letter from my lord earl, in which he agreed to take you on as a page in his service.'

'What's that got to do with…? Never mind, carry on. I'm sure there's a point to this and you'll get to it in your own good time.'

'As we might expect from our lord, he was cautious about what he was offering – you'd be promoted to squire *if* you were a good page, you'd be knighted *if* you were a good squire. Everything was conditional.'

'Yes? But he must have thought that I was good, or I wouldn't be a knight today.' He paused. 'You're going to say "but", aren't you? What is it? Nobody can take my knighthood away, not now!'

Edwin rushed to reassure him. 'It's not that. No, it's that my lord was also prudent about offering to support you financially, so your father had to compensate. In fact, the last clause in the agreement was that as soon as you turned twenty-one, your father would resign his manor in your favour. Since then, of course, my lord has made further provision for you, but that doesn't negate the original agreement.'

Sir Martin sat in silent shock for a few moments. He raised a confused hand to his face. 'So, what you're saying is…?'

'That you didn't inherit Woodthorpe this week, when your father died. It's been yours since Easter, when you turned twenty-one. I think the lord earl might have forgotten about the matter, to be honest, but Sir Richard didn't.'

Sir Martin grasped Edwin's arm, gripping hard enough that it would probably be bruised later. 'He wrote to me. Do you remember me saying? He wrote to me at Easter to ask me to come and talk about something to do with the inheritance of the manor. And I didn't come!'

'That's why I think that none of this was public knowledge. Your father didn't want to tell anyone about it, not even Jonilda, until he'd spoken to you first.'

Sir Martin stared at him, aghast. 'Edwin, what if none of this would have happened if I'd come when he asked? Have I just been forgiven for killing my mother only to find that I've killed my father?'

'You stop that, right now!' Edwin's voice was rather sharper than he'd intended, but he was going to need his friend to be fully capable of thought and action for the next day or so. 'You didn't kill your father, and you are in no way responsible for his death. That culpability lies only with the man who shot the arrow at him.'

'And who was that?' Sir Martin thumped the wall in frustration. 'And how are we to find out? We must, Edwin, we really must. I can't leave all these people here, looking to me and depending on me to keep them safe, if there's a killer out there walking free.'

There was a pause while Edwin tried to work out how much was safe to say at this precise juncture.

'What? Edwin – tell me. You've got that look on your face. What do you know? Don't keep it from me.'

He wasn't in a stable enough frame of mind to be told too much, not yet, although Edwin was becoming more certain in his own mind. It was the only really logical explanation, except for that one nagging, seemingly impossible point. 'I think,' he said, carefully, 'that I'm beginning to sort things out.'

'Who?' urged Sir Martin. 'Tell me who!'

That was exactly what Edwin wasn't about to do. The due process of law needed to be followed – and be *seen* to be followed – and the last thing anyone needed was Sir Martin engaging in a violent act of retribution before that could happen. 'It's only a suspicion at the moment,' he warned, 'and I can't make any accusations without further evidence.' He made a rueful face. 'And for that, I need to talk to Gabriel.'

Sir Martin was thunderstruck. 'Gabriel?' he repeated. You mean, *Gabriel*? Surely you don't suspect…'

'I just need to ask him something, that's all,' said Edwin, getting up. 'Something I'd know already if I'd been paying more attention.'

Sir Martin glared at him in exasperation. 'And that's it? All right, I take your word for it. You know I trust you with my life, so the sooner we get back for you to ask this mysterious question, the better.' He strode to the horse and began untying the reins. 'As soon as we get to Woodthorpe, I'll get him to the stable, you find Gabriel, and then maybe you'll tell me what in the name of God's blood is going on.'

You know I trust you with my life. Sir Martin was also trusting Edwin with the lives of all his family, and Edwin knew what a huge responsibility that was, so he prayed that his suspicions were correct. At least he had some little time to deal with the matter, as there was no immediate danger to anyone else.

It was just as the manor buildings were coming into sight that they heard the screams.

Chapter Eleven

They were high, childlike screams, accompanied by splashes, and they were coming from the direction of the pond.

'What the–?' Sir Martin's sudden anxiety was such that he dropped the reins and, heedless of the horse, ran off so fast that Edwin could barely keep up.

They reached the pond, and Edwin took in the situation at a glance. One of the older girls – Eleanor – was standing on the bank, and she was doing most of the shrieking. When she saw Sir Martin she didn't stop, but pointed to where Constance was splashing waist-deep in the water, crying out that she was coming.

In middle of the pond, a small figure was floating face down.

Sir Martin didn't hesitate. 'See to her!' he bellowed at Edwin, indicating Constance, even as he waded past the child. 'It gets deep there!'

Edwin jumped in and reached the little girl just as she slipped and fell, catching hold of her and lifting her out of the water. Her sodden gown was heavy and would have pulled her under if he'd been a moment later. 'I've got you! Hold on round my neck.' He waded back to the shallows and put her on the bank next to her sister. She was soaking, shivering even in the heat of the afternoon, and crying, but she was otherwise unharmed.

Edwin turned to look back at the pond. It really did get deep quite close to the edge: even Sir Martin was up to his chest in the water before he got halfway to his target. He reached the lifeless child – Jonny, as Edwin could now see – who had made no movement or sound in response to any of their shouts. Sir Martin pulled him close before turning round and making his way back, holding the body high out of the water and feeling his way with his feet so he wouldn't trip.

They reached the bank, and Sir Martin laid the limp form on the grass. 'Is he breathing? I couldn't feel him breathing. What do we do?' His voice rose in panic as he knelt by his smallest brother. 'Edwin, help me!'

Fire and water, Edwin, that's how the Lord chooses to bring children home to Him. Father Ignatius had said that, before he buried a drowned boy, the latest in a long line. But he'd said something else, hadn't he? *At least with water, you can sometimes bring them back.*

Edwin turned Jonny over on to his front and began pressing and thumping him.

'What are you–? Here, let me.' Sir Martin made as if to shove Edwin aside.

'No! Not you. You're too strong, you'll break his ribs.' Edwin continued pushing, trying to match the rhythm of how Jonny would breathe in and out if he were able.

More shouts sounded, and a group of men, led by Dominic, arrived. 'We saw the horse passing the field on its own,' he called to Sir Martin. 'It was only when I caught the reins and got nearer the stable with it that I heard the children, or I would have been here sooner.' His voice was agonised as he looked at the scene before him.

By now, Sir Martin was sitting with both girls swept up in his arms, trying to comfort them as they cried. 'You'll be all right,' he was saying to them, over and over again, talking into the tops of their heads as they sought to bury themselves in his neck. 'And so will Jonny. He will.' Then, suddenly, in horrified panic, 'What about Adela? Was she here too?'

Edwin was too busy with Jonny to look, but Constance must have replied in her brother's ear, because he heard a relieved, 'Well, that's something.'

Any further talk was forestalled by Jonny making a sudden retching noise and then vomiting up what seemed like half the pond. Edwin kept up his pushing on the child's back until he was sure it had all come up, and then bent his head. 'He's breathing!'

Jonny proved it by a fit of coughing, and gasps of relief, shouts of joy and prayers of thanks sounded from all around him. Edwin sat back, feeling suddenly light-headed, as Sir Martin and the girls all scrabbled to embrace the little boy.

Thank the Lord and all His saints. Edwin's mind had been so preoccupied by thoughts of murder that he'd almost forgotten that accidents could still happen. But the children were safe now, and this had nothing to do with–

Edwin's blood turned to ice, and for a moment he wasn't sure whether he really was going to faint or be sick. Surely he hadn't underestimated his suspect *that* much? Surely not even someone who would shoot a man in cold blood would be capable of–

He began to stagger towards the house, his sopping wet clothes and boots slowing him down.

But it was already too late.

'Maaaaaaar-tiiiiiin!'

Gabriel was tearing towards them. He was tripping over his own feet in a frenzy of alarm, screaming out the name of the only person who could help. He reached them and threw himself at Sir Martin, clutching at him, tears staining his cheeks, and so breathless with the running and the panic that at first he couldn't get anything coherent out.

Eventually, he was able to pant a few words, which were understood more quickly by Edwin than anyone else because he had an inkling of their content. Dear Lord, he'd had his suspicions for some while – why hadn't he acted on them earlier?

Gabriel's gasps became a little more intelligible. 'He's taken my mother – don't know where the nurses are – sent the others away so we'd be busy looking for them – wanted to take her right away – horse – Michael tried to stop him –'

By this time Sir Martin had grasped that there was danger, even if he didn't yet understand the specifics. 'Up at the house? Someone has taken your mother?' He shook the child. 'Who?'

The name came out of Edwin and Gabriel's mouths simultaneously. 'Simon!'

There was no more than half a moment of stupefied silence before Sir Martin was in motion, dragging Gabriel along with him while he fired off questions.

Edwin paused before following, looking down at the three smaller children as they huddled together. 'You must move away from this pond,' he said, 'but don't go back to the house.'

Sir Martin had already barked at Dominic that he should round up every manor man he could find and bring them to the yard, and the reeve was even now on his way, but one of the other men still standing around in shock was Bernulf, he whose hand had been wounded. 'If you will, sir, I'll take them all back to my wife and tell her not to let them out of her sight until you or Reeve comes to say otherwise.'

'Yes, do,' said Edwin, in some relief, watching him pick Jonny up and chivvy the girls. He turned to the other men. 'The rest of you had better come with me.'

When Edwin got there, Gabriel and Michael were both in the open yard that was bordered by the manor buildings. The latter had a bruise starting to show on his face.

But there was no sign of Sir Martin. 'Where is he?'

'He said he wouldn't be long,' said Michael, nodding towards the house, and indeed Sir Martin now emerged from it, his sword belted around his waist. He had also changed his hand, Edwin noticed, fastening as he walked the straps of the replacement he didn't wear too often: the one that ended in a vicious knife blade.

'They're in the hay barn,' he said to Edwin as soon as he drew near. 'Simon, and Jonilda, against her will.' His expression was very grim indeed, and Edwin might almost have felt sorry for what Simon's fate was now sure to be, if he didn't already know that the abbey bailiff had murdered Sir Richard and attempted to kill nearly all of his children.

'And Adela,' added Michael.

'*What*?' Sir Martin stared in disbelief.

Edwin called down curses upon himself. This was even worse than he'd suspected – the man was pure evil. Simon had surely condemned himself by his current actions; but, if he survived long enough to face a trial, Edwin wanted to make absolutely sure that the evidence was in place to convict him. So, while Sir Martin was issuing brisk orders to the manor men, with Michael at his heels, Edwin beckoned Gabriel aside.

The poor boy was still dazed, with tear tracks down his face. Edwin knelt and grasped him by the shoulders. 'Listen. You did exactly the right thing in coming to fetch your brother, and he'll take charge now. He's a knight who's been in battle, and he knows what he's doing. And none of this is your fault. All right?'

Gabriel gulped and nodded.

'Good. Now, I have a question to ask you, and we need to be logical again. Can you do that?'

Gabriel scrubbed at his face. 'Yes.'

'Good,' repeated Edwin, 'because I need your help. I think I've made a mistake.'

'You?'

In other circumstances Edwin might have been flattered at the boy's confidence in him, but just now it just reminded him again that he could have prevented all this if he'd only been looking in the right direction earlier. 'Do you remember when we were sitting with the chess set, and working out who might have been where at the time the two arrows were shot?'

'Yes.'

'And for the second one we placed you, Michael and Sir Martin on the road back from the church.'

Gabriel nodded. 'The white knight and the two pawns.'

'Correct. Now, that's where I made my error. I'd heard, earlier, that Simon had chased off into the woods after the archer, and I'd assumed that was true, so I placed him – the black knight – with you too. And I saw at the time that you were unsure about what I'd done. In fact, I think you were going to say something, but I moved on too quickly.'

'I should have interrupted you,' said Gabriel, miserably.

'Because that wasn't right, was it? The man who told me that Simon rode after the archer was *Simon himself*, and if there's one thing I should know by now, it's never to base my thinking on what any one single person says to me.'

'In case he's lying?'

'Precisely. I always look – or I always *should* look – for corroboration. Proof,' he added, seeing Gabriel's puzzled expression, 'from another source; either someone else's evidence or my own findings.' He took a deep breath. 'So, tell me what happened. Take your time and describe it in detail.'

'We were coming back from the church,' said Gabriel, 'when there was a sort of buzzing noise and my brother shouted for us all to get down. Then Bernulf shouted out too, because the arrow had hit him.'

'And Simon wasn't with you at the time?'

'No. It was after that that he came out of the woods on his horse, and he called out to my brother that he thought he'd seen the archer and chased after him, but he'd got away.'

Edwin expelled a long breath. The idea that Simon could not possibly have loosed the second arrow had been the great flaw in his suspicion that the abbey bailiff was the killer; if only he hadn't allowed himself to be misdirected, he could have worked it all out sooner.

'So, just to be sure,' he said to Gabriel, 'in your opinion, could Simon have been the man who shot the arrow? Logically, would he have had the time to shoot, drop the bow, get back on his horse and then ride towards you, all in the time between when you saw the arrow and when you saw him?'

Gabriel was nodding. 'Yes. And,' he added, 'if you need corr– whatever you just said, you can ask one of the others, and not just take my word.'

Edwin patted his shoulder. 'Well done. I'm not sure if you'll ever have to say that in front of a jury, but if you do, just say it all exactly like that. But now, we need to get you to safety.'

'Oh no. I'm not leaving while my mother and sister are in there.'

Edwin looked over at Sir Martin, who seemed to be having the same conversation with Michael – who, Edwin now noted, was in possession of a bow and a quiver of arrows.

'–get away from here,' the knight was saying. 'It's not safe.'

Michael shook his head, his expression stubborn. 'No.'

'That's an order.'

The two of them stared at each other, and then Michael spoke in a voice of resolute determination that belied his years. 'Tell me, what would you do if you were me, and that was your mother in there?'

Edwin saw Sir Martin's eyes widen. Then, after a few moments of silence, the knight nodded. 'All right. It's your right to stay, and it was you who stopped him getting away on his horse, after all. But you obey my orders, just like the others, you hear? Even if you don't understand *why* I'm telling you, you do what I say while we're in a combat situation.'

Michael straightened and gave a decisive nod, and the two of them turned back to look at the hay barn. It was now surrounded by a rough half-circle of carts and other makeshift barricades, with wary manor men standing behind them.

Just at that moment, the two nurses burst out of the manor house. Sir Martin sent Dominic to head them off before they blundered into danger, and Edwin added that he should tell them they'd find the three missing children at Bernulf's cottage.

Sir Martin glanced towards them while keeping most of his attention on the barn. 'I'll be having words with them later about letting the children wander.'

Edwin had an idea of where they'd been, but for now he said nothing. There would be time enough for explanations later.

As if reading his mind, Sir Martin spoke again. 'The rest will keep, but tell me now – it was Simon who killed my father?'

'Yes.'

'And you can prove that?'

'Yes. And it was also he who shot the arrow at you on the road.' Edwin paused, wondering if was altogether wise to make his friend even more angry than he already was. But Sir Martin seemed furious in a cool, controlled manner that Edwin hardly recognised, rather than hot with indiscriminate rage. So, he risked continuing. 'If he'd hit you, and wounded or killed you, he'd have had more time amid the chaos to nock and draw again, and I'm fairly certain that he would have tried to kill Michael and Gabriel at the same time.'

Sir Martin's expression grew even more horrified and outraged, but Edwin had started now so he might as well finish. 'And, just now, I think he intended for Constance, Eleanor and Jonny all to drown.'

Sir Martin did not burst with anger or lose control of himself. Instead, he spoke in a soft, sibilant voice that was even more terrifying. 'He won't see another sunset.'

'Careful,' Edwin warned. 'It would be better if the law could take its course.'

In return, he received what could only be described as a look of contempt.

He had one more try. 'Think of your family, then. I know what you're capable of, in combat; I've seen it. But they don't. Yes, they need to know that you'll protect them, but please don't let them see you perpetrating acts of extreme violence. Think what it will do to them.'

Sir Martin looked down at him, and now his voice was stone cold. 'Your advice is... *noted*.'

Edwin stepped back. He'd tried, but this was Sir Martin's manor, his family and his fight, and he must do as he saw fit. Besides, Edwin thought he could probably make out a good enough case of provocation and self-defence to save his friend from execution even if Simon did end up dead.

Sir Martin conferred with Michael, and with a man Edwin recognised as one of the house servants. 'Do we know what weapons he might have in there with him? And what in blazes happened?'

'He just arrived like normal,' explained the serving man, 'and asked to see Lady Jonilda.'

Yes, thought Edwin. *Like normal*. Simon comes here a lot. Why hadn't he, Edwin, thought it odd at the time that the abbey bailiff, a man unconnected with the manor, should be able to give him such an exact description of the layout of the buildings when he'd first arrived himself?

The servant was continuing. 'I said I'd see where she was, and he stood outside talking to some of the children while I went to find her.

Then I came back out and said he could come in, and he'd find her in the family quarters… I'm sorry, my lord, if I'd had any idea what was going to happen–'

Sir Martin cut him off. 'Never mind that. Michael, who was where, and what happened when he came in?'

'Connie, Ellie and Jonny were all out here.'

'And he spoke to them? Why?'

Michael shrugged, so Edwin broke in. 'I think he saw they were unattended, took his chance and suggested that they go to the pond. It's a hot day, after all. He wouldn't be there to make sure, but he must have been aware there was a chance they'd get out of their depth in the water. And even if they didn't drown, they would draw people's attention away from the house, and away from what he was about to do.'

Edwin saw Sir Martin's expression harden. 'But,' he added, 'don't blame them. They're good, respectful children, so of course they'd obey an instruction from an adult they thought was a friend of their parents.'

'Don't worry,' said Sir Martin. 'I know exactly where the blame lies.' His fingers touched the hilt of his sword. Then, to Michael, 'Go on.'

'Gabriel and I were in the parlour, but the others were upstairs: Adela needed to go down for her nap and Mother wanted some help with sheets on the bed, or something. Simon came in and saw us and asked why we were inside on such a fine day, and why weren't we out in the sunshine...' Michael paused for breath, looking anxiously at Sir Martin, but the knight's face was expressionless. 'I don't know whether he thought we would go out, because he didn't stop to check – he went up the stairs. And then there was… shouting, and thumping, and noises. And he came down again carrying Adela and with Mother chasing after him, asking him to put her down.'

'The nurses?'

'He shut them in the bedchamber, my lord,' broke in the serving man. 'After all this happened, we heard them calling out and banging on the door. He'd pushed them in and tied something round the latch on the outside, so they couldn't open it.'

Sir Martin exchanged a glance with Edwin. 'Not their fault, then. Keep going, Michael.'

'We knew something wasn't right, so we followed them all outside. I shouted and tried to grab him, and he got really angry and hit me, and Mother was upset. I didn't know what was going on, but I didn't want him to get to his horse while he had Adela, in case he tried to ride off – it was tied up just outside the stable – so I pulled and dragged on his arm, and I shouted out to see if anyone in the pantry or the kitchen would hear me. And I called to Gabriel to run and find you.'

Sir Martin nodded. 'But how did they end up in the barn?'

Michael swallowed. 'I wasn't strong enough to stop him, and he was getting nearer to the horse. So I let go and ran to it myself, and untied it and hit it to make it run off.'

'That was a sharp idea.'

'But,' continued Michael, his anxiety rising again, 'that meant I'd let go of his arm, the one he wasn't carrying Adela with, and he drew his knife and held it to her throat.' He choked. 'And he said to Mother, "You come with me or she's dead", and he looked around for the nearest place and they were just by the barn, so he made Mother push the door open a little bit and they all went inside.' His face was a picture of misery. 'I'm sorry, I couldn't stop him. Before I got to him he would easily have been able to…' His shoulders heaved.

Sir Martin placed a hand on his shoulder. 'You did well, honestly you did. Better they should be in the barn than that he should have taken her away the Lord knows where.' He brushed the back of one finger almost affectionately down Michael's bruised face. 'And you've got your first battle scar to show for it, though I don't think it will be permanent.' Then, in a more businesslike tone, 'So, we know he has a knife. Was he wearing his sword? Can you remember?'

Michael thought for a moment. 'Yes. Yes, he was.'

With a jolt, Edwin recalled something else. 'I'm afraid there's a bow and some arrows in there as well.'

'What?'

'I found them earlier, in the place where he shot at you. I put them in there because I wanted to see if anyone could identify the bow.' He grimaced. 'Sorry.'

Sir Martin turned to his men. 'All of you – make sure you stay behind these barricades until I say different, understood?' Then he addressed Edwin again. 'How many arrows?'

'I…'

'*Think*. It's what you're good at, remember? And it's important.'

Edwin closed his eyes as he sought to picture the scene in the woods. The bow on the ground, the quiver half-hidden in the undergrowth with the arrows spilling out…

'Seven.'

'You're sure?'

Edwin opened his eyes. 'Yes.'

Sir Martin spoke to the serving man, who was still hovering. 'Stay behind that cart and keep watch. If he starts shooting, your only task is to count the arrows. As soon as you get to seven, you call out to me.'

The man gave a nervous nod.

Sir Martin and Edwin conferred. 'We should talk to him,' suggested Edwin. 'Try to calm the situation. We don't want to make him desperate while he's got them both in there.'

'Agreed.'

'Do you want me to speak for you?'

'No, I'll do it.'

'Try not to get too angry.'

Sir Martin nodded. 'Simon!' he bellowed.

Edwin crouched behind the cart, making sure that Michael and Gabriel were doing the same as they listened. He tried to think his way around the problem, but it was hard to apply logic and reason when the criminal had none. Simon had backed himself into a corner, after his plans had gone awry, and now he had nowhere to go. The simple truth – which the bailiff had perhaps not yet realised himself – was that he was going to end up dead, one way or the other. What the rest of them needed to ensure was that nobody else lost their lives in the process.

The initial negotiation did not go well. 'Come out and stand where I can see you!' had been Simon's first call – which, knowing as he did that there was a bow in the barn, was a very dangerous thing for Sir Martin to do. He scorned to back down, however, and moved in front of the cart while cautioning everyone else to stay where they were. Edwin and Dominic complied, but shifted so they were within arm's reach of him and could pull him down if necessary.

'Why don't you come out too?' called Sir Martin. 'I'm here in the open, ready to talk to you if you're not too much of a coward to face me.'

Edwin knew that Simon wasn't going to be goaded into doing anything so foolish.

'We're fine in here, and this is where we'll stay until you let us leave in peace. All of us.'

'Never!'

There was silence from the barn. After waiting for a further reply that never came, Sir Martin returned to the others. 'What now?'

Edwin's mind had begun to work. 'For now, I suggest we don't make any sudden moves, in case it makes him panic and ki–' he looked over at where Michael and Gabriel were still sitting 'and do something foolish.'

Sir Martin nodded. 'Time is on our side. We can stay out here for however long it takes to starve him out, if we have to.'

'I'm not suggesting we wait that long,' replied Edwin, not feeling the need to say out loud that little Adela would suffer from hunger long before Simon did.

'What, then? Wait until we think he's asleep, and then attack?'

'Too risky.' Edwin paused. 'Just give me a moment.'

Sir Martin sat with his back to the cart's wheel and began to gouge viciously in the earth with the knife that was currently in the place of his missing left hand.

After a short while, Edwin began. 'I know you want to think of immediate action, but let's think of Simon, his motives, and what he's been trying to achieve all along.'

Somewhat to his surprise, Sir Martin didn't snort derisively. Instead he said, 'Sir Geoffrey always said you should try to understand your enemy.'

Edwin sent up a small prayer of gratitude, hoping Sir Geoffrey might hear it and know that he was helping them from beyond the grave. He tried to suppress the wish that the old knight were here now; he and Sir Martin must learn to stand on their own feet.

He gathered his wits and addressed his audience of Sir Martin, Michael, Gabriel and Dominic. 'Simon's aim has always been to gain control of this manor.' That much, he supposed, had been obvious, and nobody exclaimed or interrupted him. 'He's a younger son, and so will inherit nothing from his own family; he must be, or he wouldn't have taken the position as abbey bailiff. He needed to keep it, he told me, which indicated he had no other source of income. And I was reminded of that when I saw the picture of Saint Matthew in the church: I recently had a conversation with Matthew, the bailiff at Conisbrough, on just that subject.'

Three of his audience of four had no idea what he was talking about, so he moved on. 'The abbot, as we know, had no idea that you even existed. That was what made me look in the wrong direction and suspect him.' Edwin paused. 'Actually, he wants to get his hands on Woodthorpe as well, though he had nothing to do with your father's death. But, returning to Simon – your existence was also a great surprise to *him*, because he's also new at the abbey since the last time you were here. He was as shocked as the abbot was when he first met us, though I misinterpreted his reaction on the road. I thought he was just nervous in case he had to try to stop you attacking the abbot.'

Misinterpretation, thought Edwin, ruefully. *Idiocy, more like. I'm not as clever as I thought I was, but please God don't punish my friend's family for it.*

He shook his head to dislodge the unhelpful thoughts. 'So,' he continued, 'his first plan was a relatively simple one: get rid of your father, leaving – as he thought – the manor in Michael's hands. And Michael would need a regent because he's underage, which would naturally be his mother.'

'But you said she wasn't–'

Edwin cut off Sir Martin's interjection. 'She isn't. She's completely innocent in all of this – indeed, more so, as you'll see. Simon has been paying attention to her for some time, hoping to flatter her into marriage as and when your father was dead. That's why he spends more time here than he needs to.' He paused.

It was Gabriel who grasped it first. 'So, if Mother was Michael's regent and Simon was married to her, he'd be the one who was really in charge.'

'Quite. And so he took his chance. On the day he was attacked, your father had been to the abbey. Not to see the abbot, or Brother Gregory, but to talk to Simon. I don't know exactly what they said, but I suspect your father wanted to gain some idea of exactly how Simon felt about Jonilda, and that he was perhaps a bit clumsy about it, making Simon suspicious. Simon then realised your father would be riding home alone and decided to take drastic action. He's out and about so often himself that nobody would have looked twice or even noticed that he'd gone. He often carries a staff, and an unstrung bow can easily be mistaken for one of those, so he wouldn't have looked out of the ordinary, and I think he probably only took a single arrow, as that would be much easier to conceal than a whole quiver. He went out, hid himself in the woods and waited.'

'Where we saw the footprints,' said Michael.

'Yes. Your father would be moving, but it would be fair to guess that he was riding slowly, as he was in no particular hurry. Simon had plenty of time to aim, then he loosed the arrow, saw Sir Richard fall from his horse and lie still, and assumed he'd killed him. He didn't know he'd only wounded him, and that he was only lying still because he'd hit his head. Then Simon would have wanted to get away as quickly as possible, to make sure that nobody saw him in the area, and also that nobody saw him anywhere in possession of a bow. Fortunately, he was in so much of a hurry to be gone that he didn't approach your father to double check, or he might have finished him off there and then.'

He looked round. They were still with him, Sir Martin nodding slowly as he imagined the scene.

'So,' continued Edwin, 'he ran away – in the other direction from the abbey – hid the bow in the woods near the church, then kept going.

Maybe he'd also hidden his own horse somewhere so he could get away more quickly. We know the abbey owns manors on the far side of Langley and Woodthorpe, so I would guess that if we asked anyone there, they'd say they'd seen him late that afternoon. Don't forget, because your father wasn't found for some while, nobody could tell the exact time he'd been shot.'

Sir Martin let out an expletive under his breath.

'It wasn't until the next day that he found out that Sir Richard had survived, but this wasn't an insurmountable difficulty as he seemed sure to succumb to his wounds. So, all he had to do was wait, and offer his condolences to Jonilda as often as possible.'

Sir Martin added a few more choice words.

'But then two things happened. First, he became aware that Jonilda wanted nothing to do with him. She was grieving, and she loved your father deeply. She would do nothing to dishonour his memory. And she can have had no idea of the real reason he was making up to her, because she knew all about you and assumed that he did too. She had no reason to suspect his attentions weren't genuine, but she still didn't want them.'

Sir Martin sighed. 'And Father knew that, didn't he? He told you to trust her.'

Edwin nodded.

Before he could continue, there was a minor disturbance inside the barn, and they all stood up. A child's wail sounded, followed by Simon's voice calling out to 'Keep that brat quiet!'

Sir Martin tensed.

Edwin laid a hand on his arm. 'This tells us more.'

'Does it?'

'It means Adela is with her mother and Simon isn't currently holding her.'

'They're both away from him? We could make a frontal attack?'

'No, please – it's still too risky. But…' He leaned over and muttered in his friend's ear.

Sir Martin stood and made his way round in front of the cart again. 'Simon!'

'What now?'

'It must be hot in there. Let us put down some food and drink, then one of you can come out and get it.'

There was silence for a few moments, and then Simon's voice came again, his tone wary. 'All right, if it will shut the brat up. But this is what's going to happen. You will get a woman – a woman, mind! Not you or any of your men – to put the victuals down right in front of this door. Then she will move away. This door will open, and my lady here will step out to collect it. I will have my knife to the child's throat the whole time. If any of you takes one step forward, or if Jonilda tries to run away or even speaks to you, the girl dies. Understand?'

Sir Martin's fury was incandescent, but he managed to control it. 'Very well.' He nodded at some of the household servants. 'See to it.'

By now every single man on the manor, as far as Edwin could make out in the gathering gloom, was assembled around their makeshift siege fortifications. As the food was fetched from the kitchen, another group arrived: Christopher, marching at the head of a party of Langley men. He was carrying a sword, and the others a motley collection of whatever they could find to serve as weapons.

'Word reached me,' he said to Sir Martin. 'We all stand with you, and I place myself under your command.'

'You have my thanks, though I'm not sure how much you can do just n–' Sir Martin paused as Edwin murmured to him again. 'Good idea.' He let Edwin explain to his grandfather, and then the latter slipped off to the stable.

An older woman, whom Sir Martin recognised and greeted as Dominic's mother, volunteered to place the food. Both the knight and the reeve were agonised at the thought of putting her in danger in their own stead, but Simon's instructions and threats had been clear. Edwin, too, was worried, but he hoped that even the increasingly desperate and unhinged Simon wouldn't stoop to shooting her, even if it was only to save his few precious arrows.

The victuals were placed, and Dominic's mother withdrew in safety. Then, with aching slowness, one side of the barn door began to swing open.

'Don't shoot,' was Sir Martin's terse instruction to all those holding bows. 'It'll be her, not him.'

It was indeed Jonilda who emerged. Even from this distance and in this light, Edwin could see that her face was blotchy with tears. She looked fearfully behind her and kept up a running commentary that Edwin could just make out. 'The food is here… I'm going to bend and pick it up… no, I'm not looking at them, I won't say anything… I have it, I'm coming back… please don't hurt her…'

She disappeared, and the door swung shut. It opened inwards, as Edwin already knew, though surely it didn't have a bar on the inside, like a castle gate, for it would normally be fastened from the outside.

Michael and Gabriel were staring in anguish at the space their mother had lately occupied, so Edwin called their attention to his questions, learning – as he had expected – that there was no fixing on the inside, but there were various heavy items in the barn that might be pushed up against the doors if Simon so chose. Which meant that as and when they rushed forward in a frontal attack, it would take some effort and some time to open them, giving Simon the opportunity to take any of a number of options.

The waiting started anew.

'You said,' began Gabriel, once they were all seated on the ground again, 'that two things happened that ruined Simon's plans. What was the second one?'

Edwin pointed to Sir Martin. 'Your brother turned up.'

'So, Simon found out that Michael wasn't my father's heir?'

'Which was a great shock to him. Sir Martin is of full age and could take control himself, meaning that all Simon's plans about marrying your mother and controlling your brother were useless.' Edwin sighed. 'In fact, he also didn't know – nobody did, except your father – that the manor *already* belonged to Sir Martin, and not Sir Richard.'

Three-quarters of his audience gasped.

After a pause, Gabriel spoke again, sounding tearful now. 'You mean… my father didn't need to die at all?'

Edwin looked from him to Sir Martin's grim face and decided to change the subject. 'Your father was an outstandingly brave and generous man, ready to give up anything for his children.'

'What do you mean?'

It looked as though they were going to be here for some while, and Edwin was in any case awaiting a further arrival at the manor before he suggested another move, so perhaps now was the time.

As the darkness of evening began to envelop them, Edwin settled down to tell the three brothers, and the loyal reeve who'd worked on their manor since childhood, all the things they didn't know or hadn't yet understood. He prayed he would explain matters as well as he possibly could, because the whole course of their future lives, and their relationships with each other, depended on it.

Chapter Twelve

'Many years ago,' began Edwin, as though he were a minstrel in a hall rather than in the midst of a tense, life-and-death situation, 'when your father was on a campaign in France, he saved the life of Earl Warenne – that's my lord. In return, the earl promised him a reward, but instead of wanting anything for himself, Sir Richard asked if his son could be taken on as a page in the earl's household. It would mean him leaving home at a young age, but it would be the opportunity of a lifetime.'

Michael and Gabriel both stared at Sir Martin without speaking.

'But your father's selflessness went further. As part of the arrangement, he agreed that he would hand over his manor, and its income, to his son as soon as that son turned twenty-one.'

Dominic furrowed his brow. 'Then… that must have happened already? You're exactly a year younger than me.'

Sir Martin nodded without speaking and indicated that Edwin should continue.

'But what you two need to remember is that at the time, Sir Martin was your father's *only* son, his only family. He didn't know whether he'd ever have any more children, or even if he'd make it back from France alive. He wasn't trying to take anything away from you.'

'How could he?' Gabriel asked. 'We weren't even born.'

'He loved you,' said Edwin to Sir Martin, simply. 'He loved you more than anyone else in the world, both because you were all that was left of your mother and for your own sake. He saw the qualities you had, the same ones that everyone on the manor has already started appreciating since you've been here.'

There was a murmur of assent from Dominic.

'But Sir Richard did survive the French campaign, and when he got back, he married again. He had more children, and he loved all of them too. He wanted to encourage his two families to meet, to get to know each other, but the situation was… difficult.' Edwin avoided meeting Sir Martin's eye. 'And then came this Easter, and time for control of the manor to be passed over. He remembered his promise, even if nobody else did.'

'He wrote to me,' interjected Sir Martin, looking at the boys, 'asking me to come. But I didn't. If I had, all of this would have been avoided.'

After a moment, Michael risked laying a hand on his brother's forearm. 'You weren't to know.'

'It *might* have been avoided,' said Edwin, 'and it might not. There's no point in dwelling on it. Simon's ambitions were such that he might have made a move anyway.'

'It was him who shot my father,' said Michael, flatly. 'And he's going to pay for it.'

'Yes, it was. And that led to Sir Richard's greatest demonstration of love yet.'

He'd lost them, he could see. 'This is going to be difficult for you to hear,' Edwin continued gently, mainly to the two boys, although he didn't think the others would take it any easier. 'When Brother Gregory came to see your father the day after he'd been shot, he offered him a choice: should he pull out the arrowhead straight away, or leave it in place? If he removed it, there was a small chance of recovery, but the greater probability was that your father would die within the hour from the bleeding.'

Gabriel's hand clutched at Michael's sleeve and the older boy shuffled closer to him.

'In either of those cases,' continued Edwin, 'Sir Richard would have had a better resolution. Even if he didn't recover, a swift death would be preferable and Brother Gregory could have given him the last rites, so he would have died in God's grace. But he chose–' Edwin stopped for a moment, aware that his voice was starting to waver. Then he cleared his throat and resumed. 'He chose, of his own free will, to prolong his agony, to die a drawn-out and painful death, so that he could live long enough to see his eldest son again one last time, and so that he could be sure that his wife and younger children would be safe.'

'I don't understand,' said Michael. He looked at Sir Martin. 'What does he mean?'

The knight shook his head. 'I'm not sure I know, either. Edwin, do you mean that he wanted to see me, to tell me to look after them?'

'Yes, but it was more than that. I think he knew, or at least suspected, that it was Simon who had shot him – who had killed him, even though his death hadn't actually happened yet. You remember that in his final letter to you, he said he'd been murdered. And one of the things that was puzzling me was, why didn't he voice his suspicions sooner? While he could still speak? He was in that bed nearly a week before we got here.'

Sir Martin frowned. 'Well, why didn't he?'

Edwin allowed a sigh to escape him. 'He'd known Simon longer than I have, but that's no excuse for my blindness. I think your father realised much sooner than I did just how dangerous Simon is. He couldn't risk saying anything until you got here, because *there was nobody else he trusted to protect his family*. He knew he was never going to rise from his bed again. Michael is brave and resourceful, but he's very young. The men of the manor couldn't and shouldn't be landed with such a responsibility. Jonilda is a woman, and a grieving one at that. If your father had told her of his suspicions, what could she have done? Any attempt to confront Simon would have told him he was suspected, and he would have reacted with extreme violence, as we can now all see he's capable of. The consequences could have been horrific.'

'The abbot?' That was Dominic.

Edwin shook his head. 'Abbot Thomas had schemes of his own. Besides, he's a churchman through and through. If a mere woman had come to him, a woman who was anguished and under a great deal of stress, with wild accusations against one of his trusted officers, how do you think he would have reacted? It would have been all too easy for him to dismiss her as being in the grip of grief and hysteria. And some or all of what she said would have got back to Simon, putting everyone in danger. That's one of the words your father managed to say to me, when I saw him: danger.'

'And the other things are starting to make more sense now,' murmured Sir Martin. 'You said that he also told you to trust Jonilda, and then "don't let him take". Don't let Simon take the manor?'

'Either that or "Don't let him take Jonilda away",' replied Edwin, unable to avoid glancing at the barn as he did so.

Sir Martin thumped his hand down hard and made a strangled noise of frustration and anger. 'If only I'd done everything differently! If I'd come earlier, if I'd trusted Jonilda from the start. "Protect." That was what Father kept saying to me, over and over again. Protect, protect, protect. And I've failed.'

'No, you haven't,' said Gabriel, unexpectedly. 'You protected us when Simon was shooting at us from the forest, and you just saved Jonny from the pond.'

'And Constance,' added Edwin, 'who was surely about to get into trouble herself as she tried to help.' He caught Sir Martin's gaze and held it. 'I told you, your father knew you were the best and only person who could protect his family.'

'His family,' repeated the knight. He looked down at the boys. '*My* family. *Our* family. And that includes you, all the other children, and my stepmother. We're going to get her and Adela out of there.'

Michael exchanged a glance with Gabriel and straightened up. 'You just tell us what to do, and we'll do it.'

'And that goes for me too, my lord, and all your other men,' added Dominic.

Sir Martin stretched to look round the cart at the silent barn. 'Time to try again. And yes, still with words, but my patience won't last forever.'

'Wait,' said Edwin.

Sir Martin paused. Then he noticed Michael looking from him to Edwin and back again. 'Here's a lesson for you,' said the knight. 'One of the rules of command: always take advice before you act – and especially if the man giving the advice is much cleverer than you are.'

Michael cast a quick glance at Gabriel.

'There's no point in simply repeating the same demands,' said Edwin. 'We need to work out what his objectives are, as well as knowing our own.'

'Ours is to get Mother and Adela out of there, surely?' said Gabriel.

'And to bring Simon to justice.' Michael's voice was fierce.

'But which of those is more important?' asked Edwin, looking at Sir Martin.

His reply was immediate. 'The first, obviously.'

'And are you prepared to let him go in order to achieve that?'

The light was now almost gone, but Edwin could make out the agonised expression on his friend's face. 'It wouldn't be my first option,' he admitted, finally, 'but yes. And anyway, if he gets away, I can always chase after him once I know they're safe. He won't escape me.' He paused again. 'Why, do you think that's what he's going to ask for?'

Edwin put his fingers to his temples. 'Let's go back a few steps and think logically. So far he's shown himself capable of altering his plans at a moment's notice every time the situation has changed, and he's certainly not afraid of violence.'

'All right. Talk me through all that.'

'Understand your enemy?'

'Exactly.'

'Simon's initial plan, as we said earlier, was to marry Jonilda and act as regent for Michael. When you arrived, there was an additional hurdle in his way, but if he could kill Sir Richard then he could kill you too, and still succeed. He didn't think he'd get the chance, but then he saw Serlo capturing Farolf in the woods, and – crucially – Serlo leaving his quiver of arrows there. If we know one thing about Simon, it's that he isn't afraid to act quickly and take a chance. He knew you were on your way to the church, walking slowly because you had the cart, and he also knew where he'd left his bow. So he snatched the quiver, made his way to the right spot, and loosed.'

They were all leaning forward as the tale grew darker.

'But he missed with his shot – I'm not sure why, but maybe because the string was damp or damaged after being left outside. There was no time for another, so he dropped everything and pretended he'd seen an assailant and was chasing him. He hasn't had another opportunity since then, but his back-up was to have you accused of murder yourself.'

'Sorry, you've lost me again.'

'I've seen him talking to Eustace, and I'm sure he encouraged him to bring the charge, using Eustace's own avarice as a lever. "If I get the manor under my control, I'll pay you?" Or even, "The whole family will be disgraced, you might be able to angle your way into taking the place into the direct control of the sheriff?" Sheriffs can make money from confiscated estates, which would normally benefit Eustace's superior, not him, but it turns out that it actually is Eustace who renders the Nottinghamshire accounts to the exchequer, so he could easily have falsified them to benefit himself, and the sheriff would be no wiser.'

Sir Martin muttered something that Edwin didn't catch.

'And so Eustace was duped, blinded by his own greed, into making accusations – absurd ones that would never be believed, and surely never come to trial. But perhaps he thought Sir Martin might panic at the very idea and bribe him not to pursue it, so he'd make a profit either way. In either case, it was all enough to muddy the waters in the short term while Simon rearranged his plans.'

'Rearranged?'

'Yes. Because that, I think, was only the start. After all, acting as regent would give him only a few years of authority before Michael came of age. So, Simon's ambitions widened. Michael, I'm sorry to say this to you, but I think that if he'd married your mother, he would at some point have tried to kill you. Probably making it look like an accident or illness.'

Michael's scowl was the image of Sir Martin's. 'Leaving the manor to Gabriel, so Simon could do the same all over again.'

'And then…' Gabriel's voice wobbled.

'Yes. I really am sorry to be telling you this, but I think it's best you know what you're up against, so we don't underestimate Simon and what he's capable of.'

'But then why that business at the pond?' asked Sir Martin. 'If Jonny had drowned…'

'I think he changed his plans again,' said Edwin, grimly. 'I have no doubt that Jonilda either rejected his advances directly, or at least made it clear she wasn't interested. Which is when he began to think that acting as regent for a stepson would be temporary, but marriage to an heiress would be permanent.'

Sir Martin was still confused. 'But Jonilda isn't an heiress. I'm not following you.'

'I don't know how he thought he'd get away with it. The wiping out of almost an entire family within such a short space of time would be sure to raise suspicions, although children do drown quite frequently, so that could have been put down as a tragic accident.' Edwin paused to compose himself and shake his head at such barely comprehensible malice and barbarity. But he was almost done. 'When Michael said that Simon had taken Adela as well as Jonilda, at first I thought that was just because she was the smallest, the easiest to carry off and threaten. But I'm rather afraid that he's changed his mind about the identity of his future bride.'

There was silence, in the darkness, as Edwin's audience took in the import of his words.

In his fury, Michael went to snatch up his bow. 'Why, I'll–'

As he stood up there was a telltale buzzing, and Sir Martin just had time to wrench him down again as an arrow flew through the space where his head had been. 'I think that says something about his motives,' said the knight, grimly. 'Are you all right?'

Michael's face was pale in the darkness.

'Sit there and put your head down for a while.'

Edwin felt his arm being touched. It was Gabriel. 'But some of what you said, about what Simon was planning, just doesn't make sense. Not logically.'

'I know. And that's why he's so dangerous now. He's had the idea of Woodthorpe in his head for so long that he's become obsessed with it, with the thought of having power of his own. It's made him unhinged and unpredictable. But we need to use that to our own advantage if we can – I don't *want* him to think too carefully about the fact that

Sir Richard's four sons are all still alive, otherwise it will occur to him that Adela is less valuable, and she will be in even more danger. Do you see?'

Gabriel nodded, but Sir Martin was still reacting to an earlier part of Edwin's speech. 'Power?' His tone was derisive. 'I mean, of course it's a fine manor, but it's not exactly an earldom, is it?'

Edwin shook his head. 'It doesn't matter. If you'd grown up in a small village you'd know that greed and jealousy can be just as cut-throat at the bottom of the social scale as they are at the top. And it's not easy being a second son, knowing that the place you call home as a child won't be yours, and that you have to make your own way somewhere else.'

Sir Martin's eye flicked to Michael, who was now recovering and starting to raise his head. 'So, what does Simon want? What does he want *now*? He must know that his chance of getting Woodthorpe is gone, even in the state you say he's in.'

Edwin pursed his lips as he considered. 'In his own mind, he might not have given up completely,' he warned. 'And he might even think he can get away with what's happened so far. He can probably produce witnesses to say he was miles away on the day your father was shot. You're still alive, and so are Michael and Gabriel. Asking, or even pressuring, a widow to marry him is hardly a crime. And even if he thinks the children died at the pond earlier, he can easily pass that off as an accident. The only thing he's demonstrably guilty of is threatening Jonilda and Adela – and if they emerge unharmed then he might well get away with that too.'

'So?'

'So, what he will want is to get away. But whether he'll want to take them with him – either as a continuation of some kind of plan, or merely for leverage so you won't chase him – or whether he would leave them here in return for being allowed to escape, is still open.' Edwin made a helpless gesture. 'It's difficult to deal with a mind that isn't working as it should.'

It had been a long day, and it wasn't over yet. Edwin told himself that he must stay alert, especially as he'd made so many mistakes and errors of interpretation already. *Think*. 'If we make him a more tempting offer than "come out and surrender", there might be a chance.'

'What sort of offer? To let him get away?'

'My best guess,' said Edwin, tentatively, 'is that he might ask for sanctuary.'

'Sanctuary?' That was Gabriel.

'Yes. If he rides away from here he must know that Sir Martin will pursue him wherever he goes, and that he could call on the law, not to mention my lord earl, to help him. But if he claims sanctuary, that means he only has to make it as far as the nearest large church – so, the one at Rufford, which is only a couple of miles away. Once he's inside and said the words to claim sanctuary, nobody can drag him out.'

'What, forever?'

'No, for forty days. But after that time, he can choose to face a trial or abjure the realm – that means leave the kingdom, which he has to be allowed to do in peace. Either of which would be better than…' Edwin's eye caught the blade attached to Sir Martin's shortened arm, gleaming in the moonlight. 'And besides, he's still so confident that he probably thinks he'll be able to think of something to worm himself into a better situation, once he's out of immediate danger.'

'But that would mean he'd get away with killing Father!' Michael's anger was still palpable.

If he'd had the leisure to think about it, Edwin might have been amused at the fact that it was Sir Martin – *Sir Martin!* – who sought to calm the boy.

'The most important thing is getting them out unharmed,' he said. 'You've just lost a father, and I'm not letting you lose a mother as well.' He gathered himself. 'Right.'

'Do what you can with talk,' said Edwin, 'and if it doesn't work then we'll start considering… your way.'

'A few precautions first,' said Sir Martin, turning to Dominic. 'Of all the men on the manor, who's the best shot? You?'

'No, my lord, that would be Farolf, and by a long way.'

Which is why, Edwin reminded himself ruefully, he hadn't needed to waste all that time and effort wondering whether it could have been Farolf who shot at Sir Martin on the road that day. If it had been, he wouldn't have missed.

'Have Farolf fetched, then,' Sir Martin was saying, 'and let's hope he doesn't hold a grudge for being arrested and detained. Station him over there, where he can get a line of sight to the doors, and get him a bow and some arrows from the stores – broadheads, bodkins, whatever you can find. Tell him to keep an arrow nocked. If at any point he can get a clear shot at Simon, and Simon *only*, he is to loose. And he can aim to kill, you hear? I've given that order before witnesses, and nothing will happen to Farolf, or to you. But if there's the slightest chance he might hit my stepmother or my sister, he's to hold. Understood?'

'Yes, my lord.' Dominic slipped away.

While he waited for the erstwhile poacher to appear, Sir Martin surveyed the makeshift barricades. 'Let's have this cart turned round,' he said, quietly, to the nearest men. 'So that it's facing towards the barn doors, not sideways on. Wait until I've started talking, and then he might not pay much attention to it.'

'Aye, my lord. And did you want us to bring torches, now it's dark?'

Sir Martin almost let out an expletive, but he checked himself – remembering, Edwin thought, that these were field workers and labourers, not trained soldiers. 'No,' he replied, in a tone of forced calm. 'That would destroy our own night vision, and light us up as targets for him to aim at. We can see well enough in this moonlight for now.'

He stepped forward, remaining in shadow, and bellowed. 'Simon! I'm standing up to talk to you.'

'What now?' came from the barn, as the cart creaked into its new position.

'First, I want to hear my stepmother's voice, so I know that she and Adela are alive and well.'

There was a pause, and then Jonilda's voice – as steady as she could make it, but with a hint of a quaver – could be heard. 'We're both here.'

'Unharmed?'

'Yes.'

'Satisfied?' that was Simon again. 'Bring horses, let us all go, and they'll remain that way. If not...'

'You know that I'm not going to allow you to take them away.'

'We'll be staying here, then, for a while. And my knife is still sharp.'

Edwin admired Sir Martin's self-control more than ever, as he saw the movement in the shadows: the hand reaching for the sword hilt and then pulling back. The knight looked briefly at the ground and then up again. 'What if we let *you* go, and you leave them here?'

Edwin knew what such an offer must have cost his friend. To set free the man he knew was guilty of murdering his father – and all for the sake of the stepmother he'd always despised, and a half-sister he barely knew.

As he waited to hear Simon's answer, Edwin became aware of a quiet stir of new arrivals behind him. On his advice, Sir Martin had sent Christopher to the abbey to fetch both Abbot Thomas and Brother Gregory, the former in case his authority might help in the negotiations, and the latter in the event that his skills were – God forbid – to be needed.

'Think about it,' Sir Martin was now shouting. 'We know you killed my father, and that you tried to kill me and my brothers and sisters.'

'What did he just say?' said a voice right next to Edwin's ear, making him jump. The monks had brought Eustace with them.

'It was Simon who killed Sir Richard,' Edwin hissed. 'For all he persuaded you to lay charges against Sir Martin.'

'How did you–? I mean, that's a ridiculous assertion.'

'Is it.' Edwin turned away. Eustace might represent the law, but the forces of the law were not always to be relied on, and Edwin had nothing but contempt for men who used their positions for personal gain.

'You can't prove anything,' was Simon's next gambit.

Edwin noted his choice of words, and so did Sir Martin. 'You're not denying it, then?'

'Of course I'm denying it!' Simon was starting to sound rattled, which might be a good thing, but it might also make him more of a danger to Jonilda and Adela.

'Come out and face a trial for it, then! If you're so sure you're innocent, you'll be able to prove it.'

'Farolf's here, my lord,' came Dominic's low voice out of the dark. 'He's in place.'

'Good.'

Simon had still not responded to the knight's challenge, but Edwin heard another sound from within the barn – Jonilda's voice, he thought, her tone pleading. He didn't catch the content of her speech, but it could be gathered by Simon's more audible reply: 'No – she stays here too.' Jonilda was trying to save her daughter rather than herself.

The situation was becoming more tense by the moment, and Edwin didn't think it was going to be long before violence ensued. He wanted to speak to the abbot, but there were many men swirling around in the dark and Edwin was trying to keep his eyes on the barn and his ears listening out for the sound of another sudden arrow. Surely it could not be long before Simon realised that his position was untenable, and that abducting a woman and child was not only dangerous but highly impractical. Where would they go? How would he ensure they didn't get away? How would he feed them and ensure their safety?

'I have a proposal,' came Simon's voice, at last.

'Let's hear it, then.' Sir Martin was still out in the open, his size and the direction of his voice meaning he was dangerously exposed to arrows despite the lack of clear visibility.

'You will let the three of us leave, but we will ride only as far as Rufford. The child will be with me, my knife at the ready if you decide to pursue us. Once I've claimed sanctuary in the church there, and you've all sworn to abide by it – by God and the law – then I'll let them go.'

Realistically, this was as good an outcome as they were going to get, and Edwin was about to whisper to Sir Martin when another voice boomed out. 'You will not!'

It was the abbot, stepping forward himself now. 'You have shamed our abbey and deceived me, and I will *never* agree to shelter you in our church!'

Edwin winced. This was exactly what he'd wanted to avoid. After all their efforts to keep Simon calm, those couple of sentences had inflamed everything again. The abbot was no doubt angry that Simon's actions had thwarted his own designs on Woodthorpe, and once again Edwin cursed the arrogance of a man who would misuse his position for gain.

'No sanctuary!' Simon was shocked, and his voice rose almost to a shriek. 'Well, then, let's all go to hell together!'

Out in the open and in his white robe, the abbot was the most visible of the men in the moonlit yard, and it came as no surprise to Edwin when he heard the arrow. Sir Martin and Dominic did, too, managing between them to shove him out the way while a third figure lunged towards them all. But this time it was no single missile; Simon followed up with another and another, and Edwin heard two cries of pain out of the dark before everyone managed to stagger back behind the barricades.

Then there was the thud of an arrow hitting the barn. Farolf had spotted the crack through which Simon was shooting and had taken his chance. But even an experienced archer couldn't be expected to hit a target no more than a couple of inches wide in the dark, and he had missed his mark, which was only going to enrage Simon more.

There was a confused mass of bodies, shouts and groans.

'Who's hurt?' To Edwin's relief, it was Sir Martin's voice, meaning he hadn't been hit. Neither had Michael or Gabriel, who must be the two smaller figures still crouching behind a cart.

'Who's the heir to the manor now?' came Simon's mocking voice, teetering on the edge of insanity.

'I'm still here!' roared Sir Martin in reply. 'And you're a dead man!'

The laugh that followed sent shivers down Edwin's spine. 'If I'm going to die then I won't do it alone. I'll give you one last chance. You let us ride in safety for sanctuary – Edwinstowe, if not Rufford – or I'm going to burn this barn down!' He said something else that Edwin didn't catch, and then Jonilda's voice sounded, high and panicked.

'He has flint and steel, and he means it!'

'That barn's full to the rafters with tinder-dry hay, my lord,' said the serving man who'd been set to counting arrows, still at his post. He sounded panicked. 'If he sets light to it, it'll go up in moments. And not just the barn, but the house and the stables too.'

'Calm yourself!' snapped Sir Martin. 'He won't do it. How many arrows has he shot so far?'

'Four, my lord.'

The knight swore. 'Still another three to go. Stay there and keep watch. The rest of you, make way, so I can see who's wounded!' The press melted away as he strode through it.

Edwin wasn't as sure as Sir Martin was that Simon was bluffing, and the next words confirmed it. 'I will say the paternoster three times,' called the voice from the barn, 'and then if there are no horses ready, that's it. Shall I throw the child straight into the fiery flames, or let her shrivel up gradually from the heat?' he laughed again, the sound turning to a high cackle.

Jonilda screamed in genuine terror.

Edwin barged his way through the crowd. He grabbed Abbot Thomas, heedless of laying his hands on a man of the cloth. 'Talk to Simon!' he shouted. 'Do whatever you can to stop him or slow down his count!' The abbot began to protest, but Edwin was having none of it. 'You've caused enough trouble already, so make amends. I don't care how you do it, just go!'

Next, he tried to fight his way through to Sir Martin. The knight was simultaneously trying to respond to Simon and quieten the clamouring manor men around him, while also kneeling over two others who were lying on the ground. 'Torches, dammit,' he called. 'We'll need to have some light now, no matter that it marks us out. All of you, keep your heads down!'

Smoky flames and an acrid smell soon surrounded them, and Edwin could see that the two wounded men were Dominic and Christopher. Where they had been hit, or how badly they had been hurt, he couldn't make out, but Sir Martin was almost beside himself. 'Help them – do something–'

'See to him first.' That was Christopher, his voice calm as Edwin bent over him. Thank the Lord, that must mean he wasn't seriously injured. The older man grasped at Edwin. 'And– Martin?'

'Not wounded at all, thanks to you,' said Edwin. 'You threw yourself forward to get him out of the way, didn't you?'

'It's what she would have wanted. And if he's saved, then…' Edwin heard him sigh in relief, and felt the hand relax away from his sleeve.

'I'm all right, my lord,' gasped Dominic, from a few yards away, although he was evidently in great pain. 'But I've just thought–'

'Don't worry about anything now,' said Sir Martin. 'Let's just get you treated.'

'No, my lord, I mean–' the reeve reached out and grabbed Sir Martin's arm, leaving a dark smear on his tunic. 'The barn. When we used to play in it. We weren't supposed to, so we couldn't go in the front. Remember how we got in?'

Sir Martin froze. 'I'd forgotten. But maybe…'

Edwin reached to pull him away. 'Brother Gregory is here, look. Let him do his work, because I think it's time for you to do yours.'

The monk was already unpacking his bag, so Sir Martin stood up to leave him to it.

'What did he mean?' Edwin asked.

'There were a couple of loose boards, round the back. Quite high up – you had to stand on a ladder or a cart to reach them. But there was enough space to get in, and then we were in the loft and nobody the wiser. I wonder if they're still there?'

'They are!' Edwin recalled his experience of the other day. 'But you're not a child any more, and the gap is quite small. You'd never get through it, and I'm not sure I would either.'

'I'll try.' Michael had appeared.

Sir Martin looked as though he would object, but the frenzied sound of Simon shrieking out his paternoster could be heard over the top of the abbot's pleading and cajoling, so instead he knelt and spoke in a serious tone. 'Right. These are your orders, and you follow them, you understand? Your *only* task is to get quietly into that loft, so Simon doesn't hear you. We'll shout to him from here, to keep his attention in this direction. You shuffle forward – again, silently! – and see where your mother and Adela are in relation to him, how close or far away, and whether they're restrained, tied to anything. Then you come straight back out and report to me. Is that clear?'

'Yes,' came Michael's stout reply.

'Good. And you can put that down before you go.'

Michael reluctantly laid his bow on the ground and unslung his quiver.

Sir Martin turned to some of the manor men. 'Go with him and boost him up so he can crawl in the gap. Then stay there and catch him when he comes out. Wait until I've got Simon's attention again before you start.'

They slipped off into the darkness.

'The rest of you, take the brake off that cart as quietly as you can, and stand by to push it. When I give the word to ram the barn door, it needs to be done as quickly as possible.'

They murmured assent and moved into place.

Edwin found himself alone with Sir Martin, just for a moment. 'Are you all right?'

'I think so.'

'What will you say?'

'To be honest I don't even know. Anything that will keep his attention on me so he has none to spare for the back of the barn.'

'I'll come with you.'

'No, you don't need to–'

'It was my stupidity at not seeing through everything earlier that's got us into this situation.'

'I'm sure it would all be much worse if it wasn't for you, but… yes.' Edwin felt his shoulder being grasped. 'I'd feel better if you were by my side.'

'You don't have to do this alone.'

'Come on, then, before it's too late.'

Sir Martin strode up to the barricade and pushed Abbot Thomas to one side with very little ceremony. 'Simon, you coward!' he bellowed. 'Come out and face me! Are you afraid to fight a man with only one hand?'

'And lose my chance of dying in the soft embrace of your step-mother? Why would I do that?'

Sir Martin swore a vicious oath, and almost took the step forward that would have been fatal for everyone. He just managed to restrain himself, however, and shouted something indiscriminate to keep Simon's attention.

Edwin glanced down to where he'd last seen Gabriel, to check whether he'd heard the gross insult, and in the hope that if he had, he hadn't understood it.

But the space was empty: Gabriel had disappeared.

And so, as Edwin registered in shock, had Michael's bow and arrows.

Chapter Thirteen

Where had Gabriel got to? And should Edwin try to find him, or stay here with Sir Martin?

The shouting match was still going on, which was good, because it meant that Simon was distracted and had not yet set fire to anything. Edwin sidled nearer to Sir Martin, wondering if and how he should break the news, and hoping that Michael and Gabriel would return safely before he had to.

But the moments wore on, and neither of them came back.

Edwin had just opened his mouth to speak when the noise from the barn changed. It all seemed to come at once: a cry of surprise, or possibly pain; a woman's scream; a scuffle; a shout of 'You little– got you!'; another shout –

'They're both in there!' yelled Edwin. 'Michael and Gabriel!'

Sir Martin was already bellowing, 'Now!' at the men behind the cart and drawing his sword.

The vehicle crashed into the barn doors, forcing them very slightly apart. There was only enough space for one man to pass through at a time, but Sir Martin was already kicking at the splintered wood and forcing his way in. Edwin followed, scrambling through the gap.

Behind him, a group of men were pulling away the cart, moving barriers, pushing the doors further open. In front of him all was dark and chaos, struggles, shouting… he couldn't see enough to know who was who.

A shrill cry of terror told him that little Adela was somewhere towards the back of the barn, on the ground floor. 'Jonilda!' he shouted. 'It's Edwin – where are you?'

He followed the sound of her voice until he found her, tied to a vertical post with the little girl clinging to her skirts. Hastily, he drew his eating knife and began to saw through the fibres until she was free, whereupon she swept Adela up in her arms. 'Where are Michael and Gabriel? I heard–'

'Let's get you out of here first,' panted Edwin, pushing the knife back in its sheath and putting his arms around both of them. 'Can you walk?'

'Yes.'

The uproar towards the front of the barn ceased very suddenly, and Edwin paused while he strained to see what was happening. Thank the Lord, the manor men had had the wit not to bring any flaming torches inside the barn full of dry hay, but it meant that the light they were casting from outside was both dim and flickering.

Sir Martin was standing with his sword drawn, but unmoving. Michael was near him, bow in hand and an arrow nocked. But he could not draw and aim, and Sir Martin could not advance, because Simon was standing facing them, holding Gabriel pinioned in front of him and with the point of his knife pressed up against the boy's neck.

Jonilda couldn't help crying out, and Simon looked in their direction. Surely he couldn't see them properly, but he knew they were there. 'You stay where you are! One more step, and he dies.'

Edwin and Jonilda both froze. Sir Martin was watching his prey like a falcon about to swoop, but even he wouldn't be able to get to Simon before that blade could slide into the soft flesh.

Gabriel's face was wet, from what Edwin could make out when the intermittent light illuminated it, and his heart went out to the ten-year-old boy who had put himself in the path of danger to help his family. He wondered if he could creep any closer while Simon was concentrating on holding Gabriel and simultaneously watching Sir Martin and Michael.

He didn't have to.

All of a sudden, Gabriel screamed, 'Get my mother out of here!' At the same time, he lifted both feet off the floor and kicked backwards as hard as he could.

The momentary shift in weight was enough to throw Simon off balance just for a fraction of a moment, and his right arm, the one holding the knife, was flung out sideways as he sought to keep both his feet and his captive. Before anyone could move, an arrow smacked into the exposed forearm, propelling it back and causing him to drop the blade as he screamed in pain.

With a roar, Sir Martin threw his sword aside and launched himself forward, diving and knocking both Simon and Gabriel flying. Then Michael darted in among the flailing arms and legs to grab his younger brother and pull him away. Edwin moved forward to help them both, and soon he had all four members of Sir Martin's family safe away from the fight.

'Fight' wasn't really the correct word, as the result was a foregone conclusion. Within moments Sir Martin was on his feet, his right arm holding Simon in such a tight headlock that the smaller man was lifted off his feet.

'I should tear you in half!' roared the knight, the bladed artificial limb held ready, although Edwin was sure he was perfectly capable of breaking Simon's neck with no weapon at all, if he had a mind to. 'And by God's blood, if you've hurt any of them then I'll do it right now!'

'Stop!' Edwin had opened his mouth, and for a moment he almost thought the word had come from him, but in fact it was Jonilda who had shrieked from beside him. 'Don't, please – not with the children – we're all fine!'

Edwin saw flickering shadowy images of Sir Martin, his face still twisted with rage, staring across at them as they stood in a protective huddle. With the torchlight behind him, the knight could see them more clearly than they could see him. *Please*, thought Edwin. *Please do what you know is right. For their sake, and your own.* But he couldn't say anything out loud: his friend had to make his own decisions about what sort of man he was going to be.

Sir Martin held the whimpering Simon in an iron grip while he looked at the white, shocked faces, the wide eyes and the tears of his family. 'Truly? You're all unharmed?'

'Yes, yes we are,' cried Jonilda.

'Michael? Gabriel?'

The older boy threw a shaking arm around his brother. 'We're well.'

'All right. Edwin, get them all out of here.' Sir Martin bent his head to speak in a lower tone to Simon, but Edwin caught the words as he began to usher the others out the barn. 'You're a lucky man. I'll have the monk treat your wound, and then you might live long enough to hang.'

The knight followed them out, huge in the lurching shadows, half-dragging and half-carrying his captive while he shouted for rope. Simon was securely bound and taken off to the stable, there to be guarded by four men until he could be taken away at first light.

Sir Martin went back to retrieve his sword. By the time he emerged from the barn again, settling it back in its scabbard, all traces of his battle rage had disappeared. 'The law will take its course,' he called out to the crowd. 'And you–' he identified Eustace '–will see it done properly this time.'

The sheriff's man didn't dare argue.

'That was an excellent shot, Michael,' were the knight's first words as he reached his family. 'You must be even better than you think, to have hit him from that angle.'

'It wasn't me.'

'What?'

Michael's face was puzzled. 'I wanted to, believe me, but I couldn't find a way – I didn't trust myself to shoot in case I hit Gabriel.'

'Then who…?'

Edwin cleared his throat and indicated Farolf, who was hovering with a bow still in his hand.

Farolf stepped forward. 'It was me, my lord. Shoot if you can, that's what Reeve said to me, so I did.'

Sir Martin was momentarily taken aback, but then he managed, 'And you weren't scared of…' he indicated Gabriel.

'Of course not, my lord.' Farolf almost scoffed. 'At that range, and with his arm that far away from his body? I'm just sorry I didn't get him earlier, though I nearly did.' He pointed to the wall of the barn, where an arrow was still visible as it protruded from the planks. Edwin walked closer to examine it, seeing now that it was less than an inch away from the crack Simon had been shooting out of.

Farolf recollected himself. He put the bow and a quiver neatly down in front of Sir Martin's feet. 'Anyway, my lord, it don't look like he's like to die, but if he does and there's a punishment to take, I'll gladly take it. You said you'd make sure my lads were protected and looked after, so I'm glad to repay part of the debt, whatever the price. I'm ready.' He held out his hands, as though they were about to be manacled.

Sir Martin shook his head. 'You were acting under my orders, and you clearly prevented the murder of a child.'

'I'll speak for you if necessary,' came the abbot's voice. 'I saw it all.' He stepped into the circle of torchlight, his expression somewhat shame-faced. And with good reason, Edwin thought to himself.

'And as for you,' Sir Martin turned his attention to Gabriel. 'What in the Lord's name did you think you were doing? You could have been killed!'

Gabriel was rubbing at his neck, where Edwin now noticed a tiny pinprick of blood and shuddered at how close the boy had come to death.

'I was being logical,' said Gabriel, sounding as matter-of-fact as if he was adding two and two. 'You were trying to distract Simon from outside the barn, but if Michael had made a noise, it would have come from inside, and he'd have guessed what was happening. So, it made sense for me to go in too, to try to divert him from in there. If he saw me, he wouldn't notice Michael. And I brought Michael's bow in case he could get a shot at Simon while he wasn't paying attention. It was all perfectly rational.'

Sir Martin raised his face to the heavens and briefly closed his eyes. 'Edwin,' he said, in a martyred tone, 'are you sure he isn't your brother rather than mine?'

Gabriel took on a more defensive attitude. 'But you said that logic normally provides an answer.'

Edwin, to whom this was addressed, grimaced. 'Yes, but I also said that it's difficult to deal with a mind that isn't working properly. And sometimes, you know, you have to consider the danger to yourself, as well.'

Sir Martin *might* have expelled a cynical 'Ha!' at that point, but Edwin was still concentrating on Gabriel. 'But you can't have got in there by yourself – how did you persuade the men, when they'd all heard your brother giving Michael his orders?'

Gabriel shrugged. 'I told them he'd changed his mind. None of them argued about it, and I knew I'd get away with it because none of them was Dominic. He would have asked questions.'

'Dominic!' exclaimed Sir Martin, suddenly. 'He passed on my orders to the others, but then he was hurt. Where is he? How is he? And who was the other man who was hit?'

Gabriel had got away with it, and he had the sense to keep his mouth shut and drift away. But Edwin felt a sudden thump in the pit of his stomach. 'Didn't you know?'

'Know what?'

'The other man – it was your grandfather.'

'What? I didn't even see that he'd come back!' Sir Martin was already on the move.

'Yes, he was with those from the monastery. He got you out of the way just as you were pushing the abbot, and one of Simon's arrows hit him. But I spoke to him afterwards, he seemed calm and told Brother Gregory to see to Dominic first.'

The injured men had by now been removed to the house, they found, so Edwin and Sir Martin both entered the hall. Dominic was sitting on a bench, his mother fussing over a bandaged upper arm.

'Arrow just grazed across it,' he said, in answer to Sir Martin's enquiry. 'Looks like a ploughed furrow, and one that's none too neat. But don't worry, my lord,' he added, as the knight's brow darkened, 'Brother Gregory cleaned it out with wine – hurt like blazes, but he says it'll keep it clean. Then he's sewn it up neat as anything and put a salve on it.'

'Well, you keep an eye out for any kind of putrefaction,' said Sir Martin. He addressed the older woman. 'And I know you'll look after him, after all those times you fixed both of us up when we were boys. Anything you need, just ask.'

Then he straightened and looked about the hall. 'Where's Grandfather?'

'In the parlour, my lord,' replied Dominic.

There was something in his tone that Edwin didn't like, and he cast a sharp glance at the reeve. He was met by a sad shake of the head, and what Edwin interpreted as a silent plea, as Dominic looked from him to Sir Martin and back. If that didn't tell Edwin everything, the sound of Brother Gregory's prayers from the parlour did. Specifically, which prayers he was saying.

Sir Martin entered first, stopping so suddenly in shock that Edwin only narrowly avoided walking into his back.

The kneeling Brother Gregory paused in his Latin and looked up from the shrouded form. 'I'm very sorry to tell you, Sir Martin, but your grandfather is dead.'

Somehow, the exhausted and overwhelmed boys were sent to bed. Constance, Eleanor and Jonny were apparently already fast asleep in Bernulf's cottage, with their nurses to look over them, so they were left undisturbed while Michael and Gabriel were sent upstairs. Adela had already cried herself to sleep on her mother's lap, and after all they'd been through, Jonilda was understandably reluctant to let go of her.

Christopher's body had been moved into the hall, and most of the household, after taking some time for the first devastation of the evening's events to wear off, had retired. The abbot had waited long enough for Brother Gregory to treat Simon – whose wound was not fatal, the arrow, a bodkin, having passed directly through his forearm and out the other side, meaning it could be snapped off and removed – and then they had returned to the abbey. A crestfallen Eustace had gone with them, promising to return in the morning to ensure that Simon was taken away and securely imprisoned until his trial, which would now be for two murders as well as his other attempts.

By Edwin's calculations it wasn't far off dawn. He, Sir Martin and Jonilda, still cuddling her sleeping daughter, sat in the parlour. Edwin kept a little back from the others, letting them talk and marvelling at how much had changed in the four days – only four days! – since his arrival. Stepmother and stepson were speaking in low voices in a manner that Edwin could only describe as companionable, although to him it looked as though Jonilda was continually getting close to bringing up a certain subject but then losing her courage and moving on to something else.

Once more Edwin was the outsider, and once more he wrestled with his conscience over whether he should say something. But Sir Martin had gained so much in perspicacity in the last week that surely it would only take the barest hint from Edwin, without the need for him to become deeply involved. Besides, Edwin remembered one of the things his friend had said to Michael during those awful hours when they were outside the barn together.

He took it as divine approval that the subject of Abbot Thomas should come up between the others just at that moment, for it gave him his opening. 'Jonilda,' he said, 'Why don't you tell Sir Martin why you've spent so much time talking to the abbot recently?'

He was already sure he was right, but her brief exclamation, quickly stifled, confirmed it.

'What's this?' Sir Martin was alert, but his voice didn't hold any of the overtones of suspicion or accusation that it might have done a few days ago.

'Tell him,' urged Edwin, still keeping his voice low for the sake of the sleeping Adela, 'what you were willing to give up for your children.'

Jonilda said nothing, and Sir Martin leaned forward. 'Whatever it is, tell me, and if it's a problem, we'll find a solution together.'

There was now a faint pre-dawn light entering via the open window to add to the glow of several candles, and Edwin could see a tear rolling down Jonilda's cheek as she heard the kindness in his tone and began to hope.

'I knew you didn't like me,' she said. 'But I thought there might be some hope for the children – you share a father with them, so they're related to you in a way that I'm not. So, I wondered, if I was out of the way, whether you might be more inclined to let them stay here, to support them.'

'What,' he asked, with just a hint of what might become an ominous tone, 'do you mean by "out of the way"?'

'I asked Father Abbot if I could retire to the abbey as a corrodian. I knew my financial allowance was going to be very small, but I wouldn't need much if I was on my own, and I thought he might agree out of goodness.'

This time it was Edwin who couldn't help a derisive noise. 'But he didn't, did he?' he interjected. 'He had no sympathy for your position, no charity in his heart. All he did was tell you that the money wasn't enough. I assume it was because you're so young – what little you had to give him wasn't sufficient to buy food and accommodation for decades.'

Sir Martin looked from one to the other. 'Edwin, how is it that you *know* everything all the time? But never mind,' he added, holding up his hand. 'The more important thing is – you were going to leave? Leave your children? How could you?'

Jonilda burst into tears. 'I didn't want to!' she wailed. 'It would have broken my heart. But if was the best thing for them, then I had no choice…' she dissolved into sobs.

The noise and movement had woken Adela, who began to grizzle. Sir Martin knelt by them and put his arms around both. 'It's all right,' he said, in a tone that brooked no dissent. 'Hush, now. Everything's going to be all right. I'll make sure it is. I told Michael he wasn't going to lose his mother as well as his father, and I meant it.'

Jonilda sniffed and made an effort to control herself. She cast a glance upwards. 'I hope I didn't wake them. Perhaps I'd better go and check.'

'Here, give her to me.' Sir Martin settled back in his seat with Adela on his lap as Jonilda went upstairs. The little girl was awake enough to know she'd been transferred, but she saw who was now holding her and curled up contentedly, and it was only a few moments before she was asleep once more.

'Edwin,' said Sir Martin. 'I have some ideas, and I'd like to talk them through with you. You'll see it all and tell me if I'm being stupid.'

'Of course I will, though I'm sure you won't be.'

Edwin listened while his friend outlined some plans. He agreed with everything, and in fact he could have added one more of his own, just to tie up all the loose ends, but he'd wait to see if Sir Martin would eventually come to it himself before he made any suggestions.

It was only after he'd finished everything he wanted to say that Sir Martin frowned and looked at the stairs. 'She's been quite a while. Do you suppose she's all right?'

He made as if to move, but Edwin stopped him, a finger to his lips. 'I'll go. It's a shame to wake Adela.'

He tiptoed up the stairs, peered into the outer chamber, smiled and descended again. 'Fast asleep, along with the boys. She and Michael have got Gabriel between them, to keep him safe.' The mention of the name didn't immediately spark any new idea of Sir Martin's, but Edwin hoped he'd planted a seed.

Sir Martin looked out of the window at the early signs of sunrise. 'Not much point in going to bed now. And while we're alone, I want to talk to you about something else.'

'Yes?' His tone sounded serious, and Edwin wondered what else they could possibly have to discuss.

The knight looked down at the sleeping child in his lap. 'It's about Matilda.'

'Yes?' said Edwin, again, unsure of whether he needed to be wary or not.

'I mean, it always was a bit of a strange situation, but I just got on with it because I had to obey my lord earl, and of course I was happy at the thought of being your brother.'

'And aren't you still happy about it?'

'Yes, but… look, when you said about Simon maybe wanting to marry Adela, I felt sick. I didn't say anything to you before because I didn't want Jonilda to know about that – there's no need for her to find out now, is there? It will upset her too much. But… yes. And it made me think.'

'You've changed your mind? I don't think my lord –'

'Not that,' said Sir Martin. 'Or, not quite. But what I mean is, we can go ahead with the betrothal, but there won't be any wedding for a long time. Longer than my lord suggested, anyway. He said ten years…' He tailed off.

Matilda would still only be twelve at that point. Edwin knew that the nobility sometimes married off their daughters at that sort of age, but it was not the done thing in his own class. But then, Matilda wasn't his own class, was she? Even though she was his sister.

'Well,' Sir Martin was continuing, 'I say that it will be at least fifteen years, and even then only if she wants to. I'm not joking, Edwin – if she hates the idea then I'll defy even the lord earl, and I won't see her forced. I'll fight on her behalf for her right *not* to marry me, if that's what she wants.'

Edwin couldn't put a name to his emotions. 'You're a good man,' was all he could choke out.

'And that's Rochford or no Rochford. It's her manor, not mine, and although it did start to feel like home to me, I'm only looking after it. If she decides we're not to marry then I'll hand it back to her whole and entire. I can have that written down, if you like, just like Father did about his plans for Woodthorpe.'

He paused for a moment as another thought struck him. 'Edwin, I'm going to have to get a seal, aren't I? And take over my father's arms instead of wearing the lord earl's device.'

'And look after three manors and a family,' added Edwin. 'Congratulations on your majority.' A couple of years ago – no, a couple of months, or weeks, even – he would not have made such a remark to his friend. But Sir Martin had grown up, and Edwin couldn't have been prouder than if they were brothers already.

'Oh, wait,' said the knight. 'Rochford.' He looked again at the stairs, his expression thoughtful. 'I've just had another idea.'

Edwin sat back and smiled.

All the people of Woodthorpe and Langley were gathered outside the church. All, that is, except for the two sturdy men from each manor who had accompanied Eustace, two senior monks from the abbey, and Simon, bound in a cart, on the first stage of their journey. All four of them had lost their lord at the murderer's hand, and Edwin and Sir Martin trusted that they would not succumb to any kind of persuasion or bribe to let Simon go, even if Eustace was tempted by such an offer. Sir Martin had thought of that, too, and Edwin had overheard him telling the deputy sheriff, in a bland, factual tone that was more chilling than any overt anger, that he would hunt him down to the ends of the earth if he heard that Simon had escaped. Edwin hoped that Eustace might learn to think more of the duties of his position in the future, rather than the potential gains to be made from it, but he wasn't confident.

Edwin stood off to one side while Sir Martin addressed the crowd. He hadn't bothered to bring anything to stand on; he didn't need to.

'Most of you know who I am already, but I confirm that I am Sir Martin du Bois, son of Sir Richard of Woodthorpe by his first wife, Rosceline of Langley, and grandson of Master Christopher of Langley. If any man wishes to dispute my inheritance of either or both of these manors, let him speak now.'

The only sound to be heard in reply was birdsong.

'I am in the service of my lord Earl William de Warenne, as one of his household knights, so I will not be living here. My brother Michael and my stepmother Jonilda will manage both manors in my name, aided by the two reeves.'

He paused and swept his gaze over them all, trying to meet as many eyes as possible. 'Be under no illusion,' he thundered. 'They are under my protection, and always will be. They will be sending me regular reports, and I can be here within a matter of days if necessary. They speak for me in all things, and anyone questioning their authority will answer to me.'

The silence, if anything, became deeper.

'Now,' continued Sir Martin, lightening his tone. 'I wish to reassure you. All of you are also under my protection, and I take that duty seriously. Moreover, my inheritance does not mean that the two manors are now one. Woodthorpe and Langley remain separate, as they always have been, each with its own customs.'

There was a ripple of relief.

'Indeed, as soon as my brother John is old enough, he will take over the management of Langley, while Michael remains at Woodthorpe. That way, each manor can continue on its own proud path.'

There were probably some, looking at the fit and healthy young knight before them, who thought that such far-sighted arrangements might not be necessary, but Sir Martin had already explained to Jonilda that morning that it was going to be a very long time before he fathered an heir, so she displayed no surprise. Neither did she look quizzically at Gabriel, which a few others had done when Sir Martin had mentioned Jonny.

'And it *is* a proud path,' continued the knight, 'and I'm proud of you all, of the bravery and loyalty you've all shown during the difficult times of the last few weeks. Long may this continue.'

He stepped back to show that his speech was at an end, while Dominic and the Langley reeve, an older man, led the people in a heartfelt cheer for their new lord. Dominic was pale and looked to be in some pain, but he was otherwise well and both he and his mother had assured Sir Martin, when he went to enquire, that his wound had not become infected. Bernulf, likewise, had already been seen at work that morning, so the manors' losses were limited to their lords.

There followed another funeral, as Christopher was laid to rest. Abbot Thomas himself arrived to say the Mass, the peripatetic priest being elsewhere. Before he started, Sir Martin had accosted the abbot on that subject, and he'd promised to use his influence to make sure a permanent priest was appointed to see to the spiritual needs of both manors. Edwin wondered how much that was going to cost Sir Martin, for such a small parish certainly wouldn't pay for itself in tithes, but he seemed determined to dispense his new-found prosperity generously. If the lord earl thought he now had a rich knight in his retinue, he was mistaken, but they could deal with that as and when any questions arose. Edwin turned to look at the image of St Martin on the wall, filling the central, bridging space over the western door as he shared his cloak with a beggar.

After the service the church emptied, until only Edwin and the family were left. They stood around the space where Christopher had been interred, each saying their own prayers, until Sir Martin said 'Amen,' and crossed himself.

'He was content, at the end, you know,' murmured Edwin. 'All he wanted to know was that you were safe, and he said "It's what she would have wanted".'

Sir Martin's eyes fell on his mother's nearby grave.

Jonilda touched his arm. 'The girls and I will make sure she always has fresh flowers, now that your grandfather isn't here to do it,' she said. 'Roses when they're in season, and everything beautiful and fragrant that we can find, the rest of the year.'

Constance had already slipped across and was picking up Christopher's last garland, which had been knocked to the floor while the church was crowded. She placed it carefully on the effigy and then looked up as Sir Martin came to stand beside her. 'She was your mother, wasn't she?'

He nodded. 'Yes, she was.'

'I'm sorry you lost her.' Constance couldn't help her eyes flickering to Jonilda.

'So am I,' said Sir Martin. 'And I've been sad about it for a long time. But I'm glad I have plenty of other family, and that you've still got your mother.'

Constance took his hand as they turned to leave the building. 'We don't mind if you share her with us.'

They moved outside and out of Edwin's earshot, leaving him alone in the church.

He moved to Sir Richard's grave, which was next to that of his eldest daughter. 'He'll be all right, you know,' he said to the flagstone that would soon be covered by a raised tomb and effigy. 'He'll protect them all, just like you asked.' Edwin found, unexpectedly, that he was on the verge of tears. 'It'll all be different for me, of course: now that he has all these new responsibilities, we'll grow apart. But it's the right thing for everybody, and you – *we* – can be proud.'

He paused long enough to be sure that he wasn't about to bawl his eyes out, and wiped his face before he went out to join the others.

Gabriel grew more and more excited over the course of the day, and by the following dawn, when it was time to go, he was almost beside himself. He had many questions about Rochford, about what being a steward meant, about what he would be able to learn and who would be teaching him. Edwin tried to answer most of them himself, in order to give Sir Martin more time to spend with the rest of his family.

He and Gabriel were close enough to Sir Martin and Michael for Edwin to overhear the conversation as their horses were brought out from the stable.

'Aren't you taking Father's with you?' asked Michael.

Blanchart was already saddled, but Sir Martin began to check the girth and harness himself, as he always did. He spoke into the animal's flank. 'No. He's not tall enough for me to ride, and besides, you'll need a horse of your own.'

Michael was so dumbfounded that he couldn't speak. Eventually he squeaked 'Me?' in a much higher voice than normal. 'Truly?'

'Yes. If I can trust you with his manor, I can certainly trust you with his horse. Look, it's too late for you to become a page or squire anywhere, and that wouldn't work anyway with me needing you here. But I'll arrange for someone to come and give you some training, to carry on where Father left off. Proper riding lessons for a proper horse, and you can learn to use a sword to go with that bow.'

'Really?' the voice had come down a notch, but the same excitement was evident.

'Yes, really. And don't forget, there are going to be regular reports and letters travelling between here, Rochford and wherever I am, so you can always add a note to tell me how you're getting on.'

'I will,' said Michael. 'And you can rely on me.'

'I know I can.' Sir Martin, satisfied with Blanchart, finally turned. 'You're a good man.'

Before either of them could betray too much of the emotion they were feeling, he added in a brusquer tone, 'But now I need to speak to your mother.'

Jonilda was near Edwin, simultaneously trying to fuss over Gabriel and not to fuss over him, making sure he was ready for his journey while not treating him like a child, trying to show her pride without revealing her pain.

'Let him talk to Michael for a moment,' said Sir Martin, in a low tone, when he reached them. 'Go on and say your goodbyes to your brothers and sisters.' He watched Gabriel scamper off and held his hands out to Jonilda.

She took them both in her own, the one of warm flesh and the other of cold steel.

'I promise you,' he said, 'that he will be all right. And I don't just mean that it's a good opportunity for him. I mean that he will be well looked after and loved. Aelred and his wife have no children of their own, and honestly they'll dote on him so much that my main worry is that they'll be too soft on him, not that they'll be too strict. And he can write to you.'

Jonilda had no free hand to wipe away her tears, but she nodded. 'He needs to be somewhere else, where he can grow and learn – we've always known he's clever, and he needs to spread his wings. And I trust you with him, I trust you'll make sure he's taken care of.'

'Well then,' said Sir Martin, somehow expressing a huge amount of emotion in just two simple words, in a way that reminded Edwin of Sir Geoffrey. 'We'll be off.'

As the moment arrived, Michael enveloped Gabriel in a long embrace. 'I'll see you again,' he said, with feeling. 'And if you've ever got any advice for me, you send it.'

They mounted, Gabriel being boosted up behind Edwin on the horse that was going home to Rochford. Constance, Eleanor and Jonny ran after them for some way, calling their farewells, but soon they were on the main road and into the woods.

Sir Martin set a much brisker pace than he had done when they were travelling in the opposite direction, and thanks to that and the long summer's day, they reached Rochford just before sunset. Gabriel was exhausted by the unaccustomed long ride, and as they splashed across the ford, he was asleep cradled in Sir Martin's arms, leaning on him as he sat sideways across the front of Blanchart's saddle.

The manor was as orderly as it had been before, the news of their arrival preceding them, and Aelred stood ready to greet them. 'Welcome, my lord. I hope your family business was… I'll have food prepared for you and your guests.'

'Ah,' said Sir Martin, after returning the greeting. 'Edwin is my guest once more, but Gabriel is here to stay.' He nudged the boy. 'Wake up!'

Gabriel stirred and looked dazedly about him.

'Aelred, let me introduce my brother, who is to be your new apprentice steward.'

If Aelred was surprised, he gave no sign of it. 'Well, then, you're equally welcome, young man. Here, let me help you down.' He caught Gabriel as the boy half-slid and half-fell from the tall mount, and looked at him for a long moment.

By this time, Edwin had also dismounted and Gundreda had arrived. She was already making motherly noises over Gabriel, now awake and looking about him with interest. He smiled at her and allowed himself to be ushered towards the house with promises of food, Gundreda asking him what was his favourite and did he like pies or pastries or…

Aelred cast a questioning glance at Edwin as they watched the departing backs.

'He can reckon numbers more quickly than anyone I've ever met,' said Edwin, 'and he's very keen to learn Latin… and chess.'

Aelred's smile lit up his lined face. 'Well, now.'

Edwin stood with him in contented silence as they watched Sir Martin take both horses over to the stable. Tomorrow, or perhaps the day after, the two of them would be on their way back to Conisbrough. He hadn't yet mentioned the identity of the new castellan they would find when they got back, but he suddenly felt sure that he need not be afraid of the reaction when he did. The earl might have been wise to want the old Sir Martin out of the way while he made the appointment, but Edwin was also right in knowing that the new Sir Martin would take the tidings in his stride and deal with the situation calmly. He was an important man in the earl's household, and his consequence and the trust the earl could place in him would only increase as the years went by.

'*Ecce equus pallidus*…' Aelred's words were soft as he, too, looked at the knight stroking Blanchart before they disappeared into the stable. 'But he has brought new life to us, not death.'

Edwin felt a lump in his throat, and some of the same emotion swept over him that he had felt in the church the previous day. But no, this was different – his sadness was mixed with pride, joy and hope. Who knew what the future would bring? Whether he and his best friend would ever be brothers by marriage remained to be seen, but in the meantime they could each face their separate futures with confidence.

The sun was blurred as it sank a fiery blaze, but Edwin was able to smile through his tears.

Historical Note

In *A Pale Horse,* Edwin has the chance to interact with people at a level of society he has never really encountered before. The minor gentry did not own extensive estates like the great barons and earls, but they might be the lords of one or two manors, controlling a small section of a local area. This certainly set them well above the peasants in rank, but their income was not all that large, and it might fluctuate from year to year depending on the bounty of the harvest and the health and well-being of the manor workers. Some of these local lords, like Sir Richard, might scrape together enough to enable them to achieve knighthood (which was expensive in terms of the horse and equipment needed), while others, like Christopher, never aspired to that rank or lifestyle.

The manors of Rochford, Woodthorpe and Langley are all fictional, so you will not find them on any map, but their names are common ones, meaning 'rocky ford', 'settlement in the woods' and 'long field' respectively. They are the sorts of places that were to be found throughout England in the early thirteenth century, places that were home to the majority of the population. Cities and towns certainly existed, and many individuals did travel great distances, but society was still principally rural and agrarian, and plenty of people, especially at the lower end of society, lived their whole lives without ever travelling more than a few miles.

At this time the term 'forest' did not necessarily mean a forest in the modern sense. Rather, it was land legally set aside for the specific purpose of royal hunting, and it might include manors, farms and open countryside as well as wooded areas. Forest law was a specific set of regulations, which had been incredibly harsh under the earlier Norman kings, but which were softened somewhat by the Charter of the Forest of 1217. This was issued by the boy king, Henry III, and his regency in order to distance him from the unpopular rule of his father, King John.

The Charter of the Forest was a sort of cousin of Magna Carta (which was also reissued by Henry III's administration in 1217) and it was actually the more important of the two documents for much of England's population: Magna Carta dealt with the rights of the barons, but the Charter of the Forest affected the lives and livelihoods of the common people. All the parts of it that Edwin learns about are real clauses, including the all-important new law that abolished the horrific punishment of mutilation for poaching.

The laws and finances of each county were under the jurisdiction of a sheriff. This could be a lucrative position, depending on how it was approached: the sheriff owed an annual shire payment to the national exchequer, but how he organised that was left up to him, and if he collected more than was owing (as often happened), he could keep the difference. Bribes, *ex gratia* payments, gifts and favours were also not unknown.

Some sheriffs were assiduous and fair in carrying out their duties, such as Dame Nicola de la Haye, England's only female sheriff, whom Edwin met in *The Bloody City*. Others enjoyed the financial benefits but left all the actual work to deputies: Edwin's lord, Earl William de Warenne, for example, was at this time High Sheriff of Surrey, and he was certainly not running around collecting individual tax payments and arbitrating on matters of local justice. The High Sheriff of Nottinghamshire, Derbyshire and the Royal Forests in 1221 was a man called Philip Mark (or Marc), who was also firmly in this camp. Most of his duties in Nottinghamshire, and all of the accounting to the exchequer, was done by his deputy, Eustace of Lowdham. Eustace was known to be less than honest, and he was so intensely unpopular that he is actually the leading candidate to be the man on whom the 'Sheriff of Nottingham' character in the Robin Hood stories is based.

A few of the other characters in *A Pale Horse* are also based on real people, including Earl Warenne's squire Hugh and page Wil (William), the boys who were heirs to the earldoms of Arundel and Salisbury respectively. We have no evidence as to whether Hugh and Wil really were brought up in Earl Warenne's household, but it was the standard practice for noble boys to be sent away at young ages to train as pages and squires, and Warenne, Arundel and Salisbury were close allies, so the idea is plausible. Wil was the son of William Longespee, a cousin of Earl Warenne (and an illegitimate half-brother of King John), and William's wife Ela, countess of Salisbury in her own right. Hugh's father, William d'Aubigny, the earl of Arundel, had died on the same crusade as the fictional Sir Roger (though his body was brought home for burial), leaving his teenaged elder son – yet another William – as earl and his second son, Hugh, as the heir until such time as William junior should marry and father children of his own.

Earl Warenne appointed Sir Baldwin de Hersey, whom Edwin met in *Blessed Are the Dead*, as castellan of Conisbrough sometime around 1221; his brother Sir Malvesin already held the same position at nearby Tickhill.

Rufford Abbey was a Cistercian monastery founded in 1147. An abbot called Geoffrey was succeeded by one called Thomas sometime around 1220, though we know nothing of them other than their names. The Cistercian Order was extremely prosperous, trading in wool and owning large swathes of land. Abbeys could and did own whole manors, becoming the 'lord' of the people who lived and worked there, and a successful abbot was one who was an able financial administrator as well as a pious man.

A 'family' in the early thirteenth century was a complex entity that did not necessarily comprise a small nuclear group of closely related people living together. Peasant or urban families might include more distantly related individuals, often young people who were gaining experience in labouring or household management before marrying or setting up households of their own. Trade apprentices were often completely unrelated to the people they lived with, but still counted as part of the